BURNED

AMAZON BESTSELLING AUTHOR
JORDAN MARIE

Copyright © 2016 by Jordan Marie
All rights reserved.

No part of this publication may be used or reproduced in any manner whatsoever, including but not limited to being stored in a retrieval system or transmitted in any form or by any means, electronic, mechanical, photocopying, recording or otherwise, without the written permission of the author.

This book is a work of fiction. Names, characters, groups, businesses, and incidents either are the product of the author's imagination or are used fictitiously. Any resemblance to actual places or persons, living or dead, is entirely coincidental.

Cover Art by LJ Anderson of Mayhem Cover Creations
Model: Travis DesLaurier
Photographer: Corey Pollack

Interior Design & Editing by Daryl Banner

BURNED BY JORDAN MARIE
DEDICATION

I love all of my readers. Some of the best times I have are laughing and joking in my street team or on my personal social media pages. I'm so blessed with each and every one. My street team slogan is Badass Bitches for life, (#BB4L) and they truly are some of the baddest, sweetest, lovingest, funniest people I've ever met. This past year, I lost one. One who was important to me. She was a sweet soul, who deserved to laugh and live longer. A soul that the world needed because her light touched people and she made them happy. I know because she made me happy. She gave me smiles. She touched my heart. This book is dedicated to you Cka Inez Reagan-Wilson gone too soon, but never forgotten.

Your light lives on.

Xoxo
#BB4L and beyond.
J

BURNED by JORDAN MARIE
CONTENTS

PROLOGUE PART 1	1
PROLOGUE PART 2	13
CHAPTER 1	23
CHAPTER 2	28
CHAPTER 3	31
CHAPTER 4	33
CHAPTER 5	37
CHAPTER 6	39
CHAPTER 7	43
CHAPTER 8	46
CHAPTER 9	50
CHAPTER 10	54
CHAPTER 11	56
CHAPTER 12	59
CHAPTER 13	62
CHAPTER 14	65
CHAPTER 15	68
CHAPTER 16	71
CHAPTER 17	73
CHAPTER 18	76
CHAPTER 19	81
CHAPTER 20	86
CHAPTER 21	90
CHAPTER 22	94
CHAPTER 23	97
CHAPTER 24	101
CHAPTER 25	103
CHAPTER 26	105
CHAPTER 27	109
CHAPTER 28	112
CHAPTER 29	115
CHAPTER 30	119

CHAPTER 31	121
CHAPTER 32	125
CHAPTER 33	129
CHAPTER 34	133
CHAPTER 35	138
CHAPTER 36	140
CHAPTER 37	143
CHAPTER 38	149
CHAPTER 39	153
CHAPTER 40	156
CHAPTER 41	160
CHAPTER 42	164
CHAPTER 43	169
CHAPTER 44	173
CHAPTER 45	177
CHAPTER 46	183
CHAPTER 47	187
CHAPTER 48	191
CHAPTER 49	194
CHAPTER 50	198
CHAPTER 51	202
CHAPTER 52	205
CHAPTER 53	208
CHAPTER 54	211
CHAPTER 55	217
CHAPTER 56	220
EPILOGUE PART ONE	222
EPILOGUE PART TWO	226
FINAL NOTE FROM THE AUTHOR	229
GLOSSARY OF TERMS	230

BURNED by JORDAN MARIE
FOREWORD

Dear Readers:

When Skull first "came" to me and "demanded" I write his story (yes the voices speak to me, what can I say?), I never realized what a job it is to tackle three books that link so closely together. It turns out that ending with a cliffhanger is simple, compared to picking up where it left off. Especially, when the second book is about a different couple. I tried to walk a fine line with this one. I wanted you to be able to read this story and enjoy Torch and Katie even if you had never read Skull. I wanted to catch readers up on what happened from Captured, but not overshadow the main characters. I tried my best. I hope I succeeded. In the back of this book I have enclosed some samples of books from some new authors that you might not have heard of, but you should definitely check out! I've also included the Novella of Craved. Craved is Annie and Sabre's story and takes place before Torch actually. So if you haven't read feel free to scroll up to the table of contents, find it and start it first! It however, is not necessary to read it before (or even after) Burned.

Okay so that's it. Enjoy people! (I hope you do!) Please if you have the time and you've read, take a moment to leave a review. I don't really comment on them, but I promise I read each and every one and try to use them to motivate me.

As always remember this book contains adult content (umm quite a bit of it in this case) and read on with that knowledge.

xoxo
Jordan
www.jordanmarieauthor.com

BURNED

AMAZON BESTSELLING AUTHOR
JORDAN MARIE

I don't know how many times I scream it. I just keep screaming. It doesn't matter who's around or who sees or hears us; I'll deal with the fallout. I need to make sure Bethie is okay. I can't let anything happen to her or my niece.

"What's wrong?" asks an older man, pushing through the crowd that has started to form around us.

"Her water broke," I explain quickly, "and then she got pale and passed out. I don't know. Help her, please!"

He starts moving around her, puts a hand to her face, then checks the pulse at her neck. Finally, his hands move along her stomach, examining.

He takes out his cell phone. "This is Dr. Crowell. I have a pregnant female unconscious outside the Movie Vault Theater. Her water broke. Her pulse is weak and there's a hint of blood. It could be placenta previa. I need an ambulance, stat. Have the O.R. ready and meeting the bus."

His words mean nothing to me. I don't understand. I just know that I can't quit crying. I can't lose Bethie now, not when we've finally survived everything and are on the verge of being free...

Not now.

"The club is all I have. I will protect it to the death."

It's been a fucking night. Skull is trying to kill himself by hitting on Dragon's woman at the movies. He's not even truly interested in her, I can tell. I think she reminds him a little of Beth, but there's no real interest on his part, that much is clear. Fuck, he hasn't had a woman in his bed since Beth.

Beast and I help toss him on the bed and Beast grunts before going back to the woman he brought home. Maybe that's a sign of hope because that in and of itself is a freaking miracle. Beast hasn't looked at a woman since the day he lost his old lady and child. Chick he's got tonight is Dani. Smokin' hot, but something about her tells me she has more baggage than an airport. I don't know what gets into my brothers. Chicks are made to fuck and enjoy, then scrape off the bottom of your shoe. Jesus, didn't the mess with Skull and Beth teach them anything? When she died, Skull grieved himself to death. And tonight, I know he was hoping Dragon would end his misery. I could see it in his eyes.

Skull mumbles in his sleep. He still clutches the empty bottle of Vodka he had in his hand when his head hit the bar. I didn't even bother trying to take it from him. Chances are, when he wakes up, he'll just start drinking more, so I was afraid to wake him. He puts away so much alcohol these days, I don't know how he functions. Things need to change. I just don't know how to drag him out of the hell he seems to be lost in. Hell, if I lived through all of the shit he has, I doubt I'd be in any better shape than he is—probably worse.

"Boss okay?" I look up to see Pistol standing at the door. I hate this fucker. I'm not even sure why. A while back, he was making waves and trying to get enough votes to kick Skull out of his position. Skull beat the fuck out of him, and things have been quiet ever since. Hell, Pistol has been the poster child for Skull's biggest supporter since he almost lost his life after Beth's father shot him in the stomach—but there's still something about him that sets off fucking alarm bells. I'd mention it to Skull, but shit, I doubt the man cares much right now if Pistol takes over the club. That by itself is some scary shit.

"Yeah man, just a little too much to drink," I tell him, ready to get the fuck out of here and away from Pistol. I plan on finding a woman and getting fucking laid. If I'm lucky, maybe two or three women. A party is not a party until Torch shows up. Got to give all the ladies the attention they deserve.

"He's been drinking more and more lately," Pistol points out, and I can't even say his tone is bad, but I want to punch the fucker in the face.

"Yeah, well, he lost his woman and gave the order that killed her. That shit fucks with a man."

"Yeah, you're probably right. Still, having a cocked cannon leading us... That's dangerous. He could have caused a war with the Savage Brothers tonight."

"Back the fuck off, Pistol."

"I'm not saying anything, I just worry. Same as you, Torch."

"Whatever. I..." I trail off as Skull's cell phone rings. I follow the sound, coming up to the nightstand. He mumbles but doesn't wake. I don't recognize the number, but it's local.

"Shoot," I say into the phone, my eyes flicking back to meet Pistol's. I don't trust the bastard not to knife me in the back. Fuck, or *any* of us in the back.

"I'm looking for Skull?" a voice comes across the other line and it reaches down and wraps around my cock and makes it throb. Strangest fucking thing I've ever felt in my life.

"He's busy," I say, looking down at the man in question, annoyed that whoever owns this voice wants *him* on the phone and not me. I bet I could make her want me...

"Um... I'm calling for Beth."

My hand tightens up on the phone and I'm close to crushing the motherfucker. "What the fuck are you playing at?"

"Listen, I don't want to cause any problems. It's just that Beth came to Kentucky to find Skull, but before she could talk to him, she went into labor. She's at the hospital in London and there are some complications. I don't want to go into it over the phone, but could you tell him that she needs to see him? Obviously, they have stuff to talk about. We're in the maternity ward, and—"

"Listen, you fucking cunt. I don't know who you are, but there's no way Beth is in a hospital. Especially here in Kentucky. She died."

"She didn't," the woman argues back. "That's what I'm trying to tell you. If you'd just tell Skull to come down here—"

"You're out of your fucking mind. If you think I'm going to let my man walk into a fucking trap, you're crazy."

"It's not a trap! Listen to me—"

"Whoever the fuck you are," I growl into the phone, cutting her off, "and whoever put you up to this, you need to stop, or I swear to God I will make sure you live to regret it."

I end the call, breathing heavily and furious as hell.

"What the fuck was that?"

"Some twisted bitch trying to say she had Beth at the hospital in labor, of all fucking things. Probably some pissed off fucking hanger on trying to cause Skull some grief."

"Should we check it out?"

"Fuck no. And we *don't* mention this shit to Skull, either. Brother has enough shit going on in his head. He doesn't need this added to it."

"Yeah. I'm with you on this one. I'm going to check the perimeter of the club and crash, Torch, bud. See you tomorrow."

"Yeah, okay, later," I answer, just relieved Pistol is leaving. I'm pissed as hell. I'm glad that I got that call instead of Skull. Something like that would have messed my brother up even more, and that's the last thing he needs. He's on a thin edge right now as it is.

"Beth," Skull whispers in his sleep, like he knows what's going on.

The pain and torment in his voice hurts me. I put Skull's phone under my boot and grind that mother fucker on the floor until it lies in pieces. I'll explain to Skull tomorrow I accidentally stepped on it getting him to bed and have him get a new number. Fucker should have updated when we moved out of Georgia anyways. It's time he starts living in the present, even if I have to drag his ass the whole way.

PISTOL

"Pistol, baby, why are we doing this again?" asks Tammie.

"What the fuck do you care? I gave you a grand. You just do it and get the fuck out," I tell her. I picked her because she's a greedy, selfish little bitch—both in bed and out of it. I knew I could get her to do it for enough money and let her choke on my cock later to keep her quiet.

"I could show Skull a good time while I'm there, make him real happy."

"He's passed out dead to the world. Just get it and take the damn picture on this phone," I order.

"Fine, but if he gets pissed at me, I'm telling him it was your idea," she huffs, pulling the shirt she has on off her body. She's got some nice tits and some decent curves. It won't be a hardship to fuck her later, but that sassy comeback right there brings up a good point. I'll have to use a little force later to get my point across that silence means silence.

She climbs into Skull's bed. Fucking bastard barely turns over. God, I hate him. It'd be so fucking easy to end him right here, but there's no way I'd get away with it. I've been waiting, biding my time so I can take over the fucking club. I've won over most of the brothers, but there's a couple who would vote against me, so I've held back. The time is almost right, though. That's just one of the reasons I can't have Beth coming back into Skull's life. If she tells him that I helped Redmond, I'm a dead man. I don't know what that fucking bitch is doing back here, but I'm going to make sure she never wants to find Skull again. It's going to cost me a hundred grand, but if it gets rid of her and gets me closer to owning this club, it's worth every penny.

My attention goes back to Tammie, who's in bed with Skull now. She's teasing the ring on his lip, using her tongue to toy with him. Skull growls, taking her mouth. Tammie pulls his hand to her naked breast and he holds it with a groan, pulling his mouth away to kiss her neck.

"*Mi cielo*. God, I've missed you," he mumbles. Jesus Christ, he's a sad fuck. I'd be doing him a favor by putting a bullet in his head.

Tammie snaps a couple pictures with my phone. I take it out of her hand to look. Oh yeah, this will fucking destroy Beth.

"Did I do good, Pistol baby?" Tammie asks in a whisper.

She doesn't need to worry; Skull's already out again, snoring.

"Yeah baby, you sure did. Now climb out of there and head to my room for a real party. I'll meet you there in about thirty minutes. I just have an errand to run first."

"Don't keep me waiting," she whines.

"Grab Sabrina and you two girls start the party without me, then I'll meet you there."

"But Pistol, you know how rough Sabrina gets," Tammie complains. The bitch does, too. Fucking hell, she scares me when she gets that damn strap-on out.

"You'll take it like the bad girl you are. Daddy will be there soon to give you the real thing. Now go get her."

"Fine, but you better eat me out after all this."

"Sure I will, baby," I lie, walking away to Skull's office. Once I get there, I close the door. It takes me a few minutes to send the picture from my phone to the printer, then I write a quick note and stuff it in an envelope with some money. That should do it. Too bad I can't be around to watch the bitch cry. I can't risk her seeing me, though.

I'll just have to come back and celebrate my victory with Tammie and Sabrina. I grin. Someday soon, I'll celebrate being the reason Skull is no longer breathing air, and then I'll finally rule this club like I was meant to years ago... before he stepped in and fucked it all up.

Soon.

" Thank God my sister has me.
I'll make sure these fuckers never hurt her again. "

I stare at the receiver in my hand. The motherfucker hung up on me. He wouldn't even really listen to me. Who the hell does that? Even with them thinking Beth was dead, shouldn't he have at least heard me out? I rub the back of my neck as tension threatens to paralyze me.

I'm not sure what's wrong with my sister or my niece. They tried to explain it to me, but it was all Greek. Something about the baby's blood vessels and the umbilical cord... I don't know. I couldn't stop crying. I just know they took her straight back in for an emergency caesarian and wouldn't let me anywhere near her. I tried to do the one thing I knew she wanted, but apparently Skull or whoever the hell I was talking to is a moron. How do I break it to my sister that even though she wanted her husband—the father of her child—to be here with her, that's not going to happen?

I really should've went with plan A and cut off his balls.

"Miss Lawson?" A man in blue scrubs comes out of the main surgery doors using the name that my sister and I assumed last month when we made it to the states and started searching for Beth's husband.

"Yes?" I ask, terrified to hear what he's going to say.

"It was touch-and-go for a little while, but I'm happy to tell you that the mother and child are doing well. If Dr. Crowell hadn't found you when he did, it could have been a whole different story. The baby will have to be monitored for a few extra days, but everything should be fine."

"Oh, thank you, doctor," I tell him, grasping his hand with tears running down my face. "Thank you so much. Can I see her? Can I see my sister?"

"The nurses are busy cleaning her up and making sure she's okay. She'll be in room 313 if you'd like to wait for her up there."

I thank him, then he spends the next ten minutes telling me exactly how I will need to watch over my sister in the coming days. I assure him that I can, but inside, I'm in a panic. *What if I screw up? What if I do something wrong?* The last thing I want to do is hurt my sister. The mere thought makes me cringe. I do my best to shake it off and bring my attention back to the doctor.

"Thank you again, Doctor."

"My pleasure," he says. I watch him leave and think about

everything that's happened tonight. I'm worried how Beth will take it when I tell her that Skull wouldn't even talk to her. It's going to crush her—and that's the last thing I want. I don't want to hurt my sister, but I know the first thing she will ask me about when she comes to is Skull.

And what do I say?

* * *

I'm asking myself the same questions an hour later. That's how long it takes for the nurses to bring Bethie. I was starting to panic, afraid something had happened while she was in recovery. Apparently, they're just really packed solid and running behind.

"You look good, little mommy," I whisper to her as they transfer her on the bed, pulling the covers up around her.

"That's strange because I feel like hell," she answers, her voice tired and a little shaky. She keeps her eyes on me the entire time the nurses move her around to get her settled. They finally leave us after giving her more medication and checking her IV.

"Did you get ahold of Skull?" she asks right away.

Didn't I say that would be her first question? It makes me want to kill him all over again.

"Bethie... I tried. He didn't believe me. He wouldn't even listen..."

"We have to *make* him listen. He has to meet Gabby. When he sees her and knows I still love him, it will all be okay. With Redmond and our grandfather gone now, it's just—"

"It's just the family wanting us dead for killing grandfather," I cut her off. "Don't forget that, Bethie. We can't let ourselves forget that."

"So, we're supposed to live the rest of our lives in hiding? We're never supposed to have a life? What has all this been for, Katie? Why did we even hire that private detective to find Skull? Why did we go to so much trouble if I'm never supposed to have him? If we're never going to be a family? He deserves to know Gabby. He deserves to know that I'm alive. I can't just leave it alone, Katie… I can't. Not now when my grandfather is gone."

"You're going to name her Gabby?" I ask suddenly. I change the subject because I can tell Bethie's upset and that can't be good for her.

"Gabriella," she answers. "It was Skull's mother's name. He would want our child to carry her name."

Something about the way she talks about him and their child makes my throat tighten up. I've never had that. Hell, I've never seen anyone have a relationship where it felt like they needed the other person to breathe. She makes it seem that way every time she talks of Skull. I have to do everything in my power to make sure she gets back to him…

"Excuse me," comes a lady's voice at the door. "There was a package delivered downstairs for a Beth Donahue? It was addressed to a Beth Donahue, patient in the maternity wing. You're the only Beth we could find. It's from an Andre Cruz?" She's a doctor, or a resident… something. She has the coat on. As she walks towards me, I can see blonde hair pushed up under one of those surgical bonnets. Her nameplate reads: *T. Torres*. "Would that be you? He was a big guy wearing a leather vest."

"I'm sorry, we don't know any Andre—" I start to say.

"I do!" Bethie interrupts. "That's Skull. Is he here? Can I see him, please?"

"I'm sorry honey, he left. He said you would want this." The woman hands Beth the package. "I better get back to rounds. The admissions office was swamped and I told one of the nurses I'd check with you. I'm glad you and the baby are doing so well."

When she leaves, I turn to look at my sister because I know this can't be good.

"Donahue?" I prompt, knowing that dig can only mean one thing.

Bethie doesn't respond; she's too busy staring at the big manila envelope like it's a snake. Her hand trembles as she reaches inside and pulls out three things. The first is a folded note. The second, a picture, then finally a large roll of money. I won't know how much until I count, but from the hundreds and the size of the roll, I'm going to say it's easily a hundred thousand. She reads the note, then lets out the saddest cry I've ever heard in my life. It sounds as if it was torn from her body. She drops the note as the sobs overtake her. I clumsily wrap one arm around her, then pull her close while using my other hand to grab the note and read it for myself.

 Beth,

 I've known for a while that you were alive. I had hoped you wouldn't reach out to me. You were fun and I enjoyed what we had, but you've been gone a long time. I've moved on. I have a new woman now and she gives me just what I want: a warm pussy without so much fucking drama. She doesn't have to be trained, either. She knows how to make a man happy.

 Something permanent was never in my plans and your ass cost me too much. I could hate you for not warning me about your family. I guess I owe you something. I've thrown some money in here for you to disappear. I never want to see you or your child again. As far as I know, the baby is probably Colin's. I'm not about to let you blame me for it.

 Stay away from me and my club. If I even hear you've been trying to talk to me again, I'll make anything Colin would have done to you look like a cakewalk.

           Skull

That's when I see the picture. It's of a man I can only assume is Skull. He's kissing on some tramp's neck, his hand on her naked breast, while she's obviously taking a selfie of them.

 I hold Bethie and let her cry. She trembles in my arms as her dreams come crashing down around her.

 My hand trembles too… but mine is with anger.

PROLOGUE PART TWO
TORCH

"I've never seen him so broken, and I was there when he thought Beth died by his order."

**Almost 2 years later
Meeting with Colin on Paradise Ridge
(mentioned in Craved—Sabre's story)**

"I don't like this, boss."

"That's because it's been damn good not having to deal with that fucker Colin," says Skull.

"Well, yeah, that too. But fuck, man. It's been quiet. What's making him rear his head now?"

"If I knew, I wouldn't be here. Jesus, I move two states away to get away from this asshole and the memories, and here I am again. This crap is never going to leave me alone."

"We could just go, boss."

"Fuck, no. I'm not running from these motherfuckers."

"You ready, *ese?*" asks Diesel. The last couple of years have aged him, too. He's harder than he used to be.

"Ready as I'll ever be," Skull growls, then walks towards the meeting room. Sabre and I fall in step behind him. Crusher, who is now part of Diesel's crew, and another guy come up behind us.

"Jesus fuck, they let anyone in this damn place," I say to Crusher.

"They needed someone to pretty up the place when your damn mug got close."

"Fuck you," I grumble, but the smile freezes on my face as Colin comes into view.

"I thought I told you motherfuckers I wanted nothing to do

with you again," Skull growls, not bothering to sit down. "I meant that shit. I especially meant it with your sorry ass, Colin, so you better have a really good fucking reason for calling this meeting."

"Oh, come on now. You can't be that bitter or you wouldn't have agreed to this meeting," says Colin.

"And just like that, we're done. Contact me one more time and I'll cut your fucking head off. I've got a bigger reach than you these days. Believe me when I tell you, I will not hesitate to destroy you."

"I really don't want to hear your idle threats, Skull. This is a business meeting, nothing more."

"We don't have business. The guys I do business with aren't even in your hemisphere. I give them the word and you're wiped off the map. Understand?"

"I have a proposition for you."

"Not interested."

"It's something I think you would love to be part of."

"Fucking hell. It's like you don't have enough brain power to comprehend what I'm saying to you. *I want nothing to do with you.* I know Matthew said that you had nothing to do with the bomb that killed my man's family, but I don't trust you, and you didn't deny that shit when it first happened. I'd just as soon see your throat slit than talk to you. Now this meeting is done. I knew better than to even show up."

"But you did. Show up, I mean." I watch as my brother's back stiffens. Skull is on a thin line and I know that Colin is pushing it.

"Because I had to wonder what you could possibly think I'd want to meet with you about."

"My grandfather died. Well, he was murdered, really."

"Did you do it?"

"No. That's suicide in the family. There are a few men off-limits in power plays, and my grandfather, he is one. You cannot gain control and respect of the family by taking out the man who is responsible for everything."

"You're saying you fuckers have some morals, even if it is just twisted? Of course this doesn't surprise me, considering you're the same fuck who wanted to stick his dick into his own sister."

"*Step*sister," Colin growls, finally showing signs of losing control, his pale skin going pink.

"Tomato, toe-mat-toe," Skull says, then gives us boys the signal to mount up.

"You disappoint me, Skull. I thought you would at least be interested in knowing who killed my beloved grandfather."

"I figure I already know."

"Is that a fact?"

"Whoever you could manage to pay since your purse strings have been clipped. Torch," he says, facing me, "let's get going. The air here is starting to bother me."

"Sure thing, boss." I'm more than happy to get the fuck out of here myself.

"Colin, in case the message hasn't gotten to you yet, if you step foot into the state of Kentucky, let alone my territory—and that means you and your flunkies, the Chrome Saints—I will call Romanov and he will end all of you. Tempt me to call, Colin. I'd almost plead with you to give me one fucking reason to make sure you stop polluting the air I breathe," Skull warns Colin in a deadly voice.

We all make it to the door before Colin decides to drop the real reason the fucker is here.

"You're rather boring with your threats, and so predictable. My brother Matthew said you wouldn't care anymore. I thought he was wrong."

"I didn't even know your grandfather other than to know the asshole's seed had to have poison in it to have the offspring it did. So no, Colin. I do not give a fuck that your grandfather bit the dust."

"You might change your tune if you knew that he died at the hands of someone you know. Someone you know *very* well. Someone you might even want revenge on."

Skull holds his head down and pinches the bridge of his nose. I can literally feel the tension that comes off of him.

"Say whatever the fucking hell you have to say Colin, because it's obvious that's all this meeting is about. So just spit it out so I can get the fuck out of here."

"I thought you'd like to see your ex-girlfriend again after all these years," Colin says.

I think every breath in my body freezes. What the fuck is going on? If it's sending this amount of shock through me, what in the hell could it be doing to Skull? Nothing shows in his face except anger. You not only see it in his face, you can literally feel that fucking shit.

"What the fuck are you going on about?" Skull asks, his voice so low and deadly you have to strain to hear it.

That's when Colin shoves a folder at him that had been lying on the table where he sits.

"I came here only to give you a gift," he says. "Open it. You'll see how giving I am."

Skull opens the folder. I'm looking over his shoulder, and my stomach drops to my fucking feet when I see what's inside. It's a picture of Beth and another girl standing at a flower stand. She has a baby in a pink outfit on her hip—a baby with dark black hair with small curls. The baby is smiling while Beth kisses the side of the child's face.

Fuck.

"Where did you get this?"

"My men took it. This was the last known sighting of Beth and her sister Katie."

"Where? When? What are you trying to prove here?" Skull growls.

"Ironically enough, Tennessee. Just a month ago."

"What? What are you talking about?"

"I'm telling you that the woman you've been grieving—the woman you thought you killed—has been alive all this time, and hiding."

"You're fucking lying!" Skull yells, his body jerking in fury.

"Am I? Then ask yourself, Skull, why does that child she's holding look so much like you?"

"You're fucking lying!" he screams again.

I see the pain my brother is going through, but all I can do is think back to the phone call I got almost two years ago when I put a drunk and unconscious Skull to bed in his room. *Fuck.*

"After you work it out in your mind, Skull, you might ask yourself two important questions."

"You son of a bitch."

"First, ask yourself why she let you think she was dead this entire time."

"You. Son. Of. A. Bitch."

"Then ask yourself if you can find her before the Saints do, because if I find her first, she's going to die."

"You—"

"She'll have to. The family wants the blood of her and her sister. I only came to warn you because I wanted to see that look on your face."

"You son of—"

"That look right there, the one that says I just destroyed your world... *all over again.*"

With that, Colin leaves. We all stand there frozen, unsure of what to do or say. Skull screams, yanks the table up, and throws it across the room.

Fuck.

TORCH

" The biggest result can be traced back to the smallest of actions. "

"You alright, boss?" I know he's not, but don't know for the life of me what else to say.

"No. And for the record, I wasn't alright the other ninety-nine times you asked me."

We're walking from the garage back to the club. We spent the night in Tennessee, then drove straight here. Skull's barely spoken two words to any of us. He bunked down in Sabre's room last night, but Sabre just shrugged this morning when he came out. Well, no, that's wrong. He shrugged, then put the locket that Skull usually wears around his neck in my hand. It's still in my pocket, in fact. Since the day we discovered it in Pistol's hands when Beth was kidnapped, Skull hasn't taken it off. Not once. It's been almost three years and still it's remained around his neck. The sight of him not wearing it now should bring me joy because I've been hoping he would heal and move on for years. Now, it doesn't. He isn't healed. He removed it because he just learned his grief and mourning have been a *lie*. No one has mentioned it, but everyone's thinking it. It's not even a question anyone seems to be asking. We all believe that Beth is alive. Every last brother here is sure she is, and the kicker is, they don't even know what I do.

I haven't found the right moment to tell Skull about the call I got so long ago from a young woman claiming to have a message from Beth. I wish I could go back, but I can't. I wish I would have went to that hospital and met with the woman. I wish I had at least tried to find out what was going on. It didn't even fucking occur to me that it could be true. People don't just come back from the dead... It just doesn't happen.

We're all sitting around the wooden table in Skull's office now waiting for church to begin. Skull sits at the head of the table, but he's not made any move to begin the meeting. I know I need to confess what I know, and I will. I'm just having trouble finding the words. How do you explain to someone that you are probably the reason why his woman didn't contact him after all this time? If the shoes were reversed, I'd gut me.

"Torch, I need you to start intel," Skull tells me. "Find out any way you can if the picture that Donahue left behind is real. I want to know everything I can about the two women in the photo and the..." he clears his throat before continuing, "the child."

"Got it, boss. I... I wanted to talk about—"

"Start in Tennessee," he goes, "since that's where the fucker said she was. But don't waste a lot of time. Chances are, he fed us wrong information. He's playing with me. I want to say the women in the photo are fakes, but sweet Jesus, it looks so much like… like Beth."

"Boss…"

"You might could try France. If Colin told the truth and they did off the grandfather, that's where he lived. That might be the smartest way to check Colin's story."

"*Boss!*" I growl, this time demanding his attention. Skull stops and, for the first time since the meeting began, looks at me.

"What is it?" he asks.

Here it is: my opening. The time for me to confess. Fucking hell, I've been a member of the Devil's Blaze for a lot of fucking years. Before that, I served my time overseas facing down IED's, enemy fire, and certain death. Still, none of that compares to the knot that's in my stomach right now.

"Boss, do you really think Beth is alive? That she could have somehow survived? And wasn't her sister supposed to be dead, too? This could all be Colin just blowing smoke up our asses while he's starting more shit."

He holds his head down and rakes his fingers through his hair. There's still a small tremor that tells his emotions.

"I think there's a real possibility," Skull confesses. "Colin would have never come at me to rub this shit in if he didn't know for sure. I'm left here feeling fucked up because I want it to be true, but I also don't want it to be. If it's true, that means she has played me all this time. It means… Fuck, Torch, I'm so fucked up I'm not sure what it means."

"Boss, I need to tell you something."

"Can it wait, *mi hermano?* I want to get this done."

"Boss. I think… that woman with Beth in the pictures, her sister… I think she called here."

Skull's face goes cold. It literally freezes almost into stone. I'm proud of myself; a lesser man would shit himself. That's the look I've seen on Skull's face right before people die.

"Explain," Skull says, one terse word while his fists open and close.

"That night at the movie theater before Tiny and all that shit went down... remember? The fight with Dragon?"

"*Si*."

"You were shit-faced, boss. I was just about to leave you to sleep it off and... your cell phone rang. Some chick was on the other end claiming Beth had been coming to find you. She said... fuck, boss. I can't remember what she said. She said there were complications and Beth was at the hospital in London. In the maternity wing—"

Skull roars again. The scream is deep and dark enough to rival that of a wild animal. He jerks the heavy table enough to move it sideways—and that's not an easy feat. Then, he pushes away and grabs me by the neck, pushing me back quickly until I slam into the wall on the other side of the room.

"How could you not tell me that, motherfucker?? How am I just hearing about this right now??" he growls, and I'd answer him but I'm pretty sure he's crushing my trachea right now. "Answer me, you son of a bitch!!"

"Boss, I don't think he can." The words come from Sabre. "He's turning blue." Sabre sounds calm, but I can see his face and there's nothing calm about him. Skull pulls away from me slightly, but not much. I'm not stupid; I know I got a world of hurt coming my way. I welcome it. As much as Skull hates me right now, I hate myself even more. What if that *was* Beth? What if she needed us, and because of me, gave up? Why the fuck did she wait so long to get in touch with us, anyway? There's just so many fucking questions. I try to take air into my lungs without appearing to be a weak son of a bitch whose legs are about to give out on him.

"Boss... I didn't know. I thought someone was fucking with us. We saw that explosion. How could anyone survive that? I helped plant the charges myself. I know the extent of the damage. I just couldn't wrap my head around it. I was sure it was a hoax. I was just trying to prevent... Fuck, Boss. I just wanted to protect you. We all know what losing Beth did to you."

"I don't care what you have to do. You get those records, you get video footage, I do not give a fuck. You get me something I can see in front of me, and do that *yesterday*."

"I already contacted my guy that works in records there, boss. I should have it on my computer."

"Show me."

"It'll just be a file, boss. They don't keep video footage that long. It's been two years."

"Show me what the fuck you got."

I go to the computer to open the email. It's records, mainly. Twenty-year-old woman, emergency caesarian, coded on the table. What was that shit? Then, I see the child's picture and read the birth certificate. *Fucking son of a milk cow.* I print it out and take it to Skull, then wait.

He drops the papers on the table, all except one piece. The birth certificate. His hand shakes, and I know why. I just read it. His voice is thick with emotion.

"I want the original of this picture."

"Yes, boss."

"I fucking want it now."

"Yes, boss," I say again, but this time I start walking to the door. I stop when his voice hits me right before I leave.

"She named the child after my mother…"

"I'll go get the originals."

"Do it. And when you get back, pick two men to go with you."

"Go with me?"

"To Tennessee. You bring back Beth and *mi hijo*. If you can't find them, you bring back her fucking sister. She'll come out of the woodwork for her sister. I want all of them here. Every fucking one of them."

"What if they aren't in Tennessee? What if Colin lied?"

"Then you find out where the fuck they are and you drag them back here. Beast, you and Briar check the streets. See if anything is coming out of Georgia or the Donahue network. I want a full report in an hour."

"I don't think you should let her back in here. We can't survive another fight with the Donahues," says Pistol.

"When your opinion matters to me, I'll let you know. Get the fuck out of here, Torch. You have shit to do."

I nod, then take off. It looks like I'm heading out of state. I just hope it's not a wild goose chase.

Or worse, a trap.

CHAPTER 1
TORCH

"I like women. I like all women. I like them more when they have a little fire inside them."

I kick my feet up on the seat across from me. The chair scoots on the wooden floor, tilts, then rights itself as I cross my legs. Sabre and Latch are going on about some damn trip Lucy wants to go on, a semester at sea or something. They're dying, and Annie is adamant that it's a great opportunity. Those two are like old married men now—even if it is to the same woman. I tune them out.

I *should* be tracking Beth and her sister Katie down. That's what I'm in this blink-and-you-miss-it town for, but hell, I need a day off. I've been working with Diesel and his crew nonstop trying to find these bitches, but they are covering their tracks—and that's putting it lightly. I don't know who they're getting help from, but whoever it is, is damn good. Skull has me, Sabre, and Latch tracking down leads in Texas. Matthew Donahue told Skull he could find them there. Right now, I think the brothers are trying to gain control of the girls first, and using us to do it. It's all a big clusterfuck. Trusting either one of them for information is ridiculous, but Tennessee was a total wash. Skull is looking at other states too and called in some markers. My brother is in bad shape at just the thought that Beth is still alive and has been lying to him this whole time. If it's true—and so far, everything we're learning says it is—then I kind of pity her.

Skull will destroy her.

I'm not thinking about that shit now, though. My eyes and attention are elsewhere. Specifically, on the woman sitting with her back turned to me at the bar. She's got curves to make men fall down on their knees and worship at her feet. Her ass is this perfect pear shape, pushing against that tight little black skirt. It draws a man's eye and makes him want to dig his hands in and hold on for the ride.

"I bet you a C-note you can't tap that," Sabre says, reclining back in his seat.

"You make it too easy. It's like taking candy from a baby," I tell him with an easy grin.

"I don't think so, Torch, brother. Something about that woman says to back the fuck away," Latch warns me.

"You see *that*, and all I see is the warm pussy I'm going to bury myself in for a couple of hours."

"Just a couple of hours?" Sabre teases.

"Yeah. After that, I'm coming back to collect your money." I get up and saunter over to the lady in question.

"Crash and burn, Torch!" he yells out, and I hold my hand over my shoulder to flip him off.

I lean against the bar, standing beside little Miss-make-my-dick-cry-mercy. She's the hottest thing I've seen in a while, which is good because I'd never admit it to those sad fucks back there who are basically sown up over one woman. I haven't found a woman my dick has been interested in for freaking months. Two, to be exact. That might not sound like a lot to some people, but for me, it's a freaking lifetime. My cock is all-in with this little number, though. *Thank God.*

She's a gorgeous brunette. Hell, even with the smoke in the bar and the dim lights, the color glows. It falls in waves down her back and over her shoulders, and I literally ache to wrap my hands in it. Her skin is tanned, and I'd love to lick every inch and see if it tastes half as good as it looks. She's squeezed into a tight black skirt. I've already memorized every curve and pull at the fabric so I can jack off to her later.

But the top is just as good as the bottom. She has the sexiest little black top I've ever laid eyes on. Small black straps caress her shoulders, and silky fabric clasps her breasts close and draws attention to them. Fuck me, they are easily a D-cup or bigger.

Years of experience makes me feel comfortable enough to say that. Still, what really makes my balls heat up is the way her tits keep trying to bust out as if they can't be contained by clothes alone. Those breasts are made for a man's dick to slide in between. My eyes drink it all in. I have to move my hand down to stretch and shift my cock. *Sweet mother of God.* Yeah, he's more than standing at attention for that thick ass, fuck-me tits, and climb-me legs.

She's yet to notice me as she chats with the bartender. It's enough to give a man a complex. I'll have to punish her for that later. The bartender's eyes are glued to her breasts, and I think it's about time that stops. Those are *mine* tonight. He can try again tomorrow after I've finished with her.

I lean down against the bar, look directly at her instead of him. "Jack and Coke," I order, waiting for her to say something.

She stops talking to what's-his-face and turns her attention to me. Green eyes. I don't ever remember having seen eyes this particular color before. I don't think I'll be able to ever forget them now. The color of a murky sea, they draw me in. She looks me up and down while sucking on a straw. She slowly puts her glass down and tilts her head to the side to get a look at me.

I speak first. "Can I buy you a refill?"

She shrugs. "If you want, I won't stop you."

"What are you drinking?"

"White chocolate martini."

"That's not exactly a manly drink to order—"

"I'm not a man."

"Oh, I noticed, girl... I noticed."

"Here's your Jack and Coke," the bartender grumbles over my shoulder. He slams the drink down beside me in a thank-you-for-cock-blocking-me kind of way. He's more than welcome.

"The lady here will have another martini," I tell him while taking my drink and sliding onto the stool beside her.

She watches me drink and shakes her head.

"Something on your mind?" I ask, studying the look in her eyes.

"Just appreciating the fact that my drink wasn't manly enough for a Jack-and-Coke kind of guy." She leans in, smirking.

She's more than halfway drunk, which is kind of a shame, but not a deal breaker by a long shot. She has sass and, fuck, I can definitely appreciate that.

"Don't dis the Coke, man. It lets me stay sober and still get a kick from the Jack... so I can admire your fine ass longer."

"Did you just say *'fine ass'* ...?"

"Oh, yeah. You have one very *fine* ass."

She takes her drink from the bartender without even acknowledging him. I can't help but shoot him a look of victory. Fucker wants to deck me right now.

"Do these lines actually work for you?"

"They've been known to," I answer honestly.

"Damn, I thought I was drunk enough, but apparently I'm not, because so far they're not working at all on my *fine ass*."

"Ouch." I smile, taking another gulp and enjoying this conversation way more than I would have thought.

"In fact," she adds, leaning in closer to me, and I can only hope her breasts come out to play as she leans further—surely another inch and nipples will be visible. "You could even say I'm kind of... *bored*."

Those words would chill a lesser man, but the light in her eyes and the smile on her face tell me different. I put my drink down, then move my finger along the side of her face.

"I sure wouldn't want to bore you. How about we leave this place and go play Barbie?"

She looks at me, genuinely confused.

"Barbie?"

I lean in close to her ear, inhaling her scent. Sweet and sugary like cookies. Damn... just *damn*.

"Yeah. I'll be Ken, and you can be the box I come in," I whisper against her ear. I mean, really, can I help it if my lips graze against it?

She grows still, then pulls away from me.

"Did you really go there just now?" she asks like she can't

quite believe it. She's shaking her head and laughing, and she does *not* look bored.

Score one for me. "Figured I better come at you with my A-game," I joke, taking another drink.

"Good plan, Romeo. Not sure this romance could survive your B-game."

"What's your name, pretty girl?"

"Oh man, you are cheesy."

"I do try. Come on, give me your name."

She stops and looks at me for a minute, and it's almost as if she's trying to place me, but then she shrugs it off.

"We won't know each other long enough to have to worry about using names."

"Is that so?"

"That's a fact."

I lean in to whisper for her ears only. "My name's Hunter. You need to remember it so you can scream it out tonight."

She leans in to me, and her sweet scent claims me. "I'll do that very thing, Hunter. I'll scream it so hard my landlord will think someone is killing me."

"*Now* we're talking." My dick is rock hard as she gets up. She starts to walk around me and I grab her arm, unable to ignore the way her warm skin sends an electric current through my body. "Where are you going?"

"I figured I'd better hurry before the store closes."

"The store?"

"Yeah, Hunter. I'm all out of batteries. I'll need them tonight, when I'm in bed alone, but don't worry. I'll remember your name when I make myself come."

CHAPTER 2
KATIE

> *I gave up on fairytales. They're always backwards. In real life, Prince Charming might marry Snow White, but he's busy boning Little Miss Muffet two nights a week.*

He's a player. I spotted him a mile away.

But I also remember him. He's with my sister's husband's crew. What was it she said his name was? Torch? I like Hunter better. I should be running away from him, and I started to. Then, he touched my arm. In that moment, I felt connected to him. I don't know how to describe it, but I did. My life hasn't been my own from the day my father took me away from my mom and my sister, Bethie. I've learned to take my pleasure where I can find it. Something about Hunter, or Torch—whoever he is—calls to me, and I'm going to throw caution to the wind. Still, I need to make sure I've protected Bethie and her daughter Gabriella.

"I'll bring you more pleasure than anything with batteries, sweetness."

I wonder if he really thinks these lines work? He's a man, so he probably does, when really it's that fucking body of his that's working for me. He's got that 'V', I just know it. You know the one—the finely chiseled indention that starts along the hip bone and runs lower into the promise land? The one that makes all women lose their minds? It's there and, by God, I want to see it.

I just need to do one thing first. "Well, I need to use the little girl's room. So, I'll think about it. In the meantime, you just sit there and look pretty."

"I'll sit here and admire the view instead," he tells me.

That's just annoying. He doesn't realize that's the one thing he could say that would turn me off. Still, I know he's watching, and it kills me, but I wore the right shoes tonight to hide my limp, so I take all the energy and focus I have into making sure my steps don't falter. When I make it to the little foyer that leads to the bathrooms, I lean against the wall and breathe. After I make sure he didn't follow me, I head into the bathroom. Luckily it's a single-stall bathroom, so I lock the door, pull myself up on the counter, and call Bethie.

"We have problems," I tell her right away.

"What? Where are you? Are you in trouble? I told you, you need to stop running around. They can find us."

"Will you relax? I don't look anything like you anymore... or myself, for that matter. Between the hair dye, the colored contacts, and thirty pounds I've packed on my ass, I don't even recognize my own damn self in the mirror."

"It's too dangerous. You know they will be hunting for us. Especially now that grandfather—"

"Don't call him that. Anyway, that's kind of why I'm calling. I'm at the Broke Spoke and... there's this guy hitting on me. He says his name is Hunter, but..."

"But?" she asks, her voice laced with fear.

"It's that same good-looking biker that was at the movie theater that night with Skull."

"Oh God! You have to run, Katie! If one of Skull's crew is there, that means he has to know. Colin's carried out on his threat."

"Bethie, have you ever thought... maybe, just maybe, it'd be best to come clean and try to let Skull know you're alive? He might be more reasonable now."

"We tried that, remember? Three times. I can't risk it anymore, especially with the family out there looking for us. Do you really think they will let me, you, or Gabby live? After what we did?"

She's right. They wouldn't. They won't stop until we're six feet under. "Okay. Then you need to start our escape plan, tonight. Take Gabby and go. I'll meet you in the morning."

"What? No! You need to come home now. We can't chance that whoever is there might place our resemblance and start asking questions."

"That's not going to happen, Bethie. You worry too much."

"And *you* don't worry enough. Please, Katie, do this for me. Come home and let's head out together."

"I'll try my best, but—"

"'But' nothing! Just—"

Before she finishes talking, there's a hard knock on the door. "Sweetness? You in there? I'm getting lonely out here without you."

"My God!" Bethie hisses over the phone. "Is that Torch??"

Hmmm. I guess I did forget to mention which one was here, probably because she knows that fine man starred in several of my hot dreams after I saw him that one night.

"I'll be out in a minute," I call to him through the door. "Anyone ever tell you that you shouldn't crowd a woman, Romeo?"

"I'm too busy fucking them senseless to listen to advice," he counters.

"Bethie, I've got to go," I whisper. "Just follow the escape plan we set up when we moved here. If something happens and I don't show, move on to our next destination. I'll meet you there. I promise."

"No, I don't like this. I can call the cops or something, make a fake report and distract them, then we—"

"I got this, just get my niece safe."

"You and I are going to have words when you make it to our spot," she warns me.

"I'll look forward to it. Stay safe, Bethie. Love you bigger than outer space."

"Love you, too," she whispers.

I hang up, trying to swallow down my nerves. I open the door. Sure enough, there's the object of my lust, leaning against the wall with a wicked smile. He holds out a hand to me.

"Dance with me, sweetness. I want to feel you in my arms."

I let him take my hand, and I know I'm going to ignore my sister's plea tonight. I just hope I don't live to regret it.

CHAPTER 3
TORCH

"It's the thrill of the chase. It all goes downhill once you catch them."

I pull the hot little number to me. She stumbles slightly. I guess that means I have her off balance. I like that. I plan to do my best to keep her that way. I lead her on the dance floor, finding a dark corner away from the others. She comes into my arms, filling my hands completely.

We sway back and forth. At first she feels stiff, but it only takes a few minutes before she relaxes and wraps her arms over my shoulders, linking her hands behind my neck. She stares up at me with those eyes. They're gorgeous, but something isn't sitting right with them. I push the thought away, though, because my dick is loving how it feels to rub against her stomach. Fucker is standing at attention and literally crying in need.

"I thought you were going to back out on me."

"What is there to back out on? It's just a dance," she answers, and when her voice is dropped down this low, there's a rawness to it that appeals to me even more.

"Sweetness, we both know this game, and it's going to end in a bed, not on a dance floor."

"You're awful sure of yourself. Maybe I just want to dance," she responds.

"I'm giving you that. When the time is right, I'll show you the kind of dancing I *really* excel at."

She watches me without talking, our bodies moving together in a rhythm as if we've danced together our whole lives. Then, she finally speaks up.

"I'll think about it, Romeo."

In response, I let my hand trail down to the edge of her skirt. I gather the tight, stretchy material in my hand. She stumbles, looking wildly around us. It's unexpected, but I like it. She may know all about the game, but she obviously hasn't played it with a man like me. I almost regret that I can't keep her for a couple of nights. She'd be some damn good fun, and maybe she'd wake my dick up to what he's been missing.

It is what it is, though, and it's for the best. Something in her eyes tells me she might be the type to get attached.

"Hunter," she gasps.

I like my name on her lips. I like it almost as much as I'm going to like using my cock to rub my pre-cum on them. Will she taste me quickly, or use that sweet little tongue I keep getting a glimpse of every now and then to lick it up? I'm going to fucking find out tonight. That much, I can promise myself.

She's made no move to stop my hand. In fact, her hips thrust so her body rubs harder against my cock. I call that a green light, so I let my entire hand disappear under her skirt. Her hands slide down to my shoulders. I hum in approval as her fingernails bite into my flesh. I can feel the sharp sting even through my clothes. This girl is going to be a fucking wildcat in bed. I push my hand between her legs. I work my three fingers between the thin fabric and her heated center.

"Spread your legs slightly, sweetness."

"What are you doing?"

"I'm going to finger your hot little pussy."

"Right here?" she asks, but she doesn't sound scandalized at all. There might be a hint of fear in her words, but it's the excitement in her voice calling to me.

"Right here. Right now." When her legs spread just a mere inch, I smile in victory and reward her by taking her mouth and kissing the hell out of her.

CHAPTER 4
KATIE

" *I was right: he is trouble. Good thing I'm only using him for the night. I don't think I could handle him for more than that.* **"**

I thought I've been kissed before. *I haven't.* That much is clear the minute his lips take mine. His tongue dives into my mouth without asking for permission. He seeks, plunders, and owns me with just the warring of his tongue against mine. I concede. I give him victory. There's no way I could fight it. He dominates me and I can't stop the whimper of unhappiness when he pulls away, taking his wicked tongue with him. I follow it, needing more, already addicted to the taste of him.

"Fuck," he whispers.

Slowly, I open my eyes to look up at him. He's so beautiful, he makes my pussy clench in need just from the look on his face right now. His hair is a cross between light brown and a hint of gold. It's clipped short, but the top is long with the ends curly and lying lazily on his head. It invites a woman to run her fingers through it—a woman like *me*. His eyes are green, but not like mine. No, these are *real,* and they sparkle. I can see the color glisten even in this dark corner. They sparkle with a joy that says he doesn't have a care in the world. I want to experience that for just one minute. *I want that look.* What would it feel like to not have worries? To not have people depending on you to keep them safe? To never worry about monsters lurking in the darkness? *What would that feel like?*

My sister is going to kill me, but I'm going to sample this long, tall drink of sin standing before me. Bethie wouldn't understand, but then again... I'm not my sister. My life has never known a moment of certainty in it. She at least had *that* for a while. That's just not in the cards for me. So, if I can find joy in the arms of a man, I will, and that's exactly what I'm going to do tonight.

Bethie hasn't said, but I'm pretty sure Skull is the only man that she has ever opened her legs for. The bad part of that is, I don't think she will ever allow herself to be available to anyone else ever again. Guys flirt with her all the time and she doesn't even notice. I got after her about it once, but she told me all she had time for was Gabby. The sadness in her eyes called her a liar, but I let it pass. I keep hoping that maybe someday she will heal.

I pull my attention back to the man in front of me. His fingers are gently brushing back and forth against the wet lips of my pussy. They don't try to slip inside. No, instead, he just uses them to lightly pet my pussy in time with the music. It's a small tease, forecasting what's to come, and it sends delicious chills running through my body.

"What are you thinking about, sweetness?"

"You."

"Now, I don't want to call you a liar," he says, "but your face went a million miles away. That's okay. I know just what to do to bring you back to me."

"Is that so?" I ask, trying to ignore how perceptive he is.

"Definitely."

Then, I feel his fingers brush against my slick clit. My breath lodges in my chest and I can't help but look around. People are dancing just a few feet away from us. I'm in a room with hundreds of people, and when I feel his fingers glide down my wet pussy into my opening, I don't make one protest.

"You're so fucking wet. I could slam balls-deep into your pussy in one easy glide. Is that what you want, dirty girl? Do you want me to fuck you right here with everyone around?" his dark voice asks against my ear. His breath, just another sensation to the hundreds that are already bombarding me when his fingers thrust deep inside.

It takes my breath away, the feel of him sliding inside of me, despite being in this room. I know only a moment of panic. I might try to enjoy sex when I can, but I've never been an exhibitionist. I suddenly feel like I am in over my head here.

"Give me your name, sweetness."

"Why?" I gasp as he angles his fingers differently, hitting me in a way I'm not sure I've been touched before.

"I want to know it before you come all over my hand."

Fuck. I want him to say my name too, but I can't chance it. I may look nothing like Bethie anymore, but the resemblance is there. Giving him my name is just too much to gamble. I wet my lips and bite them to keep the moan of disappointment contained when he stops moving his fingers.

"Your name, sweetness," he urges, bending into me and whispering into my ear.

I swallow, prepared to lie, but it's hard. The truth is there and I want to scream it. I want to hear this beautiful man call my name all night. Being denied that is a physical pain.

"Holly," I blurt out, grasping at the first name that comes to mind.

"Good girl. Here's what we're going to do, Holly." His fingers begin petting me again, sliding in and out of my pussy so slowly he might be driving me insane. "Are you listening?"

"Yes?" It comes out as a question because I'm not listening, not really. I'm concentrating on the way his hand is manipulating my pussy and how his thumb is stroking my clit.

"Good girl. I'm going to take my hand away. I'm going to go tell my men I'm gone for the night. You're going to wait right here for me. Then, to reward you for being such a good girl, I'm going to take you out back to the supply closet by the bathrooms I found earlier and fuck you hard. When I'm done there, you and I are going to blow this joint and really party."

His words do strange things to me. Before I can even catch my breath, he takes his hand away and I instantly miss it. Suddenly the music sounds louder, and the noise of the crowd rushes into my ears. Apparently I had everything blocked out except the sound of Torch's voice. I feel heat rise in my face as I look around. No one seems to be noticing.

He kisses the top of my head, then pulls away completely. I can't help but watch him walk away and admire the way his ass looks in those jeans. He looks over his shoulder at me, catching me red-handed, but I just smile, which in turns makes his lips turn up. "This is going to be so good, Holly," he says back to me. "So fucking good."

And just like that, the excited haze he has me in is gone. *Holly*… I don't like him calling me *Holly*.

Bethie's right. I can't have him. I watch as he walks over to his buddies and they're laughing. I can't hear what they say, though I'm sure Torch is telling them he's hooking up with some chick he just met. *Me*. It's not like I've done this a lot, but it has never bothered me before when it did happen.

So, why does it bother me now?

I can't do this. I'm playing with fire. I look around the club, searching for the back exit. When I spot it, I head immediately in its direction.

CHAPTER 5
TORCH

"Fuck, she's perfect."

I'm walking towards my brothers, but in my mind, I'm seeing Holly's tongue sliding against her lips as I finger her tight little pussy. I'm thinking of the way her fingers hold onto me. Hell, they were clawing into my back. I wouldn't be surprised if she drew blood under my shirt.

"Hey, boys. I'm heading out. I'll meet you back at the motel later tonight."

"Is that a fact?" Sabre asks.

"Yeah. And you, you tight son of a bitch... you owe me money, and I'll expect that when I get in later."

"That's interesting. If you actually did hook up with her, where is she?"

"Just never mind, Sabre. I have plans for sweet Holly. If you're nice, I may show you pictures tomorrow. She's hot as fuck and begging for dick, man. Just like I like them."

"That's really weird," Latch speaks up, staring at his beer.

"What the hell are you talking about?"

"Well, if you're hooking up with her tonight, why is she sneaking out back?"

"What?" I spin around. "What the fuck??" Sure enough, Holly's sneaking out the back entrance. That little cock tease! "Son of a bitch-whore!"

Sabre and Latch laugh and laugh. *Annoying bastards.* I turn to flip them off, then take off to capture the little tease who thought she could play me, but the look on Sabre's face stops me.

"I might have been wrong, Torch, my boy."

37

"I'm not your motherfucking boy," I grumble back. "What in the hell are you talking about anyways?"

Maybe I should let the chick go. She's hot as hell, but I just need my dick wet. I ain't chasing after no pussy. I ignore the pain in my dick that calls me a fucking liar. Motherfucker will take whatever pussy I give him. He's been too fucking choosy lately.

"She might be right up your alley. Make you work for it. I can't remember a bitch turning you down in a long ass time."

"That's because it hasn't fucking happened."

"Don't look now, amigo, but looks like it just did," Latch joins in.

"We'll see about that."

I head out the front, intent on finding the bitch who thought it'd be fun to give me blue balls tonight. Once outside, I look around. It takes a minute for my eyes to adjust to the dark. Then, I see the minx walking along the side of the building and heading to a yellow Jeep Wrangler. Why does that surprise me? I don't know what I expected her to drive, but this wasn't it.

It's then that I notice something I hadn't before. Maybe I was too horny or distracted by her fucking gorgeous boobs, hell if I know, but I see it now: the limp. She has trouble when she walks, unable to support her weight on her right leg. I see her grimace in pain, and find myself worrying about her.

What the fuck is that? I don't *worry* about bitches. She owes me a fuck, and that's it. I push anything else out of my head. I move to intercept her, trying to keep my eyes off her legs. So she's limping. Maybe she twisted her ankle trying to get away from me. The thought makes me mad all over again. If she didn't want to start our little game, the bitch shouldn't have led me on.

I grab her arm at the Jeep. Her soft gasp travels through the night air and she goes completely still. I pull her back hard, ignoring the spasm of guilt I feel when she falls awkwardly against my body—another sign she has a problem with her leg. Not that it matters. This is about fucking. I don't need to know her life's story.

Not at all.

Chapter 6
Katie

" Regrets, I have a few. He might be my biggest yet. "

It's probably no longer than five minutes since I made my escape, but it feels like a freaking hour. I should have ran the minute I met him. Bethie was right. I shake my head at my own stupidity and start walking faster towards my Jeep. I'm probably too buzzed to drive, but I can hide there and use my phone to call a taxi. I'm almost to the vehicle. I can see the bright yellow glow of it under the street light's ray.

A hand locks around my upper arm and I gasp in surprise, because I didn't even hear anyone behind me. Before I can scream, I'm pulled against Torch. I may have only danced with him once, but I instantly know it's his body, his heat behind me. His large arm locks around my stomach, not letting me move an inch. His other hand pulls the hair from my neck a little too roughly, but the sting of pain only amplifies my anticipation.

"I thought I told you not to go anywhere, sweetness?"

"You took too long," I say in my defense, my voice hoarse. Even I can hear the need in it.

"Something you should know about me," he says against my neck, his voice dark and hard. A chill runs down my spine, but I wouldn't say it was from fear—*I wouldn't say that at all.*

"What's that?" I ask, trying to keep my mind on his words and not on the hand pushing my dress up.

The chill of the night air hits my ass and I swallow as I look around to see if anyone can see us. The way he has his mouth against my neck though, I can't turn. I'm about to complain when the sound of ripping fabric reverberates through the air.

Then he pulls my underwear from my body. The wind blows against my exposed pussy and my panic kicks up a notch. I try to look around again but he doesn't let me.

"I don't like to be disobeyed."

"But—"

"And I don't like to be argued with. You're going to have to be punished, Holly," he growls. His words should scare the hell out of me. Instead, I feel moisture pool on the inside of my thighs.

His hand palms my ass and he gives it a squeeze. I should hate it because he's definitely not concerned with who is around when he manhandles me. He's not being gentle either, and he's threatening to *punish* me. I don't hate it. In fact, when he pulls me back, half-dragging me about ten spaces, I feel completely at his mercy. My body must love that because I am wetter than I have ever been in my life. He turns us around and I'm standing in front of a bike. I don't get time to ask him what he's doing before he pushes me over the seat of it so my stomach is against the cushioned area. I pull against his hold, trying to get away from him, not sure of what he's doing. Blood rushes through my system and now it is a mixture of excitement and fear because he has me pinned to the seat of the bike—refusing to let me move. His other hand pulls my skirt up around my hips, exposing me completely.

"Hunter…"

"Don't speak unless I tell you to," he growls. It's then that I know I'm not prepared for all that is Torch. He seemed so easygoing, so laidback when he was flirting with his cheesy pick-up lines. He's anything but, now.

"But…" I start again, the panic rising inside of me.

His hand leaves my ass. I think he's finally going to let me go. I plan to jump in my jeep and get the fuck out of here. I try to pull myself up, but he pushes down harder on my back.

"Hunter," I growl, getting pissed off now. Bethie and I have taken self-defense classes. It's one of the first things we did when we escaped France, but I've already let myself get in this position and my brain is foggy from the mixture of booze and sexual awareness that I can't for the life of me remember what the instructor told us to do in this situation. You know, besides *not* getting yourself into this situation. That was probably mentioned. *I'm an idiot.*

Then, I feel his hand connect with my ass with a loud noise. *Crack!* The sound erupts as skin connects to skin and it feels like fire hits me.

"Hunter!" I shout, but again he spanks me. *He spanks me.* I've never been spanked in my life. My father never bothered when we were younger, and when I got older, his punishment was more about punching than spanking. "Stop! What are you doing??" I ask inanely, my ass feeling as if it is on fire.

"The more you talk, the harder I'm spanking this ass, Holly. So keep it up, sweetness, because I like it. Your ass is all pink now, but I'm still going, and it's going to be blood red. I'm okay with that. More than okay, because when I'm done, I'll fuck you so hard that every time I thrust against you, it will hurt, and you won't forget me for a fucking long time."

That shuts me up. It stops me for many reasons. The largest being: I went from contemplating a one-night stand with a man who is dangerous to me and my sister, to having my ass out in the night waving at anyone who wants to see and being reprimanded like a little girl. The thing is, it doesn't feel like that. No. With each connection of his hand, my body's reaction changes. Somewhere along the way, it's no longer a punishment. The pain mingles with other feelings, even as tears sting my eyes. When his big hand caresses my tender flesh, I can't stop the moan that tumbles out of my lips.

"Please," I whimper.

Torch bends down and kisses the top of my ass, and I can't help but push up into the touch. Then, he stretches out over top of me. The rough material of his jeans rubs against the burning skin of my ass, and the scrapes cause more pain, but somehow even that feels good. He grabs my hair and pulls so I have to raise my head, then bites the shell of my ear. His hand goes down between my legs and he drags his fingers through the creamy wetness that has gathered. I can't even manage to feel shame over that; my body loves what he's doing to it.

"Please what, Holly? Please fuck you?" he growls, and that hurt rises again at being called another woman's name. I want to hear him say Katie. I want to hear my name in that rough voice he has right now.

"Not here," I tell him. "Not like this."

I expect him to ignore me. It shocks me when he doesn't. Instead, he pulls my skirt back down over my ass and lets me up. He helps me to sit on his bike. I want to argue that I need my car, but can't seem to find the words, so I just go where he leads me. He gets on the bike in front of me and my hands wrap around him, holding on tight, my legs clenching his body.

"Hold on," he orders, then takes off. I lay my head on his shoulder and do just what he tells me to.

CHAPTER 7
TORCH

"Fuck. She's special."

Jesus Christ on a bed of nails, this woman may be the death of me. I was so pissed at her for trying to skip out that I just intended to tell her what I thought of cock teases, then go find a willing woman. End of story. Done. Kaput. Then, I touched her and pulled her body back against mine. Her little moan drove me crazy. Just a simple thing really, but coupled with the way her body felt against me and the way she filled my hands... I reacted without thought. I bared her ass right there and marked her with my hand over and over, and with each outline of my hand on her creamy ass, I knew... I knew I was playing with fire.

She's special. She makes me react in ways I haven't with another woman, which is crazy bad, because this is just a one night fuck fest. But, by God, I'm going to make sure she remembers me for a fucking long time once we're done. I'll mark her so that any man she touches after tonight can't live up to the night we shared.

That stupid pain in my chest hits me again and I'm fucking tired of that. Whatever it is, that's her fault too, and I'll punish her for that along with the rest. I take her back to the motel that the boys and I have been staying in. It's a cheap dump, but we stay there because it limits the attention we receive. These kinds of places usually operate on cash only and they don't give a fuck who stays here as long as they get paid. I thought about finding some place nicer to bring her to, then got pissed off again. This is a quick fuck—a bang it and forget it. I'll be damned if I treat her any different than I would any of the other pussy I've had.

I pull around to the back, parking outside the window of my room. Thankfully, I'm not sharing with one of the other guys. I try not to, though sometimes we do just for safety's sake. Latch and Sabre are sharing this time around, but I suspect it's for other reasons. I don't think my brothers get off with each other, though if they did, whatever, good for them. I'm suspecting little Miss Annie puts on a show for them nightly. She might be claimed by Sabre, but it hasn't escaped anyone's attention that the three of them have their own thing going.

I help Holly off my bike and walk her to the door with one arm around her. I do this partly because now I don't trust her not to flee again, and partly because I just fucking love the feel of her in my arms. We barely make it inside before I slam the door and spin her around so she's pushed up against it. My lips find hers, my tongue thrusting into her mouth, desperate for another taste of her. She's pure sweet nectar, her flavor bursting in my mouth and making me groan as our tongues fight with each other for dominance. Her hands push at my cut, pulling it from my shoulders. I help by letting one arm go outwards and pulling it free, then copying the action with my other arm. I can't use both at once; I have to touch her, keep contact with her.

My hands immediately go back to her body, holding onto her hips and pulling her against my cock because even covered up, the fucker wants her close. Her sharp little claws bite into my sides when her hands sneak under to pull my shirt up.

"Your shirt... take your shirt off," she mumbles against my lips when we break away to drag oxygen into our lungs.

I growl because I don't want to stop touching her. I do, but grudgingly. I throw my shirt to the floor. My reward is when her sharp little teeth bite into my stomach. She sucks the abused skin in her mouth, letting her tongue pet it, all while her nails dig into my back. *Jesus. Fuck.* She's so hungry for it, she's on fire. She kisses up to my shoulders, then bites me, my dick jerking in reaction. Her hands go down to the button on my jeans. They give, and then her hand slides inside to wrap around my cock.

That's my cue to remind her who's in charge.

I pull her arms up, capturing both wrists in one of my hands, then pin them above her head. My other hand wraps around her neck and I force her head back against the door. I don't squeeze, but I exert enough pressure that she opens those emerald green eyes and stares at me. Her sweet, pink tongue that I've been playing with comes out to lick her lips. Her breathing is hard and ragged when I give my order.

"You don't touch my cock until I give you permission."

In response, she tries to pull her body away from the door, pushing against me. I tighten my hold on her neck to stop her.

"Quit teasing me!" she huffs, and that's just further proof that this little girl has no idea who she's dealing with tonight.

"You want it all, baby? You can have it. Just remember, you asked for it." That's the only warning she's getting. Too bad it's too late for her to do anything about it.

CHAPTER 8
KATIE

" I had no idea ... "

Do I want all of it? Is that really a question? I want to tell him to quit talking and show me more action. I don't get the chance because he grabs the bottom edge of my shirt and pulls it over my head. Cool air meets my heated flesh and chills of excitement break out over my body.

"Take off the skirt, Holly. Leave your boots on," he orders, his voice dark. At the mention of the fake name, my excitement cools, but I do my best to block it out. I push my nerves—and my skirt—down. I can't exactly shimmy out of it. My leg doesn't allow for that, and I don't want Torch to see my injury—my weakness. My father and grandfather spent way too much time finding my weaknesses and using them against me. No man, *no person*, will ever do that to me again.

Torch has his zipper undone and his cock out, stroking it as he watches me. The sight makes heat run through me and it feels like every female part of me might spontaneously combust. I may not be as pure as my sister, but I've not exactly been with a huge number of men, either. Six, in total. Seven if you count Torch, and he should most *definitely* count. His dick is a work of art. It's large, though not huge. Still big enough that it will take effort to work him inside of me. And he's *wide*. He's so fucking thick and wide that being with him may destroy me. He's more beautiful than any work of art. As he moves his hand back and forth stroking himself, I pull my eyes up to take in his face. The obvious pleasure he gets from it and the lust in his eyes make my knees weak. Praise Jesus, I want to get down on my knees and worship at the altar of Torch. No wonder he's a cocky asshole; women probably throw themselves at him for just a small taste once they see him. Who could blame them?

"You're fading away from me, Holly. Eyes and mind, on *me*. Get rid of the bra," he orders, and it may be my imagination but his voice seems darker and huskier than before. I don't think to question him. My hands go immediately to my bra to do as he orders. "Stop. Turn around. I want to see your ass."

I look up at him questioningly. I mean, that's fine, it's even kind of hot, but is there a problem with the rest of me? I ignore the voices in my head that tap into my own insecurities and turn from him. Then I take off my bra. I hold it away from my body, looking over my shoulder at him as I drop it to the floor.

"Like this?"

He still stands there firmly stroking his cock. He's kicked his boots off, but his pants are still up. I guess I should just thank God he goes commando because at least there's nothing in the way of that beautiful cock and the show he's putting on.

"Your ass is red. Does it still burn, sweetness?"

There's no mistaking the need in his voice. It makes my pussy spasm.

"It feels… hot…"

"It looks fucking hotter," he says. I bite my lip, wanting to moan as he keeps stroking himself. I can see pre-cum leaking over the head of his cock and flowing down on his hand as he works himself. "Get on the bed. Stomach down." Nerves float through me. I lean down to unhook my boots and he growls. "Leave the fucking boots on, Holly, and the next time you bend over like that, you best be prepared to have my cock buried in your ass. Now get on the bed."

Oh, wow. Okay. I mean, I like my boots. They hide the fact that one leg isn't exactly right and they do it in style, but I never imagined wearing them while being fucked. I'm not sure what it is about Torch that makes that seem like the hottest thing ever.

I walk carefully over to the bed, hating that I'm terrified of stumbling and having him discover there's something *off* with me. I take a deep breath and get on the bed, face down. I hear him padding heavily over to me even without his boots. I twist to get a better look at him, but he stops me.

"Chin to the bed. Look straight ahead, Holly. Don't turn around." His orders are short and commanding and I obey, then wince at how easily I'm falling under his spell.

"Yes, master," I grumble under my breath, upset with myself more than him. Truthfully, everything he does is hot. I just never thought I'd be *that* woman—the one to follow commands so easily. I stop thinking when his hand comes down hard on my ass. The skin is already battered and reddened from his earlier attention, and as his hand connects with the tender flesh, tears immediately spring to my eyes and I cry out.

"Don't smart off to me, Holly. I can promise you, I'll make you regret it."

"You'd hurt me?" I ask. I hate the fear in my voice. I know more about hurt than most people. The fact that Torch might be a man who would hurt another person twists inside of me.

He spanks me, harder this time, and then again. "I'd only stretch your limits and the things I do to you will always end in pleasure. But if you ask me such a horrible question again, sweet Holly, I'll torture your body until you're begging constantly to come, and I won't let you. I won't let your body have a release for hours and hours," he says, delivering another blow.

"Hunter!" I cry out, and he does it again… and again. Each time, I know he's taking care with me. His hand connects and then soothes the skin, and he spaces each spanking out. I register that, and it does something to the inside of me. At the same time, it hurts and the pain makes my body quake. He reaches around me. I see a quick blur of white and the next thing I know he's lifting my ass up and pushing a pillow under my stomach. He angles my body by using the pillows from the bed and his hands. He gets me exactly where he wants me: head down and ass up in the air. Then, he pulls my legs apart and puts himself between them. I know because the rough material of his jeans brushes against my thighs. His hand moves over my ass, the skin cool

and feeling good against my heated body. I moan when his lips touch the same places. His tongue follows the path and I grow louder in my appreciation.

"You like that, sweetness?" he whispers.

"Yes." I can't even deny it—not that it would help. I know he can tell by the way my body thrusts towards him, wanting more attention. When his tongue glides over my ass cheek to slide in the valley between, my body stiffens. "Hunter..."

"Shh," he whispers, his hands pulling on my cheeks and widening the gap, and I know why because I feel his hot breath and his tongue slipping further towards the small round entrance to my ass. My body trembles. This is uncharted territory for me and I'm not sure what to expect. When his tongue darts around the opening and then plays just on the side, I instinctively tighten my muscles there to ward off his entrance. Surely he doesn't mean to... I mean not... *there*. Then, when I feel his mouth attack me, I forget to question *anything*. He pulls my ass into him as he uses his lips and his tongue to torture my hole. Pushing his tongue inside a little deeper and licking all around the rim of the opening, he drags his teeth over the area and bites the flesh when he can. So much is hitting me at once. It's like nothing I've ever experienced before and I'm pretty sure I never will again.

I don't think I was prepared for Torch.

CHAPTER 9
TORCH

"It's just one night..."

I hear myself, but I can't stop it. It's a one night stand for Christ's sake. Still, I find myself fantasizing about keeping her longer. *About fucking her longer. About teaching her how to please me... longer.* It's all in my head and it's fucking with me. None of it is her fault, but motherfucker, I'm going to take my frustrations out on her body.

I work my tongue around the ring of her ass, coating it. I want to fuck her ass, but I can tell from her reaction that's she's never had a cock there before. My dick is wide and there's no way I can fuck a virgin ass without preparing it. If I had more time...

I growl and bite into the check of her ass while pushing my fingers further down, finding her pussy. God, she's so wet, it feels like she already came. I let my fingers play in her cream, petting her poor swollen clit. The fucker is pulsating it needs to come so bad. Next go around, I'm going to torture it with my mouth. Jesus, I bet I could almost drown from her orgasm when I'm eating out this juicy cunt.

I bring my fingers back to her ass, pulling my face away so I can watch as I paint that perfect little hole with the sweet liquid from her pussy. Fucking beautiful, and only more so when I take my index finger and thrust it into the small hole. The opening stretches, making way for it and tightening at the same time.

"Oh, God... What are you doing?" she moans.

"You like that, baby? Does it feel good? Do you like having my fingers ass-fucking you?"

I move my finger around on the inside of her as she slowly takes it in past my knuckle. *Jesus, fuck.* It's so damned tight and it's just my finger in there. Pre-cum pours off the head of my cock, begging me to let it inside her. *How I wish I could.*

"I have a pussy!" she growls. I grin because she's testing me yet again. If I had more time, I would spend the whole night with her body on the brink of orgasm and never giving it to her.

More time…

Just thinking that pisses me off yet-the-fuck-again, so I thrust another finger inside her ass without warning.

"Fuck!" she growls, her ass going back at the intrusion. I bite down on her cheek, not even trying to be gentle. My fingers pound her tight little hole, my teeth mark her ass hard, and I pull my fingers apart inside of her, stretching her just because I fucking can. She's into it because she's tightening against my fingers trying to ride them, trying to fucking break them, she's sucking them so tight. "Hunter!" she calls out, and I can hear the break in her voice.

She's close to coming and I've barely started.

I pull my hand out at the same time my teeth release her ass. I let my tongue soothe the bite.

"Holly." She keeps whimpering and trying to thrust her ass back onto me, begging for my fingers again. "Holly!" I command louder. Her body freezes. She turns her head to the side to look at me. "Reach into the nightstand and get me a condom."

She swallows, looking at me. Fuck, I'm even entranced by the way her throat moves. How will it move when it's stuffed full of my dick? That's one thing I will definitely find out tonight. There's something in her eyes, but I don't have time to figure out what it is; my own are just too full of fucking lust. I need to come and I need to come now.

She stretches away from me, but I keep a hold of her ass, not letting her go too far. She reaches in and then throws a bunch of condoms back at me. I grin. There's at least eight, maybe more.

"That's a lot of condoms." I tear open the foil on one of them with my teeth, then slide the fucker down on my dick.

BURNED

"Oh, well, if you're not up to the challenge…"

I'm sliding my latex-covered cock around her pussy, teasing her clit while at the same time covering it in her cream. At her words, though, I decide I shouldn't be nice, so I move my dick to her pussy and thrust inside, quick and hard, and I don't stop until my balls are pushing against her wet core.

"Son of a bitch!" she shouts out, but her pussy spasms on my cock already, primed to come.

"What's wrong, sweetness?" I ask her while I use my hold on her hips to adjust her body the way I want it. I slant her so that my dick will rake her womb in a tilted direction. Then, I move over her body, stretching across her. I know my rough jeans are scratching against her tender ass and I know it stings—I can tell by the way that hissing noise leaves her lips. My hands find her breasts and I squeeze the fullness of them. She's completely underneath me, at my mercy, and her pussy is stretched to the limit with my cock. It feels fucking perfect.

"Jesus, you're packing a cannon," she groans as I pull back, then slam inside of her even harder than before.

"That's right, sweetness, and it's all fucking loaded to explode inside you. Now, hold the fuck on," I growl, slamming into her again.

"Hunter!" she calls, but I'm too far gone. I handle her breasts so hard I'm bruising them, but it's no harder than the way my cock rams her. The fucking bedpost bangs against the wall with each thrust, and Holly is so greedy for it that she is meeting each thrust just as hard. She's right there with me. I can feel heat running down my spine. I'm already fucking close to coming. I've never gotten so excited so quickly. I'm more one to torture my toy and enjoy the full meal. Holly is something else entirely, from what I'm used to, and I can't hold back. I let go of one of her breasts to bring my fingers down to her clit. It takes a few glides and a hard pinch and she fucking shatters around my dick. I continue ramming in and out of her, and even after I've emptied everything I have into the condom, I find myself still slowly gliding in and out of her pussy while my hand pets her ass.

"Damn, sweetness," I say when I can find my voice.

"Yeah…" Her voice is muffled because her face is buried in the bedspread.

"Are you okay?" Fuck if I'm not smiling.

"Give me a minute and I'll be ready for round two," she mumbles, and just like that, my bastard cock jerks in reaction.

One night might not be enough. I got a feeling I'll be getting Ms. Holly's digits and setting up another meeting. Damned if that idea don't make my smile widen.

Chapter 10
Katie

" *You get what you pay for...* "

I open my eyes slowly. My body has been used hard and I feel it. I'm sore everywhere. Hell, after round—whatever, I lost count—even my *stomach* was sore. I know I have bruises all over my body and my poor ass may never be the same again. It was perfect, I think.

I hate that I have to leave. I look over at Torch, who's still asleep. Even while he's dreaming he looks cocky as hell. Then again, after last night, I can see why he can be so cocky. I didn't think they made actual men like that. I have the strangest urge to dive down under the covers and give the sleeping beauty the best hummer he's had in his life. I don't, though. I need to get out of here before he wakes up. I don't really do the whole morning-after thing. Shit, I usually leave right after, that's more my speed. Besides, Bethie is probably worried to death. I need to get back to our apartment and get my stuff and get the hell out. Our plans have me meeting Bethie in Oklahoma. If I hurry, I can pack up, grab some breakfast, and be at our meeting spot before noon.

With that thought, I get up and go about finding my shit. My skirt is by the bed, so I slide it on first. I'm definitely going to have to shower when I get home, too. That thought comes as my legs slide together and I feel the dried remnants of my last orgasm. It should be illegal for a man to have a dick *and* a tongue that work the way Torch's does. I sit in the sad little side chair and do my boots up. My leg is sorer than fuck. Even the extra insole cushion and tight support of my boots isn't going to help with the pain today. I find my bra over by the door, but I can't bring myself to put it on; it's too fucking early to be harnessing the ladies. I can't find my shirt and I'm starting to panic. Then, I see the rolled up, black fabric peeking out from under the bed. I bend down to get it, sparing a quick glance at Torch. Yep, still asleep. *Thank God.*

I unroll the shirt and notice the dried crusty fluid on it. That son of a bitch used my shirt to dry his cum with when he shot all over my ass. The man definitely has a thing for asses and, shit, after last night, I may too. Still, I am *not* wearing that out. When I questioned why he had condoms in the nightstand drawer, he mentioned they had been there for a few days and he likes to be prepared. Kind of sucks knowing some other chick will probably be in my place tonight, but then again, Torch is a player, and I was just using his dick. What can I complain about? *Not a damn thing.* Still, I'm hoping the fact that they've been staying here works in my favor and he has some other clothes in the worn out dresser in front of the bed.

I wince as the fake wood squeaks when I pull out one of the drawers. I look self-consciously over my shoulder. Damn, he sleeps like the dead. Good for me, I guess. *Eureka!* I find a couple t-shirts. I hold one up. It's black and faded-soft. In large writing it says: *A Shaved Beaver is A Happy Beaver.* I want to laugh out loud, but I don't. It's not easy. I slide it on over my head. It falls almost level with my skirt. It even smells like him. I'll use it to sleep in. I shrug, trying not to contemplate on why I would want to wear anything that smelled like Torch. I'm about to leave, but then on a whim, I reach into the pocket of my skirt and pull out a twenty. I grab the motel paper and pen on the table, then leave him a note with a smirk.

One last look at him, then I head out.

Chapter 11
Torch

"Motherfucker!"

It fucking sucks waking up alone after the best night of sex you've had in your life.

Everything about that little brunette spitfire pleased me, except for the fucking fact that she left while I was sleeping. I should have tied her fucking ass up. I realize it was a one night stand, but hell, after you fuck a woman unconscious, you expect her to stay until you can get a goodbye round.

Actually, I'm talking out of my ass. I've never wanted a woman to stay in my bed for the night. I've never had a woman in my bed the whole night. I rake my hand through my hair. Shit, I guess I still haven't. There's no telling what time she left. I had planned to get her number, but that was stupid. She's in motherfucking Texas, and that's way too far from Kentucky to get my dick off. Still...

I shake my head and get up. I need a shower and caffeine before I can face today. I've almost made it to the bathroom when the door to my room shakes from the force of the fist hitting it on the other side.

"Guess Sabre and Latch are up," I mutter after looking through the peephole. I stand back, opening the door for them and turn away to go start my shower. I smell like Holly and, though that's a fucking awesome thing, I don't need Sabre and Latch smelling her pussy. It's an irrational thought, but it's there all the same.

"Hey man. We got a locale on the girls. Get dressed and let's get the fuck out of here," says Sabre.

I'm busy stretching my dick and planning on jacking off in the shower because the son of a bitch is hard as a rock. *Fucking Holly.* I stop short and turn around to look at him.

"I need a damn shower."

"No time. You'll have to go smelling like pussy. If the info that Diesel's crew intercepted from the Donahues is good, we need to get there before those fuckers do."

"Fuck." I go to the drawer to grab a pair of jeans and my favorite blue t-shirt. It's a cat with a fucking huge dong that says Pussy Patrol on it.

"Jesus, you and your shirts," Sabre grumbles when I turn back around zipping up my jeans.

"Don't be intimidated by the size of my cat's dick."

"Fuck you."

"Haters gonna hate," I tell him, going to my pants over by the bed to fish out my billfold.

"It's a mystery to me how you get laid wearing the shit you do," Latch grumbles while I'm putting on my cut.

"It's all about the size of the ship and motion of the ocean, brother," I brag, running my fingers through my hair. "Let's get the fuck out of here," I tell them while heading for the door. "Oh wait, let me grab my keys."

I walk over to the small table by the window and grab my keys, and that's when I notice the paper and a twenty dollar bill. I grab it and bring it to my eyes.

Torch,

Thanks for last night. You weren't bad. Have some breakfast on me.

That's it. She didn't even bother to sign the motherfucker. I just stare at it, unbelieving. *Not bad?* What the fuck is that shit? She was literally asleep during the last orgasm I gave her. Which, by the way, was like the fucking twelfth of the night for her. What the ever loving fuck? *Not bad?? Jesus!* If I had time, I'd find the bitch and blister her ass so hard she won't sit for a fucking year. *Not bad!*

"Oh, dude! You got served!" Latch is standing beside me. Before I can react, he grabs the twenty.

"Motherfucker, what the hell do you think you're doing?"

"I'll just keep this for my silence."

"Silence for what?" Sabre asks as I wad up the note and throw it on the floor, following the two of them out to our bikes.

"On the fact that poor Torch's ship sailed into waters it couldn't handle."

"Shut the fuck up, Latch," I growl, jumping on my bike and starting it up.

Shit. This is not a good start to my day. My mind should be all about finding Beth and her sister. Instead, I'm following Sabre and Latch since they have the address, and all I can do is think about Holly. That, and there's one thing that's bothering the fuck out of me: how did she know I'm called Torch?

CHAPTER 12
KATIE

"*Bethie was right...*"

"Ahh," I moan. "There's nothing in this world that can't be made better by a shower," I tell myself after finishing blow-drying my hair. I have all my things packed and I've called Bethie to let her know I'm okay. Now, I just need to get dressed. I find my most comfortable pair of yoga pants and slip those babies on. I look longingly at Torch's absurd t-shirt. What the fuck do I care if people stare at me? I want to smell him around me today. I'm not going to look at that too closely. I mean, the man rocked my world last night. What woman wouldn't want to remember that the next day? I'm apparently real adept at lying to myself; it's a skill I've honed over the years.

I finish packing my makeup and toiletries and zip my satchel with a sigh. I've enjoyed Texas. Since escaping from the Snake and leaving France in our rearview mirror, Bethie and I have called quite a few states home. At first it was just Georgia and Kentucky because Bethie was intent on finding Skull again. After the bastard broke her heart, we broadened our horizons, figuring the safest thing to do was to get as far away from Georgia as possible. So far, Texas has been the best. We're going to meet up in Oklahoma, but we have California in our sights. We figure we won't stand out quite so much in a big city. We've gone over it and over it, but it doesn't make it any easier. Then again, nothing in our lives has been easy. I used to think I was the one who had it worse, but not anymore.

Bethie loves Skull. She loves him so much I hear her late at night crying in her room over him. What would it be like to find the love of your life, only to be torn away from him? And then finding him again, only to find him with someone else?

Bethie says I'm strong, that she wishes she could be just like me. What she doesn't realize is, she's stronger than I'll ever be.

I shove all of these thoughts behind me. I'm putting off leaving. I know I am. Driving is hard on me with my leg, but I do need to get going. I check my things one last time, then grab my satchel, my laptop carrier and jacket, then head for the door.

When I open it, I freeze. The last thing I expected to see when I opened the door was Torch.

"What are you doing here?"

"Holly?" Torch says, staring at me, just as shocked. I freeze. *Fuck.* I can see the exact minute understanding hits him. "That's how you knew my name was Torch. You knew who we were and what I was doing here."

Bluff your way through, Katie. *Bluff your fucking ass off,* I repeat over and over in my mind.

"What are you talking about?" I ask, ignoring the other two who stand behind him. "You told me your name. Listen, it's cute, you showing up here and all, but I'm running late." One problem at a time, that's all I can handle. I lock the door, turning my back to him and acting like I don't have a care in the world.

"Is that a fact?" asks Torch, and the tone of his voice makes me nervous.

"Afraid so, but hey, maybe we could meet up later at the bar for lunch."

"Where are you headed... *Holly?*"

The way he stressed my fake name doesn't escape me, but I soldier through. I just have to commit to my lie; I have to get to my car and get the fuck away. I know these back roads better than anyone. I can lose them; I just need to get to my jeep.

"Headed?" I call back. "Oh, my grandmother's. She lives in Odessa and she's feeling pretty bad. She caught a stomach virus and can't seem to shake it. I'm going to go be with her for a little while, you know? Help go take care of her."

"That's awful sweet of you."

"Well, I care for her. That's what you do for family, you know?" I figure I'm about ten steps away from my jeep. Ten steps and I can find freedom. *Ten steps.*

"Yeah, I get it. But hey, I have a question." I ignore the way my heart speeds up in panic. *Five more steps, just five more.*

"What's that?" I ask, still walking. *Four steps...*

"How were you going to have lunch with me if you're going to Odessa?"

Fuck! Three steps... Deep breath, Katie... Deep breath...

"Okay, well, I guess I wasn't really planning on meeting you."

"I bet," he says snidely, but I'm jumping up and down inside because I've made it to the jeep.

"Well, you have to admit, you finding my address and just showing up here, that kind of stuff screams stalker, Hunter," I tell him, unlocking my jeep. I open the door and remove the strap to my laptop off my shoulder so I can throw it in. Torch grabs it, and that's when I realize he's beside me and not in front of me. "I could have got that," I grumble. He doesn't say anything, but he does slide my overnight satchel off of my shoulder. "Whatever, just put them in the back, will ya? I need to get going. My aunt needs me."

"Your aunt? I thought you said it was your grandmother?"

Fuck!

"That's what I meant," I insist. "You have me all flustered. Can you just put my stuff in the back so I can get going?"

I don't know what I expect, but it isn't the feel of cold metal latching around my wrist. I look down to find Torch putting a handcuff on one of my arms, then deftly latching the other to his own wrist. "What—What are you doing?" I ask stupidly, because it's pretty clear what he's doing.

"The jig's up, Katie."

My heart turns over at his words.

Fuck. I should have run.

Chapter 13
Torch

"Jesus, talk about a kick in the gut."

I watch as Katie does her best to get out of this situation. It won't do her any good. The minute she opened the door, it clicked. On the surface, thanks to hair dye and colored contacts, she looks nothing like Beth, but once my brain had made the connection, I could see it. Beth is skinnier and less curvy than Katie, but their facial expressions, the lines of their face, and the mannerisms are so similar, I could kick myself for not noticing sooner. It's no fucking wonder that I hadn't seen eyes like hers before. *The fuckers weren't even real!* The first real peace I've had all day is when I handcuffed her to my arm. She won't be getting out of this shit anytime soon.

"Hand me the keys, Katie."

"I told you I'm not—"

"Drop the fucking act. In case the handcuffs didn't clue you in, sweetness, I'm not buying. Now hand me your fucking house key."

She looks at me. If looks could kill, I'd be toe-up, six feet under, pushing up daisies. She slams the key in my hand.

"Sabre, Latch, go check the rest of the house. Find Beth," I order, tossing the key to them. I barely look at them, my eyes are glued to... *Katie.* Jesus, everything she told me was a lie.

"Bethie's not here," she announces with a look of pure triumph, which irritates the fuck out of me.

"Then we'll find her, sweetness. Just like I found you. Fuck, you can't even keep your lies straight. I'm sure there's something here that will lead us to her."

Something flashes in her eyes, which aren't green anymore. They're more gray, and it's irritating how much more I like that, even when it hits me that the emotion in her eyes right now is hurt. What the fuck does she have to be hurt over? I didn't lie to her and I sure as hell didn't sneak out on her.

"You won't find a thing. We're good at hiding from Colin and Matthew. You aren't the first assholes he's sent after us," she growls, jerking against the handcuffs.

"Jesus, you're so fucking out of your head. Do you have any brains in there? Sorry, sweetness, we're not here on behalf of the fucking Donahues. Your sister nearly destroyed my brother. The only reason we're here is revenge."

Her body jerks as if she took a heavy blow. My eyes jerk up to hers and the pain in her gray eyes is huge. I see it and I'm pretty sure I could glimpse into her soul, then it's just gone.

"Your brother is a fucking asshole. I have plenty of brains."

"Whatever you say," I tell her, tired of the conversation. I can't believe the woman who I spent one of the best fucking nights of my life with is Beth's sister. I can't believe she has Donahue blood, and the thing that really, *really* pisses me off the most right now is that my dick is hard and already wanting another night with her, even while she's standing there with hate coming off of her in waves at the mention of Skull.

"Nothing in here, Torch man, it's been cleaned out," Sabre says, returning.

"Told you," Katie hisses.

"Check her bags," I tell him, ignoring her—which was a mistake. I was looking over the property wondering if something here might give away some clue as to where Beth might be, when I hear a weird noise. I turn back around to see Katie stomping something. When she moves her leg I can see the broken pieces of her cellphone.

"Whoopsie," she says, then flips me off. "Guess I got a few more fucking brains than you were planning on."

How can a bitch piss me off and then turn me on all at the same time? I'm going to fucking set her ass on fire later tonight.

The thought only makes my cock throb harder.

"Cute, honey, but quit trying to mess with the big dogs," I tell her, bending down to pick up the ruined phone—and yeah, I might have jerked her arm a little harder. "I can get everything I need to know right off your SIM card," I tell her, already sifting through the broken pieces to get to the part that contains the things I need to get her account info.

"Golly gee, Torch, I know I don't have any brains or anything, but did you know they make burn phones that don't even use SIM cards these days?" she asks in a saccharin-sweet voice that makes my hand itch to show her who's in charge.

"Katie, I'm warning you…"

"I'm sorry, I can't hear you. You've ceased to exist now," she says, not bothering to look at me and, instead, peering off in the distance over my shoulder.

Her words serve as a dare, and I'll pick up the challenge. *Oh, she'll know I exist… and soon.*

Chapter 14
Katie

" He's an asshole. Hot, but definitely an asshole. "

I'm doing my best to act cool, but inside I'm freaking dying. How did they find me? It took me thirty minutes to walk back to my car this morning. I was in so much pain that I felt I had to come home and grab my gear and shower. I wish I could go back. I would have jumped in my Jeep and hit the road. Fuck everything else. If I don't show up today at noon or get word to Bethie, then she's going to freak. I'm not sure what Skull would do to her, but after the cruel note he gave her when she was having his child, I don't trust the motherfucker not to turn her straight over to Colin. Wasn't that Colin's last threat? Did we force him to seek help from the one man who hated Bethie as much as he did? What right does the asshole have to hate Bethie, anyway? *He's* the one who cut out her heart with a dull spoon and left her to bleed to death. It's been two years and Bethie still grieves, walking around like a shell of the woman she used to be.

"Let's go," Torch growls, pulling me along by the handcuff. I stumble hard and nearly fall before he rights me. His touch burns through my clothes. I pull away from him—or at least try. He doesn't let me, and thanks to the way he has me chained, I can't.

"Go where?"

"My bike, sweetness. Time to report back to your brother-in-law."

"I'm afraid you're mistaken. I don't have one of those."

"Oh trust me, sweetness, you do," he says, and I'd love to knock the kinky look off his face.

"What about my stuff?" I ask him, annoyed.

"You won't need it."

He's wrong, so wrong.

"I do! Torch, I can't leave my things behind."

"I'll buy you whatever you need. Now get on the fucking bike," he orders.

His tone left no room for argument, but I try. "There's things in there you can't buy. At least let me have my damned clothes!"

"I can buy clothes," he returns, his eyes going over me. I know he notices his t-shirt when he gets that twinkle back in his eye that he had last night. I curse myself for wearing it. I don't want to smell him on me now, not even a little bit. Right now, I'd like to gut him. *Well, almost.* "Nice shirt," he says. "It fits you."

Asshole. He's not talking about the size; he's talking about my Brazilian wax. The dirty talk he gave me last night about loving the fact that he could see my release all glossy on the lips of my pussy doesn't feel hot today. It feels like just one more reason to kick him in the balls. The shirt he has on today hasn't escaped notice either. If I wasn't scared and pissed, I would laugh.

"I could say the same. Let me go and you can work on finding your next pet," I huff.

"Oh, but I'm not ready to give up on the one I have," he says, and that cocky look instantly changes into one fueled with lust.

"Too bad. I'm off the market," I grumble, getting on the fucking bike because it's become clear that he's not going to listen to anything I say. I wince when I step on, putting all my weight on my bad leg. I'll be lucky if I can walk tonight, but I'll be damned if I complain to him.

"We'll see about that," he says, getting on in front of me. I do my best not to touch him. He jerks his arm while he wraps his hand on the handle bar. I'm forced to stretch to allow it. I fall forward, using my free arm to brace on his back. "Wrap your other arm around me and don't give me any flack, sweetness. It's dangerous enough to ride like this. You make me fuck up my bike, I'll take it out on your hide and you won't like how that feels."

I do what he tells me, wanting to suggest we take my jeep. I don't. I know he wouldn't listen. I look over my shoulder when the three of us pull out of my old driveway. I watch until my jeep completely fades out of sight. I can't stop it when the tears escape. All I can do is promise myself that I will dry them up before Torch ever gets to see them.

Chapter 15
Torch

"It shouldn't make me happy that she turned out to be Beth's sister, but it does."

Katie beats on my chest and yells at me when I pick her up. She pulls against her restraints and that shit stings, but I figure if she can handle it, I can. I sit her down beside my bed in the motel. She looks at the rumpled sheets and blushes. It's things like that that confuse the hell out of me and make my dick throb.

I undo the handcuffs and she sighs with relief, rubbing her wrists. I let her for a moment. Her eyes look overly bright. She has a reason to be upset, but I don't want her crying. I'm starting to fucking hate this job, but I didn't make this situation. Beth did by running away from Skull and keeping their child hidden... if it even *is* his child. She's told so many lies, who's to say the baby isn't Colin's? I'd never mention that to Skull. There's just so many things about Beth and her delicious handful of a sister that doesn't add up.

"About time! I need to go to the bathroom!" she growls, spitting fire at me. God's truth, it should be illegal for a woman to have as much fire as she does inside. She'd wear a man out if he tried to take her on fulltime. Good thing I'm not that stupid. I don't do fulltime *ever*, no matter how intriguing a bitch might make the prospect seem.

"Too bad. I got shit to do. You'll stay here." I see the light bulb go off in her eyes. Does she think I'm dumb enough to leave her behind unwatched? Did I make it so easy for her last night that she thinks I'm a sucker? I'll have to work harder now. My dick is practically nodding in agreement. Jesus, maybe it was better when he went a couple of months without pussy.

"What kind of business?" she asks. I could talk with her all day, but I'd rather go get shit done and "speak" with our bodies later. I grab her wrist and bring the red area to my lips. Then, I kiss the underside, letting my tongue dance along the delicate veins before kissing it again with my lips. I look at her and her breathing has changed slightly, her eyes watching me, the gray color so fucking stormy-looking my balls tighten with need.

"All better?"

"What?" she asks, distracted. I like that she can't hide her reaction to me. Even if she tried, her body would give her away. Right now, her nipples are so fucking hard they could almost cut through my t-shirt.

This is going to piss her off more, and I'll have to work overtime to get back between her legs tonight, but it can't be helped. I use my other hand to grab the cuffs I had put in my back pocket and then, before she has time to react, I connect one of them back to her wrist.

"What are you doing??" she screeches.

Oh yeah, I'm going to have to come at her with my A-game to get that pussy tonight. I take her hand and kneel down on the floor. It takes some doing, but I latch it against the metal railing of the mattress frame.

"Sorry, sweetness. Honestly, I am, but I can't trust you not to run away."

"I can't even stand up! You can't leave me like this!"

"You can lay down and watch television. You'll be fine until I get back," I tell her, situating her on the bed despite her protests. Then, I put the remote control beside her.

"You can't do this! What if the motel catches on fire? You could kill me!"

"I'll be gone an hour, tops. You'll be fine," I tell her, annoyed when her plea manages to make me *actually* worry.

"Don't do this, Torch. If you leave me tied up alone, I will hate you," she whispers, her voice deadly still.

"One hour, sweetness, that's it. Behave now," I tell her trying to keep my voice light while dismissing her. I need to know more of Katie's secrets, I think, but not right now. I open up the door to find Sabre and Latch waiting not so patiently.

"Are you ready?" Sabre asks.

"Yeah, in just a minute."

"Torch," Katie shouts from the bed. "If you leave me like this, I will scream until the police come!"

"No one will hear you, but hey, go ahead. It'll give me a good reason to gag you next time," I respond.

She screams. When I turn around to tell her that she just bought herself punishment, the remote control comes whizzing at my head. I barely have time to duck before it shatters against the door frame and busts, falling into pieces like it was confetti.

Sabre and Latch laugh their heads off.

"I hate you, you limp-dick motherfucker!!" Katie screams louder. That only makes Sabre and Latch laugh harder.

"That was your last chance," I tell her. "We'll see how limp you think my cock is when you're choking on it tonight." With that, I slam the door on her screams.

Sabre and Latch are still laughing. Hell, I think Sabre's laughed so hard, the asshole has tears coming out of his eyes.

"This trip back to Kentucky ought to be fun," says Latch. I ignore the motherfuckers and jump on my bike.

"Hey, Torch. Before we head back to that spitfire's house, let's run by the pharmacy we saw in town."

"What the fuck for? You know Skull's waiting for a report."

"Aye, that I do, brother, but I'm more worried about your dick. Maybe they can find you some little blue pills to help you out with your problem. I've never needed them, but I hear they can work wonders for men like—"

I start up my bike to drown the motherfuckers out. I'm going to kill them, then give Katie something to scream about later.

Chapter 16
Katie

" Why do men think it's okay to tie me up and leave me defenseless? Why does it hurt more when Torch does it? "

I lie here in shock. I can't do much else. I hate the feeling of being tied up and having no control. *Being abandoned.* It's a feeling I'm more than a little familiar with and I fucking hate it. The fact that Torch is the one to do it this time is just salt in an open wound.

I spend a few minutes trying to calm my breathing. I hate that being confined makes me panic. There's nothing I can do about it, though. There's just been too much water under the bridge.

To get my mind off of it, I concentrate on the things I need to accomplish. I need to get a message through to Beth, and that's not going to be easy. I need her to keep running. She'll want to come after me, but I can't risk the fact that Colin might get his hands on her, or worse, Gabby. There's a phone in the motel room. I could call Beth's cell. I figure that they may have the number monitored, though, and I have to decide if it's worth the risk. Can I pretend to fall under Torch's spell? Maybe if he thinks I'm sewn up over him, he'll relax his guard enough so I can escape, or at least get a message out. Would that be safer?

I feel panic nipping at my heels. I should have listened to Bethie and fucking ran. No dick, however spectacular it is packaged, is worth it. I let myself forget that with Torch and I fell for his pretty eyes and the promise of fun he offered. It *was* fun, but at what cost? It sure as hell won't have been worth it if it destroys the two people I love the most in the process. I don't know what Torch's club and Skull's endgame is. If Colin is to be believed, he wants his child and, in return, he's going to turn me

BURNED

and Bethie over to him. It pisses me off. Skull pushed Bethie out of his life in the most brutal way possible. What right does he have to come back and destroy her further after all this time? The only thing important here is Bethie.

With that in mind, I reach over and pick up the motel phone. I hope and pray I'm making the right choice.

"Hello?" Bethie's voice comes over the line.

"Bethie, it's me. I need you to listen."

"Katie! Where are you? You were supposed to check in before you reached—"

"Stop. Bethie, this phone isn't secure. Listen to me because we have to hang up quickly. I don't know if they can trace you and I'm not taking the chance. Skull's crew showed up at the house and they have me—"

"I warned you! Okay, Gabby and I will turn around and—"

"No! That's exactly what they want. You know what the next step in our plan was. Do it. I'll bide my time and get away from them. I'll be in touch."

"Katie, I don't like this! I could—"

"You could *listen to me*," I cut her off. "This isn't about me—or even *you* anymore. We have to keep Gabby safe. So go through with our plans, understand? I'll contact you the minute I can. Destroy this phone like I showed you and switch to your back up. I'll use that number when I get free. Do it now, Bethie."

"Katie…"

"Just do it. I have to go now."

"Okay," she whispers, and I hate that I can hear the tears in her voice. "I love you bigger than outer space," she whispers.

"To the moon and back," I tell her, then hang up, praying I didn't stay on the line too long.

I stare at the receiver for a while afterwards. I need to figure out what my next step is and I need to know if I'm strong enough to play Torch, because it will take a lot of playing to get out of this mess. I *will* get out. I don't have a choice. I will do it…

For Gabby.

Chapter 17
Torch

"She needs to learn who's in control now."

"What do you know, amigo. Your woman's been using the phone," Latch says, but I tune him out. I'm still pissed at him and Sabre. They've been laughing enough at my expense. Today, for the most part, has been a total bust. We went back to Katie's and ransacked the place, but didn't find anything else. I grabbed her jeep and we went by the local bike store and bought a box trailer. I can't trust Katie not to be stupid with my bike, and I need to keep her cuffed to me the whole time. Okay, that last part might not be necessary, but it sure as fuck makes me feel better.

I also went through her shit and there was next to nothing in there. I'm not so sure what she was throwing a fit about. The only thing I found that might hold any value for her was a picture of Beth and Gabby. Gabby was in a high chair and her little face was covered in cake. Beth was crouched down beside her, smiling. She looked beautiful, but she looked so different from the Beth the guys and I remembered. There was a sadness in her now that echoed even through the photo. One thing was clear: she loved her daughter, and though I doubted it, after seeing the photo, I am more inclined to believe that Gabby is Skull's. The little girl looks too much like him. I snapped the photo with the camera on my phone and texted it to Skull. He didn't respond, but then I didn't expect him to. It's been almost two hours, and I know Katie will be pissed. I would have been back on time, but she pissed me off, so I've been chilling in Sabre and Latch's room for the last hour. I had hacked into the motel's system and checked out the phone calls placed from my room. I was sure

Katie would contact her sister; it's almost disappointing that it would be so easy. I get the number and write it down. Then, I switch to my software and set about trying to triangulate the signal for Beth. I'm surprised when that doesn't turn up a hit.

"Looks like your girl might know a little bit about hiding her tracks," Sabre says over my shoulder. He might be right, but I'm not ready to give up on it yet. I do some number searches and then carriers. Prepaid cell, of course; *that* I was expecting. I hack into the carrier's database and try to do a search on the phone. The number has been disabled. I'm not finding shit on how to hack into it again. I can't even turn the number back on.

"Look at that, Latch. Our boy not only met his match everywhere else, I think she can out-hack him on the computer."

"Fuck off. I'll find it. It may just take a bit."

"Whatever. We're going to go out and find food. You want to go with us, or are you going to get back to your woman?"

"She's not mine. If she was, I'd sure as fuck bring her to heel. She runs too fucking wild," I grumble. "Bring us back some burgers and fries. I'll go see what other shit our little captive has got into." I do my best to sound like I'm dreading it, but if the truth was known, I've wanted to get back to her for a while now. Fuck, I didn't even want to leave, if I'm being honest.

When I get back to the room, Katie is turned on her side, staring at the wall. She doesn't turn around to acknowledge me and she doesn't say anything.

I guess I'm getting the cold shoulder now.

"I brought your stuff back," I tell her, starting with a peace offering. It's met with silence. "I also got your jeep. We'll ride in it when we take off for Kentucky tomorrow. It'll make it easier." I just keep talking and ignoring her silence. I commend myself for not already spanking her ass. "We could go pick up your sister and her daughter first and make things easier on everyone, if you'd rather."

"Go fuck yourself."

Well, it's not what I wanted from her, but hey, at least she's talking.

"I see you're still cheerful." I walk over to her. Even standing right in front of her, she refuses to talk to me. "I like your eyes much better this way," I tell her, for lack of something better to say, bending down to unhook her from the bed.

"My life has meaning now," she says.

"Do you need to go to the restroom?"

"Wow. You mean I actually get to go to another room all by myself?"

"I can tie you back up if you'd rather," I offer with a snide smile.

"You really are an asshole," she mumbles, pushing off the bed. It's then that I notice she's limping. It seemed a couple times last night like her leg bothered her. I thought I might have been imagining things, but it's definitely more pronounced today. I follow her into the bathroom, making sure there's nothing she can use against me and double checking there's no window. "Hell no! You're not staying in here while I use the bathroom!"

"Wouldn't dream of it, grouchy. Was just making sure there wasn't anything in here you could use to slit my throat with when we sleep tonight."

"Now there's a thought to cheer me up," she says as I start to close the door.

"Words wound, you know, Katie."

"I think your ego could take it, Torch."

"I think I liked it better when you called me Hunter."

"I think I liked it better when you were buried between my legs and couldn't talk."

"That could be arranged again," I tell her.

"I could twist your dick until something pops while you sleep tonight too," she says with a fake smile, then slams the door.

Damn.

CHAPTER 18
KATIE

" It'd be too easy to let my guard down. "

"Do you really think these are necessary?" I ask Torch yet again. He's got the one cuff on his wrist and one on mine and it's really starting to piss me off. "I mean, we're in the same room. It's not like I'm going to be able to get away from you or outrun you."

"Speaking of which, what did you do to your leg?"

Fuck. I've been so relaxed, I forgot to hide my limp from him. Yes, I know how absurd that sounds since I've spent the day screaming at him and threatening bodily harm and being chained up. Still, it's not like my life has been normal, or sadly, that this is a new occurrence for me. Quite the opposite, really. It's just that I kind of like the guy who has me tied up and is being a douche this time. That's me, though; always getting into stupid situations just to keep things interesting. I *really* should have listened to Bethie.

"I don't know what you mean," I tell him sounding bored, as he swirls another french fry that one of the other men—Sabre, I think Torch called him—dropped off a bit ago.

"Whatever, Katydid."

"What did you just call me?"

"Katydid. It's a—"

"I know what it is. I'm just wondering why you think it's okay to nickname me after an insect."

"Open up," he says, holding the fry close to my lips.

"I could feed myself, you know." For some stupid reason, I'm enjoying him feeding me. I've decided to ignore it and give myself a break. My brain is probably still trying to catch up from all the orgasms last night and still views him as a friend and not an enemy. I'm sure it will recognize the difference soon. I lick my lips at the thought, hopefully before I make the mistake and sleep with him again.

I take the fry from him to try and concentrate on something besides how much I want sex...*with him...again...tonight...all night...*

"Katydids are cool. They—"

"Are ugly grasshopper-like things that chirp," I finish for him. "I know you're the king of pickup lines and all, but I've got to tell you, being compared to a bug is not what a woman wants to hear from a man."

"I'll keep that in mind. So, your leg?"

"I injured it," I tell him vaguely, taking a drink of my soda.

"I really need you to be more forthcoming, Katie."

"Why?"

"Because I want to know more about you."

I freeze with the straw to my drink right in front of my lips. "Why? We spent one night fucking each other's brains out. It was hot and damn good, but it was just sex. It's not like we need to become friends now, as if we even *could*. You're holding me hostage, remember?" I take another drink.

"You're a hard woman, Katyd." I give him the mean look and he holds up his hand in defense. "Katie," he corrects himself. "So, at least tell me how you managed to erase all signs of your burn phone," he says, holding out another fry to my lips.

I stop. So, that's his game? He wants to act like my buddy and pump me for information? He doesn't realize I've spent my life with men who mastered mind-fuck games.

"Nice try," I tell him, turning down the fry. "I don't think I'm hungry anymore. I'm suddenly really tired."

"You sure?" he asks, sounding surprised.

"Definitely."

He shrugs and starts bagging up the trash. He reaches over with his free hand and puts it on the table. I hand him my coke.

"Do you think you could maybe unhook us so we can sleep?"

"I'm not real tired," he says, ignoring my request. "Think I'll watch some TV."

"Great, but how am I supposed to sleep when you're attached to me?"

"You didn't complain last night."

"I can't remember last night."

"I could remind you."

"Something you should know about me, Torch. I have this rule. It's a small one, really. I don't sleep with men who hold me captive. I'm weird like that."

"I could make you like it," he says, and I'm beginning to hate that cocky grin he wears.

"Probably. I mean, you're obviously a man-whore, so you have enough experience to make me like it. It's part of what made last night so great. But, after it was over, I'd want to put my head in the oven and die."

"Damn."

I give him an over-the-top smile. "Will you please unhook us now?" I ask again, rattling our hands.

"Afraid not, Katydid. Can't risk you trying to make a break for it in the middle of the night."

"God, I hate you."

"Now, is that any way to talk to the future father of your children?"

"Jesus, you've gone insane!"

"Let's go brush our teeth. Got to keep those chompers pearly white."

He stands up, pulling me along, then puts one hand on my ass, pushing me into him. He starts pulling me up his body. I'm forced to use my free hand to brace on his shoulder.

"What are you doing?" I gasp, trying to ignore the fact that his cock is hard and pushing into my stomach.

"Your leg's hurt. Climb on me. I'll take us to the bathroom."

"I can wa—" I stop when he shifts me, trying to do it all himself. "Okay! Okay! Stop before you dump us both on the carpet." I help him lift, then wrap my legs around his waist. Our linked hands make it so he holds my ass, my other arm down at my side. Not the most comfortable position, for sure. "Are you planning on brushing my teeth for me too?" I ask sarcastically.

"We'll brush together. The couple that brushes together, stays together."

"Was there crazy pills in our food?"

He actually kisses my *nose* in response.

We brush our teeth, *together,* and then I somehow manage to make him unhook us and turn his back so I can take off my yoga pants. Luckily, his shirt I'm wearing is long enough it comes to just above my knees. I climb under the covers before I finally tell him.

"Okay, you can turn around now." He walks around and gets in the bed beside me. "There's another bed you know. You could sleep there."

"Yeah, that'd be kind of hard to do," he says, and I try to concentrate on what he's saying but he's taking off his clothes. *All. Of. His. Clothes.*

"What are you doing??"

"Getting ready for bed," he says, sounding bored.

"You can't sleep with me naked!"

"It's how I sleep. You know that. Remember last night?"

Like I could forget it. "Yeah, well, that was just last night. Tonight, I'm not here willingly. So, if you are sleeping with me, you're going to do it with your clothes on!"

"Not happening," he says, slipping into the bed. "Hand me your arm."

I don't know if I could take him, but it'd be close. Still, if I try it so quickly and I fail, it won't work. I need to plot this out carefully. So, as much as I'd rather junk-punch him, I hand him my arm. He secures the handcuff once again and links our hands together like we're going to sleep holding hands. I roll over as much as I can and ignore him.

Then, I hear moaning. I look over my shoulder. The TV has some woman on her hands and knees, sucking some man's cock like it's a lollipop. Some other guy is fucking her ass. Two more are standing around watching and jacking off.

"You're watching porn?"

"Yep. You want to watch? This one here is a classic. She came to the garage to get her car worked on and instead they service *her*."

I roll over, throwing the pillow over my head. "I hate you." Then I spend the next hour trying to block out the moans and screams from the TV.

Chapter 19
Torch

"I've never been accused of being a saint."

It's three in the fucking morning and I'm lying handcuffed to the hottest woman I've ever met in my life. I've got the world's largest hard-on in the history of hard-ons and I'm slowly dying.

On second thought, watching porn might not have been such a good idea. Who would have thought Katie could go to sleep with all the moaning and shit going on? Who would have thought having me naked in bed beside of her, *obviously willing*, while all the moaning was going on wouldn't affect her?

Shit, apparently I'm losing my touch. She's lying there looking so fucking sexy that it should be illegal—in my shirt, too—and she's just sleeping away. Meanwhile, if I don't come, I will probably be foaming at the mouth while rocking back and forth speaking gibberish.

I get that she's mad at me and I should stay away from her. There's something about Katie, though. I don't think she has a mean bone in her body. I don't. Her faith and love in her sister Beth is evident. That means I'm missing something here. Worse, it means that Skull is missing something too. I think Katie holds the key and I need her to open up to me. If it will help me figure out what's going on as well as get my brother his daughter, don't I owe it to Skull to try? That's really all I'm doing. I'm just making sure my brother knows the full story and helping him get the daughter he was denied.

That's the pep talk I give myself when I unlatch the handcuff from my wrist. Next, as delicately as possible, I pull the covers off of Katie's body. My shirt has gathered up around her hips.

She's wearing this sexy red piece of cloth that hides her pussy from me. That's the first thing that has to go. I move to the foot of the bed, hooking my fingers in her panties and pulling them down as slowly and as carefully as I can. My eyes watch her face the entire time. She mumbles in her sleep, but shows no signs of waking up.

Now, I'm a man who loves pussy. I've made a point of worshipping at the altar of pussy. I'm a fucking connoisseur. But Katie's pussy is something special. It's bare, so fucking smooth, the lips are plump and soft, and the color is this delicate pink, all feminine and gorgeous. All that, and then the aroma. Fuck me, if I could smell nothing for the rest of my life but the scent of Katie's sweet cunt when she's horny, I could die a happy man. I haven't touched her yet, but even now in her sleep, her pussy is begging for attention. Her arousal coats the lips of her entrance. I take a minute to just take this sight in. Her hips are flared out perfectly, and she's got this curve in her waist with this sexy little pouch that I just want to nibble on. She's all woman and I don't think I've ever had the pleasure of sampling a more beautiful one.

I place a line of soft kisses along her hip bone. I keep the pressure light, as I don't want to wake her right away. I need her to be on the verge of a climax before she does. It's underhanded and sneaky, I can admit it, but I'm hoping if I play my cards right that she'll return the favor and suck my cock. The poor fucker has been craving her all day and night.

Katie moans and her hips thrust up just enough to show me that even in her sleep she's receptive to me. I kiss down to her pussy. I nearly groan aloud at the taste of a light hint of cream there. I pull her lips apart and then moan at the beautiful dessert bared in front of me. I blow softly against the tender exposed flesh. Katie whimpers, but luckily doesn't wake up. I flatten my tongue and lick her slowly, humming as her sweet taste gathers on my tongue.

Even asleep and relaxed, I can feel her clit easily. I zero in on it, licking in short, fast strokes. I can feel it grow larger in my mouth from my attention, demanding more. I suck it into my mouth, capturing it and focusing all of my attention on it.

"Hunter," she moans from above me. I feel her fingers dive into my hair, pulling me to her in want.

Hunter.

I've had that name forever. I never really liked it. I embraced the name Torch when Skull gave it to me. All day long, since I discovered who she truly was, Katie has been calling me Torch. I accepted it, didn't think a thing about the change from the night. Except for now. Now, in this one small moment with nothing but complete honesty from our bodies, it's different. Katie is still more than half asleep, and yet the first thing she does is wrap her fingers into my hair, lift her legs over my shoulders, and tilt her body to bring her pussy closer to me. All that would be enough, but she gives me my name on her lips. My name while she's caught up in passion. My name... *Mine.*

I let that sink in, humming my pleasure against her clit before releasing it with a wet, popping noise. I look up to find her eyes on me—hazy gray beauties filled with sleep and lust. Definitely better than the emerald she disguised them in yesterday.

Definitely.

I drag my fingers through her pussy, letting her desire coat them. I go back to manipulating her clit, this time with two fingers pinching and kneading the little nub. I'm rewarded when I feel it harden and swell even more against my fingers. Her body shudders with hunger.

"Hunter," she moans again as I move my fingers down and thrust two inside of her tight channel.

"You like that, sweetness?"

"Oh, oh... fuck!" her sweet voice stutters. Her fingernails clench against my head, biting into me. Her feet push down on my upper back as she opens herself up more to me. She tries to push up to meet the driving force of my fingers.

"You've got the hottest pussy, Katie. So ready to be fucked," I growl, pushing my thumb against her clit while I continue finger-fucking her at a steady pace, priming her for more.

"Hunter, please…" she gasps.

"Do you want my tongue again, Katie?" I question her.

"God," she moans, her head pushing back against the pillow in abandon. Her cream floods over my fingers, so sticky, hot, and wet that my dick would sink inside of her tight depths easily. Motherfucker, I want that, but for now, this isn't about me and what I want.

"Tell me you want me to eat out your hungry little pussy, Katie. Do it and I'll give you what you need."

She moans, but ignores my demand. I pull my fingers out and then ram them forcefully back inside of her. She cries out, but I don't move them. I hold them still inside of her. My thumb does the same, pushing hard on her clit but not moving, just giving her constant pressure. Her hips lunge up, her feet press down, and her body curls up off the bed as she twists and turns, trying to take control. *I can't allow that.*

I pull my fingers from her sweet honey. I use my fingers to stretch the lips wide open, then deliver a hard slap, reprimanding her. Her moans break into a cry and then a soft gasp as I see her pussy contract with hunger while more sweet cream gathers. *Jesus.* Watching that and hearing the noises she makes is all so sexy and hot that I spank it again.

"Tell me, Katie," I demand, refusing to let her move. Showing her that I'm the one in charge.

"I want you to fucking eat my pussy!" she screams in frustration when she realizes I'm not letting her move.

If I wasn't so fucking turned on, I'd laugh. That's beyond me right now. In reward for giving me what I wanted, I slam my fingers back inside her pussy. At the same time, I let my tongue lash her clit, flicking it over and over before curving around and sucking it into my mouth, owning her, tasting her, *devouring her.*

I can feel the way her muscles are rippling around my fingers, signaling that her climax is close. I keep torturing her clit and pussy, but take my other hand and find that small, snug entrance to her ass. Someday before our ride ends, my cock is going to claim that ass. *Someday soon…*

I stop sucking on her clit long enough to capture it between my teeth, applying light pressure, just enough to cause a little pain while I torment it. Then, I slip my finger into her ass past the knuckle. I curl it, scraping her tender walls as her muscles tighten up against the unfamiliar invasion. She cries out as I let go of her clit and bury my face in her pussy, devouring it. My fingers and tongue discover every inch of her sweet cunt, all while my finger possesses her ass. She detonates. Her pussy tries to ride my face, her thighs tightening up against my head and trying to smother me in her creamy cum.

I don't stop even when her orgasm is done. I keep at it until she goes over the edge again. This time when she climaxes, she does it screaming my name.

Hunter.

Chapter 20
Katie

" No, damn it! I can't. "

"Good morning, sweetness," Torch says, licking his lips and looking like it's just another day.

Like he didn't just give me two mind-blowing orgasms. Like he wasn't still between my legs. Dear Lord! If Beth could see me now, she'd kill me. How did I completely lose control?

"What was that?" I ask Torch like an idiot.

"You don't know?"

"Okay, I know what it was, but why? Why did you do that?"

"Because I wanted to. Because you wanted me to. In fact, I think we should do it again. You're way too uptight. Let's go for round three," he decides, pulling my body back to his mouth. I start kicking in a downward motion, hitting his back with the bottoms of my feet.

"No! *Stop that!* Will you get up from there??"

"That's not what you were saying a few minutes ago."

"Torch..."

"No. You called me Hunter. I think the correct phrase was, 'I want you to eat my fucking...'"

I whack him over the head with my pillow to shut him up. That's when I see the handcuff that he conveniently unhooked himself from hanging on my arm. That's a good reminder. *A great one, really.* He grabs the pillow midair and grins at me.

"Stop! Stop giving me that look!"

"What look is that, sweetness? The one that says I know what you taste like first thing in the morning? That I can still taste you on my tongue?"

I jump off the bed, needing to get away from him to think. "You don't get to do this. This doesn't get to happen now!"

"Why the fuck not?" he asks, and his easygoing attitude is definitely missing now.

"Oh, gee, I don't know, Torch, maybe *this!*" I growl, shaking the arm that still has the handcuffs attached to it. He stands up, his cock rock hard and his body a piece of art, and I'm doing my best not to get distracted. *But it's hard!* And, yes, the pun was intended. I'm dying to give in, but know I can't. At least, not yet. I need to figure out my next move, and whatever it is, it has to help me escape and get to Beth, not get laid.

"How about you let me show you how women love it when I cuff them?"

"How about you cover up your boner and let me go back to sleep, where I was quite happy before you woke me?"

"You weren't complaining, earlier."

"I was asleep!"

"The fuck you were!"

"I was, in the beginning! And will you cover up, damn it?"

"Why, sweetness? Does the sight of my cock bother you?"

"Yes!"

"Does it make you hungry?" he asks, shaking it.

That does it. It's time I stopped plotting. If Torch wants to be a dick, then it's time I show him what happens.

"Fine! It does. Is that what you want to hear? I liked fucking you. I enjoyed it."

"Enjoyed it?"

"*Immensely*," I tell him, disgusted. "But that doesn't change the fact that we were a one-night stand and you're holding me here against my will."

"It doesn't change the fact that we still want each other, either, or are you going to deny that you're turned on right now?"

"No. I'm not. I'm big enough to admit that I like sex and you're pretty good in bed."

"Pretty good?"

"Will you get over your gigantic ego? Jesus, it's a bigger

choking hazard than your cock. You're a man who's had a lot of sex. Of *course* you're good in bed. but there are others out there who are just as good. You're not special because you know how to give a woman an orgasm."

"I think I gave you more than that, but maybe you need a reminder."

"What are you going to do with me, Torch?"

"I've been trying to tell you…"

"No, I mean what's your endgame here? You have me. So, what now? Are you going to drag me back against my will to my cousins so they can finish what my fucking grandfather and father started?"

He seems taken back by my question, and I have no idea why he should be.

"We don't make deals with the fucking Donahues," he says.

"Then what exactly are you holding me for?"

"Your sister nearly destroyed my brother!" he growls. "Do you know what it did to him to think he killed the woman he loved? Do you know what it did to him to discover Beth was alive and to find that out through a man he fucking hates? Throw in the fact that he has a *daughter* he didn't know about…"

"Bullshit!"

"What?"

"You heard me! Bull-*fucking*-shit! Your 'brother' knew Beth was alive and had his daughter, but when she reached out to him for help, he paid her to disappear!"

"You're fucking insane. That shit did not happen."

"Really? Because I was there, Torch, and let me tell you, it happened and it nearly destroyed my sister. So, if you think I'm going to sit around and wait for you to drag me back to Kentucky just so your brother can fuck Bethie all over again, then you're the insane one."

"Damn it, Katie, I'm telling you that… that did not…"

"Save it. I was there. You weren't. In case you're wondering, pretty boy, if it's between trusting you and your overused cock and protecting my sister, *she* wins every damn time."

With that, I limp into the bathroom and slam the door, since I couldn't stomp like I wanted too. Once I lock the door, I slide down to the floor and stare up at the ceiling. I have to get out of here and find Bethie and Gabby. I can't let my stupidity be the reason she loses Gabby. Colin said he made a deal with Skull. He hired Skull to bring us back to him and in exchange, Skull gets to keep his child. Bethie and I were convinced he was lying, but it's clear now that he wasn't. It's also clear that I should've listened to my sister and never spent the night with Torch.

I just hope Bethie's not the one who ends up paying for my stupidity.

Chapter 21
Torch

"something is rotten ..."

"So you're taking me back to Colin," Katie says dejectedly.

I refuse to feel guilty here. I have nothing to feel guilty about and she's not even trying to believe what I'm telling her, which pisses me off.

"Damn it, Katie. Skull will not turn you or Beth over to Colin," I tell her for the hundredth time. It's true, he won't. I conveniently leave out that Beth might prefer that to what Skull will do with her; that's a battle for another time.

"Yeah. Sure. You have such faith in your *brother*. Whatever. When are we heading out?"

I don't know if I want to shake some sense into her, or kiss her. "In a few minutes. I just need to say goodbye to Latch and Sabre first," I tell her, throwing my t-shirt on and rolling it down my chest. I'd hoped she'd change her mind about sex, but it seems she's intent on not having sex again. I don't know why that fucking pisses me off more than anything else, but it does. And the fact that it does, pisses me off even more. I mean the least she could have done was sucked my cock, after I gave her *two* orgasms. Her outrage didn't even bother coming out until she got hers. Women. Fucking hell. This is why I will never do a relationship. *Never*.

"They're not coming with us?" she asks, confused.

"No. They have to get back to Annie. Latch's sister got into some kind of trouble. They're going to drive straight through. Skull wants us to take our time while he gets things ready there," I tell her, refusing to look at her.

"You mean he wants us to drag our feet to give my sister time to come out of hiding and try to save me?" she asks. "And who is Annie?"

Really the fucking woman is too smart for her own good.

"I'd deny it, but you wouldn't believe me anyway, and Annie is their woman," I tell her, slipping on my boots. "I'll be back after I say goodbye to my brothers."

"They share a woman? Are you guys, like, polygamists? Shit. Bethie has no idea what sick fucks you guys are."

"Just because they happen to love the same woman doesn't make them sick. They're completely sewn up over her and treat her like a queen. If Annie's happy, you don't need to fucking judge her," I growl, really pissed off at her now. Shit, I don't think I'd ever be able to share a woman I loved fulltime, but it works for them, so what-the-fuck-ever. I don't ever intend on having a relationship that lasts more than a few weeks. Month, at the most. So it's not like that fucking matters.

"Of course Annie's happy. That's, like, every woman's fantasy. Shit I want to be her."

"You just got all self-righteous about it!" I don't like the idea of two men sharing Katie at all.

"Only because I thought they had, like, six wives or some shit. What you just described is hot as hell. Hmm, you seem to have a lot of brothers. Maybe you could hook me up with a couple to play with. If I'm going to be held there against my will, I might as well have fun."

"Sorry, baby. I offered you my dick last night and you turned it down. I'm the only option available to you. So, all of this," I say, making a sweep over my body like a game show model, just to piss her off, "I'll just give to someone else. You'll just have to go without any while you're at the clubhouse."

"Not likely."

Those two words bother me. Is she planning on fucking some of the other brothers? That shouldn't get to me; she's just a one-night stand. I'll most definitely be finding a replacement tonight since she seems to have her legs closed permanently. No matter my plans though, the thought of Katie fucking any of my other brothers pisses me off.

I'm jerked out of my thoughts when her voice brings my attention back to her. "You cannot seriously be contemplating wearing that t-shirt out of this room."

I look down at my blue t-shirt with the yellow writing that says *Choking Hazard* and has a yellow arrow pointing down to my dick. I look back at Katie with a smile. "You inspired me."

"Where the fuck do you get these shirts? And how do they let you out at night by yourself?"

"Don't be jealous, sweetness. I'd let you choke on my cock tonight over the chick I'll end up picking up. You're the one who told me no. If you change your mind before I head out, the offer still stands," I tell her with a wink. "At least, for a couple more hours." She throws a pillow at me, but I just grin. "I'll be right outside. Don't make me sorry I didn't chain you back up," I tell her, leaving my parting shot. I close the door just as she starts screaming. Good times really. I'd be lying my ass off if I didn't admit that I love sparring with her.

"I hate you!" the muffled yell broadcasts through the door.

"Sounds like you guys are getting along just great," Latch says. He and Sabre are standing over by their bikes, looking impatient.

"I always like to leave them screaming for more," I joke as we say our goodbyes and slap each other a little too hard on the back. I still say I hit harder. *Bastards.*

"You sure you're gonna be okay?" Sabre asks me. I swear, since he hooked up with Annie he worries over everything.

"I'll be fine. I'll drag my feet a day or two just to see if Beth is going to follow us, and it's not like the Donahues know I'm bringing Beth back anyway."

"Yeah, I know. I just got a weird feeling about this shit."

"You always have feelings lately. You're worse than a fucking mother hen. *I'll be fine*," I reiterate.

"Whatever, fucker. Just don't let your dick get in the way of the big picture."

"Shit, it *takes* a big picture to actually hold my dick."

They shake their heads and Latch's laughter is loud, which is good. Something is going on with him. He and Sabre haven't said a lot about it, but Latch is going back overseas soon. Shocked the fuck out of all of us that he'd leave Sabre and Annie, let alone Lucy.

"Check in, asshole," Sabre orders.

"Will do, mom."

"I'm serious, man. Something about this whole damn thing isn't sitting right with me. I'm not sure what it is. You mentioned Katie thinks Skull pushed Beth away. We know that shit didn't happen. So what the fuck really did?"

"You think it's the Donahues?"

"Maybe. Hell, I don't know. It just seems like the Donahues have always been one step ahead of us, even when we were at war."

"A mole," I answer, and it is an answer, because I've had the same thought. We all have. Skull and I have had that discussion often. Pistol was the number one suspect, but he tried to save Bethie and got himself gut-shot in the process. Fucker almost died. The fact that he put his life on the line for Beth is the only reason Skull hasn't killed the motherfucker himself.

"Maybe. There sure is something going on. You better watch your fucking back."

"Will do. You do the same."

"Always. Later, bro," Sabre says, starting up his bike.

He and Latch wave as I turn back around to look at the motel room where Katie is. It shouldn't make me fucking happy that I'm alone with her for a few days.

But it does.

Chapter 22
Katie

" I have to get away... "

He's watching me like a damn hawk, but so far he hasn't handcuffed me again. So there's that, at least.

I've been trying to be on my best behavior while being an ass to him so I don't rouse his suspicions. We've been driving all day and we're just now in Oklahoma. I was worried when he started driving, afraid he had somehow found out that Bethie was here, but he's too relaxed and laidback. Still, if I could get away from him now, it would be perfect.

We pull into a truck stop diner. I have a look around, secretly jumping up and down. These are my people. I can totally use that to my advantage. It's a giant gas and shower station with big rigs parked everywhere in the back, and there's a diner stowed away behind the main store. The trick here will be to get away. It won't be easy. He may not be chaining me to him for now, but he's not taking his eyes off of me either. I need to play it smart.

"Gee, Torch. You think you could spring for a steakhouse or something?" I complain.

"They have steak," he defends, shutting off my jeep.

"There was a steakhouse down the road that looked great. I bet they even show you to your seats and bring you peanuts."

"Poor Katie, having to rough it with the regular folk. Sorry, sweetness. We'll eat here and you'll enjoy it. Besides, it's barely noon. I want breakfast."

"Whatever."

"Just be on your best behavior. If I have to, I'll put you back in cuffs. Don't test me."

"Yes sir, master."

"Damn, I think I'd like that. Tell me, Katie, would you be a good little slave or would I need to punish you?"

"If 'good' means biting your dick off and leaving you in a pool of blood, sure," I return. I could almost grin at the way he rubs his cock.

"You're a vicious woman, sweetness."

He really has no idea. He's not prepared for the thoughts running through my head. I'd hate to do it, really, but I'm desperate. I'll feel bad for him after it's done. First, I'm going to eat. Fucker took all my stuff and I can't get it from the back of the jeep when I make my break. If I did that, he'd catch me again. No. Whatever I do, I have to do fucking quick. I'm going to eat because who the hell knows when I'll get food again. Probably not until I meet up with Bethie, and that could be a while. I really am surprised that he's leaving me out of the handcuffs. But then, he has no idea I've made a living out of escaping from men who have held me prisoner. He's pretty, but it's sad; he might not be as smart as I'd given him credit for. Maybe all his brains are in his massive dick. My insides quiver at the thought of his cock. I'd never tell him because he's an ass and, on top of that, his ego can't take much more inflating. The truth is, I wanted to throw myself at him last night. Even now as I plan my escape, I'm dying to be with him just one last time. He's so damn addictive. I wanted to scream when he talked about finding my replacement tonight. *Fuck him.* That, right there, is why I never needed a man. I will not fall into the same rabbit hole that my sister did. I can see just how well that worked out for her.

We sit down at one of the booths. A waitress comes by, instantly flirting with Torch. *Like his ego needs that boost.* He's eating it up like a kid diving into the birthday cake. I hide behind the menu and roll my eyes. He keeps looking at me, so I know he's trying to see if it bothers me. Why should it bother me that some woman's flirting with him like a bitch in heat? I mean, could she *get* any more obvious?

"Looks like you've found my replacement for the night," I tell him when she leaves after taking our order. I busy myself with arranging my silverware and putting the laminated menu back in the holder, refusing to look at him.

"Jealous, sweetness? All you have to do is say the word."

"What word would that be? Male whore? Oh wait, that's two words."

He leans into the table. I can't stop my eyes from locking onto his green ones. He really is like a giant man-child and I would love to get caught up in this happy enthusiasm that he has bundled up inside of him. I think it's what drew me to him in the first place.

"I didn't see you complaining about me when you were opening your legs and begging me inside," he says, and his voice changes. He's not happy-go-lucky right now, not even a little bit. Now, he's pissed. His eyes sparkle, but there's anger in them.

Gee. Did I hit a sore spot? He can go fuck himself if he thinks I'll apologize. I shrug. That's the only response he gets. I ignore the part of me that wants to apologize and laugh again. That part is what got me in this mess. I need to get back to Beth, not get caught up trying to… shit, I'm not even sure what I'd be trying to do. Torch was a one-night stand. A bad decision. A really bad decision, that's all he is and all he will ever be.

My mind's made up. We finish eating our meal in silence.

CHAPTER 23
TORCH

"she's tempting me."

"If you keep giving that fucking trucker those looks, I'm going to tan your hide, Katie," I warn her after she smiles at the trucker in question for like the hundredth time. She's clearly offering him a taste of her honey and the fucker is all set to take her up on that. I may have to kill the asshole before it's done.

She looks at me innocently. "What are you talking about?"

"Don't play stupid. You know what the fuck you're doing and it's not going to work."

"Maybe I'm just finding *my* good time tonight, since you're planning one already."

"That's not going to happen. I told you, the only dick you have on the menu for the foreseeable future is mine. So if you need cock, you tell me. Other than that, you're in for a bit of a dry spell."

"That's not hardly fair, is it?"

I lean into her because I like that her eyes are on me. I enjoy that I'm the fucker who holds her attention. Most of all, I like that she's not looking at that hairy fucker sitting across from us.

"It doesn't have to be fair. It just has to be true. Which it is. You know what I think your problem is, Katydid?"

"I told you to stop with that horrible nickname. But please, do tell me what my problem is. Unless it's you insisting on dragging me back to Kentucky and closer to the men who want me and my sister dead, because I already know that problem, stud."

"You've run too wild. You need a man who can contain you. Show you boundaries while also showing you how fucking far your body can stretch to receive the pleasure it's capable of."

"Let me guess. You're the man to do that?"

"I've never wanted to be. That kind of training takes longer than I've wanted to invest before, but…" I trail off, studying her face. She's beautiful. I can see something flare in her eyes at my sentence. I'm not sure what it is, but I'd like to pretend it's hope.

"But?"

"But I think, with you, I'd like to play a lot longer than my usual timespan."

"Timespan?" she asks, taking a drink of her soda. "Do tell, what *is* your usual timespan?"

"Few days. Couple weeks at most. You're different, Katie. I think I could take my time with you and not grow bored. At least, for a month or two," I admit. I'm being totally sincere, which is fucking hard for me, to be honest. I don't know what it is about Katie, but I do know I want more time with her.

"Be still my beating heart. Do you even listen to yourself when you talk?"

"What? You can't tell me you ever envisioned being with the same person for more than a couple of months."

"Maybe I have. Maybe I want the white picket fence, babies, and a minivan. The whole damn thing. What makes you say that I don't?"

"Because you're too much like me."

This time, it's her who leans in closer, and those gray eyes get that stormy look again that I'm coming to crave. Usually that look means she's horny. This time, it's something else: a deep emotion that she doesn't mean to let me see. *But I do.*

"Maybe the reason I appear not to want the normal things any girl does is because it's not in the cards for me."

"Tell me another one. Any man you smile at would want to give that to you."

"Says the man who's intent on taking me to someone who wants me dead."

"Skull isn't planning to do that. He won't let anything happen to you." *I won't let anything happen to you,* I add silently.

"Your faith in Skull would warm me, if I didn't know what a miserable fucker he is. I need to use the restroom."

I want to growl, but I let it go. It is what it is, and there's not much I can do to change the path we're on. I throw some money down for the food, plus a tip for the waitress. "Let's go."

We walk towards the back of the diner where the bathrooms are located. When we pass the trucker's table on the opposite side of the aisle, it might be my imagination, but I can totally admit I'm fucking jealous, which is upsetting enough. But when we walk by, it seems like Katie's steps slow down, extending the time she comes in contact with the other man.

"Hey there, little lady," the guy says as we pass. I already have Katie by the hand, but I move my hold up to her shoulder so there's no mistaking my message.

"The little lady has a man," I growl, and it's fucking true. At least for now, damn it. He needs to know, that son of a bitch, as long as Katie doesn't undermine my fucking claim.

"Hi," she whispers with a giggle. *A fucking giggle!*

I practically pull her away from the damned table. She's been walking better today, but she stumbles twice as I pull her. I don't give a fuck. I want her to do her business and then get her the fuck away from that asshole. Then, if I don't change my mind, I'm going to spank her ass so red that she won't be able to sit down for a fucking month without crying out. Damned cock tease. It was bad enough when it was me she did that shit to, but I will not have her trying to get another man's attention. *Fuck no!*

I open the door to the one-stalled bathroom and practically shove her inside. "Get done. You have five minutes tops, then I'll come in after you. If I have to do that, Katie, you won't like it," I threaten, slamming the door shut.

I wait against it. I wait longer than five minutes, which makes me a liar. But, motherfucker, I need to get a hold of myself. She's been in there a good ten minutes when I hear her gasp, followed by a loud noise I can't really describe. I start banging on the door. "Katie, you need to get your ass out of there or I'll break the motherfucking door down. We need to get going."

BURNED

"I don't like the way you're talking to that girl," the trucker from earlier says.

He's standing in front of me, apparently taking it on his own to follow us back here and check on Katie. Well, hell, it looks like I'm going to have to beat the asshole down. I'm not worried. I'm pretty sure I can take him… until two of his butt-buddies join him. The three of them look at me like I'm next on their list of things to fuck up.

If I survive this shit, I'm going to strangle Katie.

Chapter 24
Katie

" I will not feel guilty. I will not feel guilty. "

I think I'm losing my touch. I gave that trucker enough of an invitation that he really should've walked over. He didn't. That's Torch's fault too, since he looks pretty damn formidable. Well, if you discard his damn t-shirts.

Shit. I have to get away. I have to.

There's a tiny fucking window in here that is way too small for my ass, and he'll give up waiting on me at any moment. I try to push it open, but it's not budging. My finger snags on the rusty metal handle and it stings like hell. It starts bleeding right away. I'll probably die of tetanus and it'll be all the asshole's fault.

I take a deep breath and try to look around for something, *anything*, that can help me get away from him. As if he can hear my thoughts, he pounds on the door, yelling. I ignore him. I have to think.

That's when I hear *him*. A second voice; I'm almost sure it's the trucker. Now's my chance. I need to make sure when I come out that I get him completely on my side. I can't take the chance that Torch will talk the Trucker into his side. The man has a golden tongue… in more ways than one.

I look in the mirror above the sink. I look down at my Black Crowes t-shirt and mourn losing it. I pull at the collar. Luckily, I had already taken scissors to it and made it into a V cut. I hate the round collars that most t-shirts spout; it feels like it chokes me, and Lord knows I've had that feeling enough—I don't need it from my clothes. I rip it so it falls down on my shoulder, enough to show the silky red bra beneath, because let's face it, men get distracted by boobs. Satisfied with that, I muss up my hair just a little. At first, I grieved losing my blonde locks. The longer I have this dark color, the more I like it. I doubt I'll ever go back. Not to mention, I like looking different from Bethie. With that done, I look a little roughed up, but it's not enough. I need signs of violence. Torch is talking to the trucker. I need to hurry before the trucker leaves.

I take a deep breath, make a tight fist like I learned in self-defense class, then hit myself along my jaw and the corner of my mouth. *Jesus.* Okay, that hurt, but I know I've pulled my punch some. I don't really like pain. Isn't that ironic? After three more punches, I can see the red inflamed skin. Eventually, it will swell. That'll work, except for...

I take my ring off. It's a small diamond surrounded by pearl petals so that it looks like a daisy. It was a gift from Bethie during our first Christmas together after she found me. I use the diamond to cut the corner of my lip. It doesn't bleed much, just a little bit. It's enough though, because I'm about two steps away from joining the crazy train now. I use the blood from the finger I cut earlier and smear extra along the bottom of my lip making it look like it's bleeding a lot. One last look in the mirror and then I walk to the door.

"She's my woman," I hear Torch say.

"Didn't look to me like she wanted to be your woman anymore."

"It's just a lover's tiff. She's mad I forgot her birthday. It's not bad enough she's busting my balls over that, but she's also on the rag. You know how women get."

"Yeah, I guess..."

Fuck. I knew he'd talk his way out of it. I guess it's show time. I put both hands on the door, take a deep breath, then push it open.

Chapter 25
Torch

"I'm going to kill her."

I've just about gotten the guy calmed down, and the other two seemed to have relaxed as well. They're about to go back into the dining area of the store when Katie opens the door.

Only she doesn't look like she did when she went in. Someone beat the hell out of her. I'm about to charge into the bathroom and find out what the fuck is going on. I thought it was empty, but obviously it wasn't. I'm going to kill a motherfucker for even thinking about putting their hands on her. One thing stops me—and it stops me cold.

"I'm here, I'm here… Just please don't hurt me again," she says, her voice breaking, her eyes bright. She looks so pitiful and frail standing there like that with unshed tears and her body trembling. I know I'm going to kill someone, until it clicks in my head: *she's talking to me.*

I'm slow because it doesn't take He-Man and his buddies as long to figure it out. I know this because a fist barrels into my nose as I'm making these observations. *Motherfucking son of a milk cow!* A fist slams into me, spraying blood from my nose. I hear a crunch in my ears. Skull and the brothers would have my fucking ass for being caught so unawares. I can't help it, though; my brain was all about Katie being hurt. *How the fuck was I supposed to know that the bitch was setting me up?*

I know it now, though. There's not a doubt in my mind. I can see her out of the corner of my eye, curled into one of the other men, scared to death. Looking at her cost me as I'm cross-cut with another left. *Fucking bloody hell!*

That's it. I'm going to tear this asshole's arms off and beat him to death with them, then I'm going to strangle that damned brunette.

I deliver a blow to the gut. When he bends down to protect his weakness, I deliver shot after shot under his chin and to his face. He backs up a good five feet because he wasn't expecting me to fight back so violently. I don't have my cut on because I'm trying not to broadcast I'm in the area, so motherfucker has no idea who he's dealing with. I could eat men like him for breakfast and spit on his grave. I'm feeling pretty fucking great about it because Goliath here falls back against the wall, going down for the count. I'm about to turn my attention back to Katie when I'm brought to my knees with a heavy thud on my head. The room swirls in circles and goes precariously gray. I try to fight through it. *I can't go down like this. I can't lose Katie. That's not an option.* I try to fight, but I'm sinking further down, falling on the concrete floor with a thud.

I look up. My vision is blurry and I'm seeing double, but one of the truckers is standing over me with a huge metal rack in his hand and there's sales books all around the ground. The fucker hit me from behind with a magazine rack?? That was a punk-ass move, getting me from behind like that. I'll remember that for when I get up from here to kill the son of a bitch.

"Is he alright? Oh my God, did you kill him?" Katie's voice reaches me. I'd like to think that's real fear in her voice, but I know better. After all, I'm in this situation because of her, the lying little cunt. I'll make her pay too, as soon as the room stops spinning. And what's with all the gray?

I'm losing focus. Son of a bitch, nothing I can do will bring it back. I know I'm going out. I keep trying to fight it, but it's pointless. My eyes flutter closed and, right before I go out, I see Katie walking out with one of the fuckers. She looks over the man's shoulder at me and I think she's mouthing the words, *I'm sorry.* I can't be sure.

It doesn't matter. When I catch up to her, she will be sorry; that much I can guarantee.

Chapter 26
Katie

" Why should I feel guilty? "

Guilt is eating me up inside and I hate it! I never meant for Torch to get so hurt. I hope he's okay. Surely someone has found him by now. Probably that damned waitress who was already panting after him and drooling. Somehow, I ended up with a different trucker than my original mark. I liked the first guy; he had a kindness in his eyes. Torch managed to take him down though and that left me with Mr. Hands over here.

I've gone along with him though because after everything I've done, I *need* to get away from Torch. I have to get to Bethie, but more than that, Torch is going to be pissed as hell at me. If he gets a hold on me again, I'll never get away. He has a right to be pissed, I guess, but he was holding me captive! He was forcing me into a situation that would put my niece and my sister in danger, and he wouldn't even try to understand. He's an asshole and I should *not* be feeling guilt.

I try to breathe and consider my next move. When I climbed up into the rig, Mr. Hands made a big show of helping to boost me up. In reality, it was just so his hand could cup my ass, hence the nickname I gave him. Since then though, he's been okay. I'm just letting him drive and tell me about how little women like me need to be careful, how I need a man to protect me, and how if he was my man, he'd spoil me like a queen. Do women really fall for this stuff? I don't get it.

Then again, I've never had use for a man past one night. Never even thought about it. I ignore the way an image of Torch comes to mind. Okay, so I thought of keeping him longer than one night. I would have never done it. *Never.* He's a player and I will never fall under the spell of a man like Bethie did. *Never.* Did I mention never? Because it's true. Definitely true. *Never, ever, ever. Freaking never!*

"Wait. What are you doing?"

"You're too keyed up, sweetness. I'll show you how a real man works that out of you. Then, we'll see about getting you some clothes."

Fuck! Suddenly, I'm reminded of how my shirt is ripped and my bra shows through. I'm also reminded of Torch calling me "sweetness" and how I kind of like it, but when this guy says it, I don't like it. I don't like it at all.

While I'm reminded of all this, Mr. Hands is pulling off into a seedy motel. If this is how he treats the women in his life that he wants to make his *queen,* it's no fucking wonder the man is single. Though, I bet if the truth was known, he has some poor schmuck of a wife sitting at home who has no idea what her man is up to while on the road.

"Listen, I appreciate your help, but I'm not going into that motel with you. This is where I find another ride," I tell him, and before he can say anything else, I unlatch my seatbelt, open my door, and climb down.

I'm thankful I have my boots on because, honestly, I've done more on my leg in the last few days than I have in months. The pain is constant, but I've dealt with it, and my boots give me extra support which helps. Still, when I jump from the bottom step of the eighteen-wheeler to the ground, I land wrong and my ankle curls. Pain shoots up my bad leg and it's so fucking intense that I cry out.

"Whoa there! I got you. You should have waited on me. A woman like you with that fine little body, you aren't made to handle big rigs like this," Mr. Hands says, and surprise, his hands go around me and hold me by my *ass.*

I jerk away from him. "I'm fine. Like I said, this is a no-go for me. I'm going to go find a different ride. Thanks for your help back there, but I think I'm done with men for a while."

I push away from him and turn to walk back to the road. Hopefully the next person to pick me up won't be some horny trucker with an overactive libido. Or an axe murderer; not really wanting that either. I make it a few steps when he grabs me from behind. This time, his hands are on my boobs. What is it with my luck lately?

"I've got a ride for you, sweetness. I got a nice long hard ride for you."

Oh, God.

"Listen. You don't really want to do this," I warn him.

"I do, and I can guarantee you that I'll make you want it too," he says, and yeah, that pretty much seals his fate.

No one is *making* me want shit.

I bring my elbow back and slam it into his abdomen. I stick my ass hard into him while he's bent down. My hands go up behind my head to lock around the back of his neck and I use the force of my body and his motion to propel him over my head. Really, my self-defense instructor would be proud. He falls to the ground in a puff of dust, looking up at me like he can't believe what I just did. I use that same foot to slam down on his crotch, grinding the steel-toe so damned heavily, I figure his balls might burst. He cries out, which brings me a small level of joy. He's curled into a ball now, but I know he'll get up quick, and because Torch has my clothes and took away the weapons I normally carry, I've got to move fast. Shit. Shit. *Shit.*

I run—well, mostly hobble—to the big rig. I climb up on the driver's side. The key is still in it. I can drive a six speed dually; surely this can't be that much different, right? Luckily, it's old-school; no fancy push-buttons, so I'm not completely lost. I'm ridiculously helpless at backing up anything with a trailer, even my jeep, so I cut the wheel deep and pray. I manage to only side swipe the back end of one car before I complete my turn, then go back onto the road. I won't be able to drive this for long because soon, I'm sure the cops will be on my ass. Still, if I can manage ten minutes, that should get me on the freeway and off to the next exit. Hopefully I can find another ride, or else a less conspicuous car to hijack. It takes some gear-grinding, and each time I have to use the clutch, my foot screams in agony. Despite it all, I find my groove and get the hell out of dodge.

Today is not starting off well. Then, I notice the trucker's cellphone on the dash, and smile. Maybe it's getting better.

Chapter 27
Torch

"Skull is going to have my ass."

"What the fuck do you mean you lost her??" Skull screams over the phone, and when I say scream, I actually mean it's more like a cold, monotone question that's meant to leave the person he's talking to dead. *That'd be me.*

I just had to break it to him that Katie got away. I questioned the diner and found out what route that trucker normally takes. The waitress helped me where the others just looked at me like I was insane. The waitress made it clear that she'd like to nurse me back to health—especially my damned cock—and it pisses me off that the fucker crawled up and hid! My cock has always been a shower, strutting his magnificent self like a proud peacock and demanding the ladies' eyes. The last two months, he's changed somewhat. Nothing interested him—until Katie. But never in my life has he revolted when a woman reached out to pet him. Shit! That crap has got to change. Maybe they have electroshock therapy for your dick. I could get that desperate.

"Are you listening to me asshole?"

Shit, Skull. I don't think he'd like to hear me say no. "I am, boss," I lie. "I promise you, I got this. I already have her hunted down. I'm heading there now," I assure him, and yeah, I'm lying out of my ass. I know a general vicinity though, and really, how hard can it be to hide a yellow eighteen-wheeler? *Shit.*

"You better, motherfucker. If I lose my chance to grab ahold of Beth—I mean, my daughter—I will *end* you. *Entiéndeme?*"

"I got it, boss. I'll have her by nightfall."

He hangs up, and I hope like hell I do have her, because if I don't, I wouldn't put it past Skull to come down here and hunt down Katie himself. I still have the urge to protect her and that's fucked up. But boss isn't thinking clearly. He might say this is to get his daughter, but I know it's to get Beth. He wants his daughter, I don't doubt that for a second. But... Beth. He wants Beth. What the fuck he's going to do with her when he gets her all depends on exactly what the fuck caused her to run in the first place.

The damn jeep is sucking fumes, so I decide to take the next exit. Just another fucking reason to hate cages. If I was on my bike, I'd have already eaten up the interstate. I make a right towards the Shell station, groaning at the backed up traffic. There must have been a wreck. Hopefully I don't run out of gas while I'm waiting for it to thin out; that'd be the fucking cherry on top of the shit pile that has been my day. My knuckles are bruised, I've got a headache from hell, and my fucking ribs are sore. Motherfuckers must have kicked me while I was out.

Traffic slowly starts moving. There's a policeman directing all the traffic into one lane. As I get closer, I can see why, and I feel a moment of complete and utter fucking joy. There, surrounded by cops in the far lane, is an eighteen-wheeler. Not just any eighteen-wheeler, but a fucking bright yellow one.

I negotiate Katie's jeep to the median and jump out to see what kind of fucking mess she's gotten into now, because I have no doubt that she's in the middle of whatever it is.

"What's going on here?" I ask.

"Sir, I'm going to have to ask you to return to your vehicle. We're trying to prevent traffic from being backed up."

"Oh, I hear ya. It's just that at the Waffle King in Brownville, that very fucking truck was there, and I saw its driver force a woman into the truck with him. I tried to tell the police there. They wanted me to come in and make a report. I did, but I don't know if they did anything about it."

"Shit. You're kidding me!" The officer goes off running to one of the other men there. I walk closer, expecting to get a glimpse of Katie, but I don't see her anywhere.

"There wasn't a woman in the truck?" I call out, and I try not to let my inner fear free. Shit, if she got herself hurt by pulling her damn stunt…

"There wasn't anyone here," the officer answers. "Witnesses say they saw a brunette limp out of the truck and start walking towards Casey. They reported her limping heavily and looking like she'd been in a fight."

"David! We don't release details of the case," another cop says, which is kind of stupid, though probably a hundred percent true—and smart. Dumbass. For all he knows, I could be the owner of the truck.

I need to find Katie. Shit. I hope she's okay. I start to turn away when I hear one of the cops yell.

"Hey! Sarge! Dispatch just got a call from the Angel Drop Motel, said some woman stole his rig."

"Have one of the men go to the motel and get this guy. Tell them to treat him like a suspect. We have a witness who said this guy might have kidnapped a woman over in Brownville."

And cue my time to leave. As much as I want to make sure that trucker gets his ass sewn up, if I have to stay around and be the motherfucker to help do it, Katie will get away. I back away until I'm out of sight, then jump in my jeep and drive off. I take the back road and hold my breath until I find a little mom-and-pop gas station and fill up. There's been no sign of Katie. I might have picked the wrong route. I thought driving on this back road would be the way to go, but—

I stop when I see her. She's limping hard, walking along the side of the road. My heart squeezes in my chest.

Motherfucking raindrops in Hell! Until this moment, I refused to acknowledge the fear I felt when I saw the eighteen-wheeler abandoned and Katie nowhere to be found. I didn't fully believe that she had stolen the damn thing. Jesus.

I pull up beside her. The window is already down. It's an older model jeep, so the windows zip. How she could like such a thing is beyond me. "Get in," I order, and my voice might rival Skull's in being cold right now.

Chapter 28
Katie

" *If it wasn't for bad luck...* "

Did I break a freaking mirror? I don't think I've ever had such a continuous run of bad luck, and considering I spent most of my life being a prisoner of my father and grandfather, that's saying something! When I think someone is finally offering me a ride, only to find Torch sitting in *my* jeep, I want to scream.

I look around, trying to figure out how I can get away.

"You even think about it, Katie, and so help me God, I will make sure you regret it. I have a headache from fucking hell after getting my skull bashed in by that magazine rack, and I'm *not* gonna put up with anymore of your shit."

I want to at least make a run for it, but with the agony in my leg, I know it wouldn't do any good. "I hate you," I grumble, then get up in the jeep. My leg protests even that small feat, and I grimace from the pain.

"The feeling is starting to be mutual," he growls, then makes a hard U-turn, squealing my tires.

I grab ahold of the dashboard, trying to brace myself. "Will you slow down? This isn't the Daytona Speedway!"

"Shut up, Katie."

I don't respond. Something about the tone of his voice tells me it wouldn't be wise to prod him. I've survived knowing how far I can go. I haven't always listened to the warning in my head, but I'm still here. I guess I should trust my instincts. Instead of going off on him like I want, I sit quietly and rub my leg. It's cramping and I've been without any type of medication for a couple days. The pain is intense.

"Are you even listening to me?" asks Torch, jarring me out of my thoughts.

"I thought you told me to shut up," I respond.

"I asked what's wrong with your leg?"

"It hurts."

"Jesus, does everything have to be like pulling teeth with you?"

"I'm sorry I'm not more accommodating to the man who is intent on taking away the freedom it took my whole life to gain."

That makes him go silent. Good. He can chew on that for a little while.

"Sweetness, I know you don't believe me, but we aren't going to hurt you."

"You might not be planning on it, but you will."

"Skull deserves to see his child, Katie. Beth and he need to talk."

"He doesn't deserve shit. He lost that chance when he turned his back on her when she almost died. She needed him there. He decided to send her money and a nice goodbye note with a picture of him and his new woman."

"What are you talking about?"

"Just let it go. Nothing I tell you will make you change your mind."

"Skull would never do that, Katie. Jesus Christ, I don't think the man has been with a woman since Beth's been gone."

"Yeah, I'm buying that."

"I'm telling you it's the truth. I mean, there might have been a few while he was grieving and drunk off his ass, but there's been no one he's bothered having a repeat performance with."

"Oh well, that makes it all better."

"What the fuck did you expect? He thought she was dead! He thought he killed her!"

"And I'm saying *he knew better!* I'm saying that while Beth was delivering her daughter, she almost *died*. I called to let him know that she needed him, and one of your brothers hung up on me!" I'm watching his face the entire time, so I see the exact moment when his face changes. "Oh my God. It was *you*. You're the fucker who hung up on me that night!"

"We thought she was dead," he says. "We thought—"

"I know what you *thought*. I know exactly what you *thought*."

"Katie…"

"You and your brother both thought you could send Bethie a goodbye package that would rip out her heart and a hundred thousand thrown in the mix and you'd be done with us."

"I'm telling you, Skull didn't do that."

"And I'm telling you, I was there so I know he did."

"I give up. I can't win with you. While you're sitting over there being a bitch and being mad at the world, Katie, why don't you ask yourself one question? Why don't you ask yourself why, if Skull was in such a hurry to get rid of Beth and his child a couple of years ago, he would even bother trying to find them now? And while you're puzzling over that one, why don't you remember who the fuckers are that have given you and Beth so much trouble from day one. Because I think if you remember that, you might discover that person has never been a member of the Devil's Blaze."

I stare at the window and ignore him, or at least I'm trying to appear that way. The problem is, he's making sense. Could the package have not been from Skull? Does it even matter? The picture in it, Bethie confirmed, was Skull. I lay my head against the window of the jeep and close my eyes. I'm tired of thinking. I'm tired of fighting—*at least for now.*

CHAPTER 29
TORCH

"I cannot understand my reaction to her. I just know I want her with me."

"Wake up, sleepyhead," I whisper to Katie as I'm picking her up in my arms. She's been sleeping all evening. I woke her up so we could grab some drive-thru. She ate, then went back out.

I've been driving for the last five hours in silence. By rights, we should almost be home, but Skull told me to drag my feet and that's what I'm doing, which explains why we're only halfway through the state of Oklahoma instead of in Missouri. He thinks Beth will follow her sister. He's so sure of it, he's planning on meeting us when we cross over into Missouri.

I have mixed feeling about it all. I don't want my time with Katie to end. As pissed off as I was at the stunt she pulled today, the relief I felt when I found her was different for me. Profound, even. I'm a lover of women. All women. I just don't believe in monogamy, or that it's even possible. Katie pulls strings inside of me I didn't know were there. I'm not tired of her. Not even a little bit. Instead, I keep remembering our night together and I fucking want more. It could be just sex, but the thing is, I enjoy just talking to her and spending time with her almost as much as the sex, and that shit right there, that has *never* fucking happened. That has to mean something, right? I don't know what it means, but I do know it makes me curious.

As I watch her stretch, her shirt pulling taut over her breasts and that sweet little noise that escapes her lips, I know it's more than that. *Katie is different.* Fuck me running. She's got a hold on me and I'm starting to wonder if I'm ever going to get free.

I pick her up in my arms and something settles inside of me.

She's made for my arms. *She fits.* It's sudden, but I feel it in my fucking blood. The same blood she heats. I made fun of Sabre, Latch, and Skull. Called them pussy-whipped and a million other things, but fuck me if it's not starting to sink in that I might be trapped and just as hard and as quick as they were. The scariest thing about that shit isn't the thought of being tied down with one woman my whole life. Fuck, no. That's how far her claws are in me. The scary thing is how Katie will react when Skull gets Beth in his clutches again, because my brother is fucked up.

I'm not even sure what he's going to do.

I checked into the Ken's Bargain Motel before I went back to collect Katie. It's a small, out of the way motel where there are five rooms attached to the main office all in succession, one right after the other. I asked for the room on the end out of habit. I don't need Katie screaming and alerting the front office, either. She's given me a big enough headache as it is.

I carry her inside and put her on the bed. With all of the shifting and moving around, she finally wakes up. She stretches her hands above her head, yawning. She probably has no idea how fucking sexy she looks right now. At least my dick is waking up and appreciating the fact.

"What time is it?"

"Late. We'll bed down for the night and get up early in the morning."

She scrunches up her nose and combs her fingers through her hair while yawning again, but not quietly. I'm freaking smiling over that. I was right; I'm going down just like my brothers were. Shit, and within just a couple of days. I might have fallen quicker than they did.

"I need a shower," she mumbles, looking around the room, probably for an escape route. How the hell did I get here? What happened to the good ol' days when I wanted rid of a woman and they were crying, wanting to stay?

"Fine, but let's hurry. I'm killed," I tell her, yanking off my shirt.

"I meant me, as in singular."

"Sweetness, after the merry chase you've sent me on, you're not moving two feet away from me. We either shower together or we don't shower. The choice is yours."

"But I'm dusty and sore."

"Then we shower."

"Hunter, I can still feel his hands on me. Please? Chain me to the shower somehow, I don't care, but I want a shower and I want it alone."

Mother-fucking-Hellfire! "He put his hands on you?"

She jumps. I don't know if it's from the tone in my voice or the look on my face. Both, probably. I'm going to hunt that bastard down and cut his balls out with a rusty spoon and feed them to the motherfucker before I do the world a favor and put a bullet between his eyes.

"My boobs and ass," she answers. "He was definitely an ass man. Can I please wash without you watching? I promise to be on my best behavior. Scouts honor."

"Sweetness, I doubt you were ever a scout."

"Please, Hunter?"

I'm starting to see differences in Katie. When she's sweet and more honest with me, she uses my real name, and I doubt she even realizes the change—but I do. I'm a card player from way back and it's good to know that I'm learning Katie's tells.

"Let's go. You look too tired to do much running anyways," I tell her.

She slides off the bed with a groan. "You have no idea," she whispers, but it breaks off in a cry when she tries to put pressure on her leg. She nearly crumbles to the floor before I make it to her side and hold her in my arms.

"Sweetness?" I question, unsure of what happened.

"I'm fine," she whispers, but we both know it's not true. I put my finger under her chin so I can see her eyes. At the sight of her tears, I know it's no longer me just worrying. I've fallen under this woman's spell, hard. I sunk just as hard and just as fast as my brothers. "*Motherfucking-son-of-a-whoremonger!*"

"Did you just say, whoremonger?" her quiet voice whispers

and she's trying to smile, but I see the tightness in her face and she still has tears falling.

I hadn't realized I said it out loud. "I have a habit of adding flair to my cursing. I like to think of myself like the Batman and Robin of cursing. It makes it more fun."

"Cursing is fun?" she asks as I help her back on the bed. I drop to my knees and start unlacing her boots. She jerks her feet away from me, but I hold onto her foot, not letting her pull away.

"Yeah, like *'Holy Anagram, Batman!'*"

"You're a strange man."

"Be still and let me look at your foot."

"It's fine. It's not really your concern."

"It doesn't look swollen."

"Just let it go, Torch," she says, and there's her tell. I'm only just starting to discover this woman. I'm not afraid to say that fact excites me.

"Where did you get the scars on your body, Katie?" I ask, letting my fingers massage into the skin of her legs.

"Where do you get those God-awful t-shirts?"

"Always giving me crap. Okay, sweetness, hold tight."

"Why?"

"I'm going to start a bath. You need to soak this leg. The ankle is puffy."

"Thank you."

I don't bother answering. She's taking a bath alright, but I'm getting in that fucker with her.

Chapter 30
Katie

" Why did I let my guard down? Stupid, Katie ... Stupid. "

I take a chance to breathe and calm myself. Feeling Torch's hands on my body is enough to totally wreck me. Feeling him bring my leg comfort does something else entirely. It makes me want to let my guard down. He seemed concerned. Other than Bethie, there has never been another person to give me that, which is bad. I mean nothing to Torch. He *can't* mean anything to me. So what the fuck am I doing?

He leaves to fix the bathwater and I'm left staring at the door. I should make a run for it, but I'm hurting so bad, I'm not sure I could make it. He threw the keys to the jeep on the dresser. He seems so unconcerned. It's like he's trying to trust me. Maybe it's the pain or the softness I'm feeling towards him, but I can't bring myself to leave. I ignore the voice inside that says I don't want to hurt him. That can't be it... *It can't*.

He returns to me. "Stand up, sweetness," he says softly, and the tone of his voice makes something flutter to life inside of me. Torch helps me stand up, then his hands brush my hair on each side of my face before slowly moving down my neck. Torch's thumbs pet the front of my throat, igniting flames of awareness in my blood.

"Hunter... I'm not sure we should be doing this," I whisper, wetting my lips since my throat seems to have gone dry. Desire floods through my system and I can feel my heartbeat echo in my ears. For some reason, he smiles. It should be noted that when Torch smiles, those green eyes of his could melt the panties off of a nun. "Why are you smiling?" I ask, unable to stop looking at him. If you can get away with calling a man beautiful, Torch definitely is.

"I like it when you say my name, Katie," he says as his hands travel over my arms and come to a rest on my hips. I have to force myself to take a breath as he moves to my waist and unbuttons my pants. My hands go to cover his as I halfheartedly try to stop him.

"Hunter…"

His lips come down and gently grazes mine, drinking from them in the softest kiss I've ever had in my life.

"Let me take care of you, Katie."

"But—"

"Katie, I can't explain what happened the night Beth had the baby, but I know that whatever happened, Skull wasn't part of it. I'm asking you to trust me. Let me show you that my brothers are not the *Big Bad* here. That *I'm* not. Trust me, Katie," he says, pushing my pants down off my hips.

His words hit me hard. I can't trust him. I don't think any woman with my history could ever trust a man. Torch makes me want to, though, and that's more than I've ever felt. He doesn't know that I've already called Beth. I arranged to meet her in Tennessee in one week. I used the trucker's phone, then threw it over a guardrail when I abandoned the truck. Just talking to Beth allowed me to breathe and regroup.

It also gives me a few days to give in to what my body wants.

I'm not sure what's changed between us, or when it did, but the softness he's showing me is something I didn't know I wanted, but it's something I crave… apparently. I want more of it. I think I need it. I study him for a minute. Then, in answer, I pull my shirt off and wait.

Chapter 31
Katie

" *Finally.* "

"Jesus, fuck," he whispers before crouching down to rid me of my pants.

"What?" I ask, nervous and worried I did something wrong.

"Just hoping I can hold it together long enough to let you soak in the tub," he says.

"Well, that's… disappointing."

"Stop it, woman. You need to soak that leg."

He pulls my body close to him, his hands grip my hips, and he places a kiss on my pussy. His body vibrates as he breathes in deeply.

"What are you doing? Did you just… *smell* me?" I ask, suddenly wishing I had put on panties this morning.

"There's not a better aroma in the world than the smell of my Katie aroused," he says.

I don't respond. I can't. Does he even realize he called me his? Why do I like that? Why does that make me happy? *Crap.*

"Stop it. You're weirding me out," I tell him. By "weirding me out", I mean he's totally weakening my defense system. I've already softened towards him; I can't weaken even more.

He stands up. Right back in its place is that easy, cocky grin I'm so used to seeing on him.

"Really?" he asks. "Because I think I'm making you wet."

He's not wrong. Before I can respond, he pulls me up in his arms and carries me off to the bathroom. He lets me down, unlatches my bra, then tosses it to the ground. The tub is small, but larger than others I've seen in motel rooms, especially for the dive this one is. I sit down. Torch slides in across from me minutes later. This is a new experience for me. I've never bathed with a man before, unless you count the shower with Torch that first night. This seems more intimate, though. Apparently not intimate enough for him; he situates my legs so that they overlap his, then pulls my hips so we're mere inches apart.

"That's better."

"Is it?" I ask, confused and distracted by the sight of this man devouring me with his eyes. *Me.*

"Now, I can take care of you," he says with a grin.

"You could have done that in the bedroom," I tell him, not really kidding.

"I meant wash you, dirty girl," he says taking the soap and lathering it between his hands. For some reason, my eyes are glued on his every movement. Watching how the soap slides between his hands, the white foam emerging between his fingers, I soon find out that's nothing compared to the way it feels when his slick hands caresses my body with the soap. He starts with my neck, leaving magic in his wake as his fingers tease and torture every inch of what might be the most erogenous zone on my body.

I hold my breath, waiting for him to move on to my breasts. He doesn't, though. Instead, he goes down my shoulder, then my arm, and finally arrives at my hands. He uses his thumbs to massage the palms of my hands.

My eyes close in pleasure. "That feels so good," I whisper.

"I have been told I have magic fingers," he says. I'm not watching him, but I can hear the smile he's wearing on his face right now.

"Please, do not tell me about the millions of women who have stroked your ego," I tell him, half-joking. For the first time I can remember, it bothers me to hear about the women this man has had before me.

"You make me forget them all," he says softly.

The importance of what he just said makes me open my eyes. He doesn't look up, though. I'm not sure he's aware he said that out loud. His hands move down to my leg, the one that's been hurting so bad I could barely walk. He begins to massage it, and I can't stop the groan that escapes as he kneads the flesh there.

"How did you get the scars, Katydid?" he asks, his finger brushing against the faint scars and following their line down. They aren't as bad as they used to be, and definitely not as bad as they *could* have been. Still, they make me uncomfortable. I'm not use to putting myself out there with a man.

"Why does it matter?" I ask, trying to divert him. "If they turn you off..."

He stops me from pulling away. "I didn't say that, sweetness. There's not a fucking thing about you that turns me off. I just want to know how you got them. They remind me of some of the scars my brother Beast has."

I swallow. Bethie has talked incessantly about the club. She thought of them as her family before Skull's note. I know right away who Beast is and I know what scars he would have. They would be very much like mine, I'd imagine, except Beast got his heroically. He got his willingly. I was just a guinea pig, a way to further my father's great plan. *Collateral damage.*

"There was a fire..." I tell him, which isn't the truth, but close enough.

"Sweetness," he groans, the word sounding haunted. My legs are in the water, but because they're draped over his, the tops are out. He bends down and kisses the scar. I swallow in response.

I'm feeling self-conscious and on-display—neither emotion is good for me. I need to divert him, and fast. "Torch..." He looks at me. I see the disappointment in his eyes, and just like that, the moment's broken.

"Hold your head back, Katydid," he says, grabbing a plastic cup off the edge of the tub. It's white, but has the motel name on it. I hold my head back just as Torch pulls me up on his lap.

"What—?"

"I just needed you closer for this. Now, hold your head back," he instructs me again, and I do it, but it's hard to concentrate when I can feel his dick pushing against my ass.

How much torture can one woman take?

He pours water through my hair over and over, making sure it's all wet. When he stops, I look up to find him pouring shampoo in his hand. He rubs it in my hair and then massages it in my scalp. I've never had a man wash my hair before. Even when we showered together, our hands were much too busy doing other things. Now, I suddenly wonder why. *It's amazing.* I groan at the feel of the way he rubs the shampoo into my hair, taking time to massage and knead my head in the process, which relaxes me.

"That feels good," I moan, grinding my ass against his hardened cock. He's been priming my body for him and I'm not even aware of it. Suddenly, I'm dying to have him inside of me. "Hunter," I growl, my nails biting into his shoulders so hard I know they're leaving marks. If he doesn't hurry up and give me what I need, I'm going to draw blood.

"I have something to make you feel better," he says, starting to rinse my hair now.

"Show me," I urge him, shifting so I can take his cock in my hand and hold it still. I slide down on him, our eyes locked on one another, and I don't stop until he's completely inside of me.

This time, his groan mingles with mine.

CHAPTER 32
TORCH

"she matters."

I watch as Katie guides me inside of her. I had forgotten just how fucking wonderful she felt. She slides down on my dick, squeezing him inside her tight little body.

Fuck, I want to come right then.

I give up all pretense of rinsing her hair. More important things are on my mind now. I capture her breast in my hand and run my tongue over the nipple, slowly at first, looking up to watch her face the entire time.

Her head is thrown back in pleasure. Her hips make this fucking turn as she grinds down on my cock, causing the muscles in her stomach to flutter and my eyes are drawn there. I'm hypnotized by that one movement. That's when it hits me.

Fucking-nails-in-my-coffin! I didn't suit up. I didn't even think of suiting up. Jesus. What is going on with me?

I hold her hips. "Katie…"

Nothing. If anything, she picks up her speed.

"Fuck, Hunter, you feel even more amazing than I remember. So fucking big inside of me. It feels like you're going to split me apart. Stretches me so good," she moans, and Christ Jesus, what the hell am I supposed to do here? I don't want to stop her.

"Katie, sweetness, we have to stop… We can't do this."

"I think we should do it harder," she moans, then lifts off my cock and slams back down onto it, grinding on me and squeezing my cock so fucking tight, I wouldn't be surprised if the fucker doesn't break in half.

"Katie… We're not protected, sweetness. I didn't put on a

glove," I tell her, giving one last Hail Mary before I say fuck it and get lost in the Promised Land.

She freezes mid-grind. I want to kick my own ass.

"What?" she asks, her eyes clouded with lust, her voice a mere whisper compared to the noises she was making earlier.

"We forgot the condom, sweetness. We need to stop."

"Oh my God!" she cries, then practically pulls my dick out of her. She stands up, nearly falling because of her bad leg. I grab hold of her to keep her from slamming back against the tiled wall.

"Will you slow down before you hurt yourself?" I growl. Her reaction isn't making me happy. I mean, I know we didn't need to risk it, but damn it all to hell, she's treating my dick like it has crabs or something. It's enough to wound a man's ego.

"What have you done?" she cries, pulling away from my hold and getting out of the tub. She wraps a towel around her, as if to shield her body from me.

I think that's about enough of that. I stand up too, and when I get in front of her, I'm rather proud of the way my dick is standing out, demanding attention. *Demanding her attention.*

"I think you're the one who put my cock inside of you, damn it," I remind her.

"You told me to!"

"I did not!"

"It was implied! Jesus! If I get knocked up, I will fucking kill you!" she huffs, turning away to march back to the main room.

I march right after her. I've been treating Katie with kid gloves. Time to show her how much I like being in charge.

I stop her at the bed when she's looking around for her clothes. I grab her shoulder and turn her around. It annoys me that I do it carefully because of her leg. She's treating my dick like public enemy number one; I shouldn't worry about her hurting, but I do.

"That's about enough of that," I grumble.

Katie looks at my dick, then back at me. "Will you put that thing away?"

"You know what I've noticed, Katydid?"

"I don't care! I need to go to a pharmacy. Do they still make a morning after pill?"

"You have got to be kidding me."

"Torch! I'm being serious! Get dressed! We need to go!" she cries, trying to pull away from me.

"No, we don't. First of all, I was barely inside of you, and I sure as hell didn't come. Second of all, if I *do* knock you up—as you so sweetly put it—you will *not* be getting rid of my baby."

"Oh my God! Are you listening to yourself? We can't have a kid! Even by accident! I don't want kids!"

"You... what?" I ask her, totally floored.

"I don't want kids! Ever! I'm never having kids!"

"Wait. Are you on birth control?"

"Of course I am!"

"Then why the fuck are you freaking out?"

"Because you can get pregnant even on birth control! It's not a hundred percent!"

"You can get pregnant with a rubber too!" I growl. The fucking woman is making no sense.

"It would be harder! And as cocky as you are, your little swimmers wouldn't rest 'til they tried to swim to the right place and then *bam!* No-fucking-thank-you!" I put my hands on her shoulders and walk her backwards to the bed. She stops when her legs are pressed against it. "What are you doing?"

"That's easy, sweetness," I tell her before pushing her back on the bed. She falls ungracefully, bouncing on the mattress. "I'm about to show you just how much *harder* I can get," I tell her, then lie down on top of her and pin her to the bed with my body.

"What? No! We have to—"

"Fuck, Katie. We have to *fuck*. Then, after I've fucked you hard and stretched that tight little pussy until my cock is satisfied, I'll let you suck it because, sweetness, I have to tell you, your mouth is *pissing me off*. Maybe if you're choking on my dick, I'll forget that I'm pissed off, I'll be nice, and just spank you for pleasure instead of blistering your damned ass."

"Torch..."

"Don't even say it."

"But you don't know—"

"I know that whatever is about to come out of your mouth is only going to piss me off more. So do us both a favor and spread those fucking dynamite legs of yours before I roll you over and fuck your ass instead, and you're busy screaming instead of pissing me off."

"My ass?" she asks, her voice raspy. As pissed off as I am, even I don't miss the interest that's mixed in with her outrage and fear.

Fucking hell. I could be with her for years and not grow bored. She makes me want to scream, but she's the first woman in history that makes me so fucking hard that I don't know which way to fuck her first, and I'm already dying for more before I'm even finished.

What is she doing to me?

Chapter 33
TORCH

"I own her. She just isn't aware of it yet."

"You have to wear a condom," she tells me, unable to keep the fear out of her voice.

"You have some kind of disease I should know about?"

"What? *No!* If anything, your dick gets more traffic than a New York subway."

"I'm clean," I tell her knowing it's true; I get tested regularly, plus I never go ungloved. Never wanted to before now.

"I'm supposed to trust that?"

"You are, but I know you won't. So instead, you're going to just take it, because that's the way I'm giving it to you."

"What?" she asks, confused.

Before she can figure it out, I push my cock back inside of her, not stopping until the fucker is curved and resting as deep inside as I can get. I've never thought of settling down with one woman in my whole life. Katie changes those thoughts. The fact that she went so fucking crazy at the thought of having unprotected sex chafes me, but not as much as hearing her say she doesn't want kids. The hell of it is, I don't want kids. Or I didn't. Just like I didn't want one woman. *Until Katie.* Fuck me running. She's changing all the rules and doesn't have the faintest idea.

"Hunter..." she whispers, but it's not a protest. It's all need in her voice.

My hand goes to her upper throat, not exerting pressure, but holding her still. My thumb pushes into her mouth while I pull my cock back through her depths, only to push back in.

"That's it, sweetness. Take my cock. Feel how fucking good it is to have me bare and raking the inside of your pussy."

She moans as she sucks on my thumb, wrapping her finger around it. I thrust into her, slow and steady, grinding my body against her sweet pussy every time she takes all of me. I pull her good leg up, bending it at the knee and forcing it back so she takes my cock deeper than before.

"Oh, fuck! That feels so good," she whimpers. Her hands start to go to my back, but I stop her.

"No, Katie. Put your hands above your head. Grab the headboard and don't let go."

"But I want—"

"This isn't about what *you* think you want. That's over. I'll give you everything your body wants, and more. It's in my control now. Don't make me tell you twice. Grab the headboard, and don't let go. If you do, you don't get to come."

Her eyes go wide, and I hold myself still to see if she does as I order. I push my thumb further in her mouth, gliding it against her tongue. Then I see the acceptance in her eyes. She puts her hands above her head and holds on like I instructed. It feels like I've won a fucking war. She closes her lips around my thumb, sucking it like her pussy is ravenously eating up my cock. I thrust in and out of her. Each lunge is harder than the last, her body unable to do anything but take it. Her breasts sway with the force of my thrusts. I lean down and use my free hand to guide one of her breasts into my mouth. The hard, plump nipple puckers even more under my tongue as I play with it before sucking it and as much of her tit as I can in my mouth. Her skin is a sweet honey taste with the saltiness of her body's exhaustion added into the mix.

"You're going to take everything I give you, Katie, and you're going to fucking beg for more, aren't you?"

"Hunter…"

She hasn't given me the words I want yet, so I change the angles of my thrusts as I bite down on her nipple. She screams out in reply, her hands relaxing off the bed and starting to make their way to me before stopping and going back to their previous hold. I look at her eyes and she's watching me.

"Give me what I want, Katie."

She swallows hard. My thumb moves down to slide over her lip. My thrusts slow into a softer, loving movement. Maybe I read her wrong. Maybe I...

"Fuck me, Hunter."

Something clicks into place. This is different from our one night together. This is new territory. This makes her *special*, a part of me. I don't know if she grasps that. Knowing Katie, she may fight it, but I'm not planning on letting her go. The mess with Skull and her sister, we'll work out when we get back to Kentucky.

"Hold on, sweetness," I tell her, my hand going down to her pussy and finding her clit. I focus my attention on it while fucking her hard. As hard as I slam into her body, she still manages to thrust up to meet me, wanting more. "That's it, baby. Take it all," I groan. I can feel my cock swelling inside of her, but I can't let myself come, not yet. I pinch her clit with my fingers before working the swollen nub harder.

"Hunter! Oh fuck, I'm going to come!" she cries.

"That's it, sweetness. I love it when you come all over my cock. I can feel the way your sweet cream bathes me, running down my shaft. It's so fucking hot. Who owns your body now, Katie? Who does your pussy belong to?" I growl, my thrusts getting rougher and more demanding, still working her clit and not allowing her to come down.

"Hunter!" she cries, and I can hear the fear in her voice. I can't allow her to run.

"I own your pussy, Katie. I own your orgasms and all of your pleasure. It's mine to give you. Tell me. Give me the words." I order, while at the same time using my hand to pull up on her hip to hit that spot that she needs fucked the hardest. I know the minute I hit my target because her body comes apart in my hands. Her forceful thrusts are erratic and out of control. Her body pushes almost completely off the bed while her hands come to my shoulders and her nails claw into me. I would punish her for that, but her next words soothe me.

"It's yours, Hunter. It's all yours!" she screams, coming again. She pulls me over the edge with her, and the nails biting into my back only make me harder. My cum rockets inside of her, and I hiss as her nails draw blood.

I love it. I love how wild she gets, but next time, I'm tying her to the fucking bed. That thought makes my cock, which had just emptied inside of her with one of the best fucking orgasms I ever had, already begin to harden again.

It's going to be a long night.

Chapter 34
Katie

> "*What have I gotten myself into?*"

"Fuck," I whisper. "What just happened?"

Torch is behind me, his arm thrown around my waist. He tries to pull me further against him, even if that's not physically possible. He kisses the side of my neck, moving up to my ear before kissing the shell. "You just gave yourself to me," he says, and the combination of his beard raking against my sensitive neck and his warm breath tries to bring my body back to life.

"We need to clarify that," I tell him, but I don't sound confident. Instead, my words end in a moan as his teeth rake against my shoulder and he bites me gently, lovingly.

Jesus. I like everything he does to me.

"Okay. I'll clarify," he says. "You gave me your body. I'm taking it. I'm taking it as often and in any way I want. There. We've clarified."

"That's a little wide-open for my tastes," I reply. "Especially considering our circumstances and, well, your *past* proclivities."

"Proclivities?"

I look over my shoulder at him to find his smiling face, his hair sexily tousled, and his eyes shining with something new, something different. I don't know what, but it's a damned good look on him.

"Hello? Man-whore, anyone?"

"Katie! I'm hurt," he says, but his tone says otherwise. "Besides, sweetness, considering the way we met…"

"And what are you saying?" I ask flopping over on my back, suddenly defensive.

"Throwing stones, glass houses," he says, still not aware he's upset me. Instead, he pulls the sheet down, exposing my boob.

I pull it back up. "Oh, please. I couldn't hold a candle to the number of women on your bedpost."

"Are we comparing bedposts? Because I'd rather tie you to them instead," he complains, going back to kissing my neck, which feels amazing. Annoying, but amazing.

"Freak," I tease him, trying to remember why I'm upset.

"Oh, you have no idea, but you soon will." He climbs on top of me.

"I'm not sure this is a good idea."

"Too late."

"I'm serious, Torch. We can't forget the elephant in the room here."

He's placing kisses on my neck and shoulders, working his way down under the covers to my breasts. The feel of his lips and tongue on my body nearly makes me orgasm right there on the spot.

"I know my dick is big, baby, but I'd hardly call it an elephant."

"Will you stop?" I groan as he nibbles down my stomach. "Torch..." I hope I can be forgiven for the way my hips thrust up towards him.

He pushes the covers back so it reveals his face and looks at me. It's annoyance I see on his face now. He lets out a hard breath and looks my face over, searching for something. I'm not sure what, and I have no idea if he has found it.

"Okay, fine," he says with a sigh. "I get you're hesitant here. What can I give you that will let you give whatever this is between us a chance?"

"My sister—"

"Don't go there, Katie," he says at once. "What's going on with Beth and Skull is on *them*. They both made choices that put them where they're at. They need to work that out."

"She tried. You don't—" I start to defend, but he doesn't let me.

"She didn't try hard enough. She should have come to him and demanded he tell her that shit to his face."

What he says hits me hard, maybe because I don't disagree with him. I wanted to do that very thing. Beth wouldn't, and she wouldn't let me. Still, Torch wasn't there. He didn't see the devastation on Beth's face. He didn't experience all of the pain and betrayal first hand…

"What he's doing now is wrong," I say. "Hunting us down like dogs, just to give us back to a family who never wanted us and now want revenge. They'll kill us."

He straightens back over my body and then flips us so I'm over top of him. His hands go to each side of my face, his thumbs brushing along my cheekbones as he watches me.

"I'm not giving you to anyone. And Skull, as pissed off and as hurt as he is…"

"He doesn't have a right…"

"He has every right, Katie. He thought he killed the woman he loved. Killed her. He mourned and grieved for her and spent *years* living with the guilt only to learn it was all a lie, and he has a child he has never met. That would fuck anyone up."

My stomach clenches at his words. I had only seen things from Beth's side, but if what Torch is saying is true… if Skull never knew he had a child, then…

"He didn't seem to be grieving that night at the movies."

"The movies?"

"Beth and I had tracked you guys down when we finally got free. We went to the club. Or, well, *I* did. Beth didn't want to meet Skull there. There was someone there she knew couldn't be trusted. And—"

"Who?" he asked, cutting me off.

"I don't know. Beth's the one who knows, not me. That's not the point, anyway. I went to the club, and they told me where we'd find Skull. We went to a theater in that small town and, when everyone came out, he was hanging all over some blonde. There was no grieving in sight."

"You're kidding me. Why didn't Beth confront him then?"

"She tried! She went into labor!"

"Jesus Christ eating popcorn..."

"Your swear words are really weird, Hunter." He stops and looks at me and, for a minute, the softness in his eyes is back. He even gives my lips a small kiss. "What was that for?"

"I'll explain someday. But back to this. That woman was no one to Skull."

"Yeah, I figured that when he sent a picture of him and his *girlfriend*."

"I don't know what kind of picture you got, but I know for a fact that Skull didn't send it. I also know he's never had a girlfriend. Shit, he wouldn't even call *Beth* a girlfriend."

"Whatever, I know what I saw."

"Yes, and you just admitted there was someone in the club Beth couldn't trust. So, don't you think you should have checked it out a little bit better?"

"You probably don't get this, but when you get enough men slamming doors in your face and hurting you, you learn when to fucking throw in the towel."

"Someday, you'll tell me all about that."

"I doubt it, since this—whatever *this* is—will end soon."

"I don't see that happening," he says.

"You're deluding yourself."

"So you're not even going to try?" he asks. "I never figured you for a quitter, Katie."

"I'll give you a week. One week to show me whatever *this* is between us, and to convince me that you really do have my and Beth's interests at heart."

"That seems like a lot to accomplish in a week."

"Are you not up for the challenge?"

"I didn't say that, sweetness. We need some ground rules, though. First of all, you'll not try to run away. If we can't have that trust between us, I can't let my guard down around you and vice versa."

"Done."

"That was awful easy."

"Done, for one week only," I qualify.

"We will be in Kentucky in a week."

"I'm not opposed to going to Kentucky, but I'm not about to give Beth the okay until I know it's absolutely safe."

"Okay, then. One week. Next, you do whatever I ask of this body. You trust me to take control and give you exactly what you need."

"Umm… are you about to get freaky on me? I watched that movie, you know. The one with the red room."

"I can promise you, however freaky I get, you'll like it."

"I want a better safe word than the lame one they used."

He seems shocked at my reply, but smiles. "That's doable. What word?"

"Bastard."

"Bastard?"

"It'll be the easiest word to remember if you piss me off."

"Fine, whatever. It's not like you will use it, anyway. So, are we making a deal here?"

"Do we seal it with a kiss?"

"Well, we can start with a kiss," he says, taking my mouth.

I hope I didn't just let my hormones make a huge mistake.

Chapter 35
Torch

"Damn straight."

"I want to know where Beth is."

I wince as I hear Skull's voice. He's pissed. He's more than pissed.

"I'm not telling you," says Katie. "Torch says you won't hurt my sister, but I don't trust you."

"You will tell me what I need to know."

"Not 'til I know for sure that you're safe. I have my sister and my niece to look out for."

"Listen, *perra*..."

"I've been called worse. But I'm not the fucker who gave the woman who loves me a pile of cash and told her to get lost with my child. So you can back the fuck off. I'm already regretting agreeing to this," Katie growls, throwing the phone back to me.

I make a judgment call. I hope I'm doing the right thing. "Sweetness..."

"He's such an ass. I have no idea why my sister loves him."

"She loves him?"

"Don't be an asshole. Of course she does."

"Two years is a long time."

"It's been longer than that, and of *course* she does. She hardly gives anyone but me and Gabby the time of day. Men throw themselves at her and she's oblivious. When she got his note that night in the hospital, it almost destroyed her."

With that, I carefully turn the phone off without drawing attention from Katie. "Let's talk about something that doesn't make you so tense. I have plans for you today."

"Plans? That doesn't sound cryptic at all."

"Nothing for you to worry about, remember?"

"It came back to me when you demanded I not wear underwear and put on a skirt this morning."

"You look amazing."

"I'm not used to men telling me what to wear."

"You're not used to having a man around at all. I'll make you like it."

"You keep saying that."

"I'll prove it," I tell her, pulling into a parking lot.

"You have got to be kidding me," she says, finally seeing where we've pulled into. "A dildo shop?"

"Shame on you. It's *adult novelties*," I correct her. "They sell much more than dildos. Of course, if that's what you want, I'll be glad to get one of those, too," I add with a wink.

"I am not going in that store with you."

"I never pictured you as a prude, sweetness."

"I'm not. I have toys. I just tend to order them."

"You have toys? I didn't see them in your things."

"I planned to buy more when I got settled."

"Then we can pick them out together because, sweetness, I'm definitely the only man who will use them on you."

She turns away from me, but I can see the way her breasts harden under her shirt. That tells me all I need to know.

Time to go shopping.

Chapter 36
Skull

"*Suficiente.*"

I listen to the woman—*Beth's sister*—blather on until Torch obviously turns the phone off. I look at my cell for a minute, then hurl it across the room. I take no pleasure in the way it shatters. Fucking hell, I'm so tired of going in circles. Torch called me earlier to tell me about the traitor I have in my crew. The only drawback is, no one has given me a fucking name. My gut tells me it's Pistol, but I can't be sure. He took a bullet to protect Beth. *Maybe...* Shit.

I'm so fucking tired of going around in circles. My life has been a fucking mess since I found out Beth is alive. I hate her. *I puta la odio!* Yet, I still want her. She's a poison in my veins and nothing I do has gotten rid of her. I get her back in my hands and—*Christ!* I have no idea what I will do. I just know I want to take every minute of the hell she has put me through out on her. I want to make her suffer.

The phone on my desk rings. I pick it up, ignoring the way my hand shakes. "What?"

"Brother. Tried your cell, but it just goes to your voicemail. I got some intel you might want."

Dragon's voice hits me. As much as I've come to like the motherfucker, his voice right now's unwelcome. He's a reminder of what I should have had, of what has been denied to me.

"What's that, *hermano*?" I ask, tired as fucking hell.

"My boys decided to check out the people on duty the night your woman was there."

My woman. Isn't *that* a fucking joke.

"Tried that route," I spit back. "No one in the admitting or the maternity wing could tell me one damn thing I didn't already know."

"Well, it just so happens, we have a friend who works there. A doctor, Teena Torres. She patches up the members sometimes when Poncho isn't available. Nailer has taken a liking to her, so we see her pretty often, and we got to talking to her."

My stomach churns. I know Teena. I know Teena well. I haven't talked with her about this shit for *many* reasons…

"And?" I ask shortly, being an asshole and just wanting this conversation over.

"She delivered a package delivered by your crew to a young woman. She didn't remember names, but she remembered the Devil's Blaze cut."

"Son of a bitch."

"You can say that again, amigo. It doesn't stop there. Teena didn't work the emergency room. She was on break that night, but she talked to the man."

"I want to talk to her."

"No need. I had Freak dig up some pictures of you and your men. By the way, that's a fucking ugly mug shot you got on file with the KPD."

"Fuck you." Dragon laughs. If I didn't like the son of a bitch, I'd hate him even more.

"Guess which man she ID'd?" he asks.

"Fuck. I already know, don't I, *hermano*?"

"That you do. Pistol. I told you, you needed to take that motherfucker out years ago."

"That, you did. I shall take you up on it now, however."

"Make it hurt."

"*Que es un hecho*. Thank you, Dragon."

"Holler if you need us," he says, and I know he means it. He's been a strong ally the last year or so. After he had Nicole sewed up, that is.

I don't answer him, however. I grab my gun off the table and walk straight into the main area. Pistol is standing by the bar nursing a whiskey. He turns to see me and notices the gun in my hand. His eyes go wide as I take aim. I empty two rounds into one knee and two into the other.

Pistol screams out along with a few other muffler bunnies. Briar, Beast, and Shaft all come into the room at about the same time. They look at Pistol and back at me. Pistol is cursing and screaming. I can't stand to hear him anymore. It's a big temptation to finish him off, but instead, I take the butt of my gun and slam it against the side of his head. If that kills the fucker, so be it. I hope it doesn't, though. I'm going to take revenge out of his hide so fucking slowly he'll pray for death, but it won't come. That'd be too easy.

"Chain him up," I order my men. "Get a man to patch up his legs, enough to keep him alive for a while."

"I take it we've found out who our traitor is?" Briar asks as Beast and Shaft drag the unconscious bag of shit away.

"Wait," I tell them once they get him halfway up. I yank his cut from his body and throw it on the ground. I spit on it and throw my knife, watching as it hits the Devil emblem on the back and pins the vest to the floor. "I want that fucker *burned*," I demand. "But save the ashes; I'll feed them to the asshole," I growl, walking back out.

In the distance, I hear Briar answer his own question. "Yeah, we found him."

I slam the door on him, on all of them. One down. Next is Beth. *I will find her.*

CHAPTER 37
TORCH

"I have so much to teach her."

"Explain to me again why we're going out tonight?" Katie asks, sounding put out, but I think she's enjoying dressing up. She should. That little outfit I picked out for her was made for her. It's green and sets off her brunette hair perfectly. It's got thin straps going over her shoulders that invite a man to pull them down. The silken material curves perfectly over her breasts. Her large globes stretch the fabric tight and very little is left to the imagination, especially since I forbade her to wear a bra. The dress fits the rest of her body just as well, including the way it hugs her ass.

When I see her from behind, my dick jerks in reaction. I want to bend her over the bed and fuck her hard. I don't, but the need is definitely there. It's short and stops nearly at the top of her thighs, reminding me of what she wore the night we met.

"I want to show off my woman," I tell her, only telling her half the truth. No, there's a reason we're going out tonight. Katie is about to have her first lesson in being owned by a man, *by me.*

"Shit, Hunter. If I bend over, you can see my panties," she says, peeking at her ass in the mirror.

"Katie, lie on your stomach on the bed."

"What?" Her head raises up and she looks in the mirror, but I know it's my face she sees there.

"Bed," I order. "On your stomach. Now."

For a minute, she looks like she might argue with me. It's almost a disappointment when she doesn't. She gives me what I ask. I get up and slowly approach the bed. We're checked into a nicer hotel tonight and have a king-size bed. I'm definitely going to give that a workout later. My hand brushes over her ass. *My* ass now. She gave it to me. She gave me her body to use as I wish. She has no idea what that means, *but I do*. I reach over for the bag we left lying on the table from our shopping excursion at the local adult store. Some of the things I bought, she saw. Others, I wouldn't allow her to. I take out the items I will need, line them up on the table, then push her dress up.

"Hunter, we'll be late," she whimpers.

She's called me Hunter almost all day. I doubt she notices the difference. Still, it's not her place to tell me I'm late. So, I deliver a smack across her ass, half of my hand delivering on the bare skin, the other half on the silky black material of her panties.

"Fuck," she whispers, as my hand brushes over the already reddening skin.

I reach over and rip the cleansing wrap from the container. I see Katie trying to lift her head to see what I'm doing. "Keep looking straight ahead, Katie. Don't make me punish you."

"I don't remember you being this bossy our first night together. I mean, okay, you were a *little*, but—"

I slap her ass again, and I'm glad she can't see the smile on my face.

"Ouch! What was that for?"

"Just wanted to," I tell her, using the cloth to clean the small butt plug I bought at the store. I put it back on the table and take the tube of lube I also purchased. I squeeze out some onto two fingers. "Did I tell you, sweetness, how much I love your ass? It was one of the first things I noticed about you. It reminds me of a plump, juicy peach and I want to take a bite out of it," I tell her, leaning down to run my tongue over the edge of her ass cheek that's exposed from her panties.

"Hunter," she whispers, thrusting her ass up. In reward, I bite the rim of her ass. She moans and the sound nearly drives me wild. When I lift up to see my mark on her ass, my dick pushes against the zipper of my jeans, demanding more.

"You're so perfect, sweetness. You were made for me."

I'm starting to believe the words, too. I push her panties down over her hips to her knees, leaving them there. My hands palm each cheek of her ass, and I groan at the way she overfills my hands. I push into the cushiony flesh, groaning out loud at the way it feels. I pull the cheeks apart, loving the dark valley that's exposed. My eyes zero in on that bright pink rosette opening... a small, dark, virginal paradise.

I'm claiming that ass, and soon. *Perfection.*

The lube I have on my fingers, I slowly paint around that little hole. Katie whimpers, but she doesn't tell me no. Carefully, I push one finger in until just the tip disappears. Her muscles immediately latch on, squeezing.

"Hunter." Need and indecision wars in her voice.

In answer, my fingers move to her cunt, already wet and eager. I rake them through the creamy wetness I find there. I gather her desire on my fingers and bring it back to her ass, mixing it with the lube and working my finger in further.

"Relax your muscles for me, sweetness. I promise, you're going to like where I take you," I encourage her, stroking her back from her neck down to the curve of her ass. When I feel the give in her body, my finger sinks in past the knuckle. I leave it there, letting her become adjusted. "That's it, baby. You're doing so good. Soon, you'll be ready to take my cock in this tight little ass of yours."

"Jesus," she whispers, but her ass pushes back towards me, wanting more. I move my finger around before pulling it almost out and thrusting it back in. "Hunter!" she cries out, but she doesn't have any idea what she's asking for. I can tell in the frantic way her body is trying to find more. I want her on her knees, but I can't risk her hurting herself more. I make a note to order a swing. I've always wanted to play with one and the idea of having Katie suspended from the ceiling for my pleasure is definitely a must.

Instead, I pull out completely. I hadn't planned this, but Katie is different. I slap her ass hard. "Get up," I command. She looks back at me, her face a mixture of disbelief and anger. She gets up, though, and for being such a good girl, she deserves a reward.

I lay down on the bed, then look at her. "Climb up here, sweetness, and ride my face."

"Just when I was about to scream at you, you show me you are smarter than I give you credit for," she mumbles, wasting no time in doing as ordered.

"Be careful of your leg."

"I got it," she says, and I can tell she doesn't like that I know her weakness. She suspends herself over my face. I look up at that beautiful, drenched cunt. *All mine for the taking.* I grab her hips and bring her down further, diving my tongue through her folds. Her clit is swelled so fucking big, already demanding attention, and since we're short on time, I give it exactly what it wants. I latch onto it, sucking it hard against the roof of my mouth, then releasing to lick and torture it with my tongue. I do this harder and harder, shaking my head and pulling on her clit as relentlessly as I can. Katie starts riding on my face, her hips moving in an eager and fast-paced rhythm. I reach behind her and find her ass. Her movements falter as my finger searches and finds entry. I don't stop until her ass has completely swallowed my finger. Then I finger-fuck it while still eating her juicy cunt. I wait until her pace is steady again and she's completely lost to the rhythm we've started before I add my second finger.

"What are you doing to me?" she cries out, nearly breaking my fingers because she bares down on them so hard. It's all she needed though to completely throw her over the edge. My fingers fuck her ass hard while her cum smothers my face. I fuck her over and over, my fingers sliding through her tight channel and stretching it apart, widening her ass for me while bringing her a sting of pain and enough pleasure that her whole body is shaking.

"I'm coming. Oh, God, Hunter, I'm coming…" she tells me unnecessarily. I know because her cum is covering my tongue and running down my face. She tries to lift off of me, but I don't let her. I keep her right where she is until she comes again. Only when her second orgasm hits its peak do I finally allow my tongue to slow down, nuzzling her pussy, allowing her to ride it out and calm down. I keep my fingers inside her ass, though, no longer fucking her but keeping them inside the channel and pulling the fingers apart forwards and backwards while widening her tight opening to get her ready for the next step, and ultimately, my cock.

When she's done, she slumps down against my stomach. Her head is near my cock and the fucker is killing me, wanting out to play. Now is not the time for that, though. I maneuver out from under her, smiling at how exhausted she looks. It's enough temptation not to go out tonight, to just keep her here and fuck her a hundred different ways until she's unconscious from the pleasure. But I have other fun to introduce little Katie to tonight.

I get the plug and lube from earlier and settle down behind her. I pull her lower body onto my lap, grateful she pulled her panties off when she straddled my face. She won't be needing those again. Katie's eyes are still closed and she's humming. *Damn, maybe I already fucked her unconscious.* I lube the small plug and then drag my fingers through her pussy and back to her ass again.

"I can't, Hunter," she whimpers. "Let me recover first."

I smile. Looks like I'm going to have to work on Katie's stamina, too.

"I need this, sweetness. Just lie still," I tell her. My answer is another hum, and shit, has a woman ever made me smile this much during sex? Never. It's always been about the act. This is different. Katie... *is different.* But then, I determined that earlier, didn't I?

Content that her ass is as lubed and wet as I can get it, and the plug is covered too, I slowly begin pushing it inside.

"Fuck!" Katie hisses.

I hold her still by her lower back and push the plug in further. It's only gone in about halfway when I notice Katie gripping the sheets.

"Breathe in and out slowly, sweetness. Just relax."

"Easy for you to say," she huffs. "I'm not trying to split *you* in two." But she starts breathing in and out, as told.

"This is just a small plug, baby. We're going to work you up to my cock. I don't want to hurt you. I only want to make you feel good."

"Small?" she squeaks as I push the plug into place, seating it inside of her. Just the sight of it is demanding I roll her over and fuck her while it's inside.

I don't, though. That would end the plans I have for tonight. Instead, I place two gentle kisses on each of her cheeks.

"Good girl. Now, it's time to get ready to go out. Oh, and no underwear," I tell her, getting up and going to the bathroom to wash up.

"What?"

"You heard me, sweetness."

"I can't go like this!"

"You can and you will," I tell her, coming back out and throwing on a shirt.

"I smell like sex. At least let me put on—"

"Not happening. Get up from there and go brush your hair. I kind of messed it up."

"I *have* to wear panties! What if this thing falls out? What if they... *smell* me?"

I stop myself from laughing—just barely.

"Trust me, sweetness, that plug isn't going anywhere. As for smelling you, if they do, they'll just wish they were me. Besides, trust me, before the night is over, you won't give a damn."

"How did I not know how sadistic you are?" she grumbles, getting up to fix her hair. She stops after taking two steps. "Oh, shit..." Her startled eyes go to mine.

"You're in for a long night, sweetness," I tell her, and this time, I don't stop the laugh.

Let the games begin.

Chapter 38
Katie

" Good Lord in Heaven. "

"I can't believe you didn't tell me you were meeting friends tonight," I mumble in Torch's ear.

The way he had me dressed, I thought we were going out dancing and drinking. Nope. We're in the middle of a steakhouse in a corner booth eating steak and drinking beers. Which would be okay, fine even, except we're sitting across from a large man named Drake—and by large, I mean if he was painted green, he could double for the Hulk. Drake has his arm over the booth and has a bitch-faced redhead pulled up next to him. Her name is Angie, which should be noted rhymes with "gag me". Okay, maybe not completely, but close enough.

"You didn't ask," he says, squeezing my leg. "You want another beer?"

"No. If I keep drinking, I'm liable to slap that look off *Angie's* face."

Torch addresses the table. "I think I'm going to take my girl out on the floor for a dance." Then, he pulls me from the seat. My hand goes desperately to my dress, trying to pull the small fabric down so I don't flash the entire free world. I know I'm blushing when I look up to find Drake grinning at me.

"Can't say I blame you," he mutters, his eyes roving over me appreciatively. I don't know what kind of relationship Drake and *gag-me* have, but apparently it's quite open.

I look away, not wanting to encourage him. I have one too many men on my hands at the moment as it is. I walk carefully behind Torch, constantly reminded that there's a plug inside of me. Every step I make is like mini-torture. I've been wet since before we left the hotel room and walking just makes me wetter. I might as well announce to the room that I'm ready to be fucked. The insides of my thighs are coated in my wetness. It pisses me off as much as it excites me. I should make him lick it up, right here in front of everyone. He's obviously into that kind of thing. Too bad I'm not.

"Not enjoying yourself, sweetness?"

"I would if gag-me would quit staring at you like you're fresh meat on the grill. Doesn't Drake realize what a ho-bag he's with?"

Torch throws his head back laughing. My heart squeezes; I love seeing him happy and laughing. Hell, if I'm going to be honest, I also love being the cause.

"I don't think he sees what a bitch he's with," he admits. "Drake's a good man. I served with him overseas, but he's pretty damned clueless about Angie. She's good in bed, and Drake is letting his dick think for him. He'll wise up eventually."

"What do you mean 'she's good in bed'? You've slept with her?"

"How do you think Drake met her?"

"Hell, I don't get you men. But you're definitely going back to using condoms," I grumble. "I may have to completely cut you off. No wonder gag-me is looking at you like she could eat you alive. She's already had her claws in you."

"Hell no. No more condoms and definitely not cutting me off. Angie may have had my cock once, but that's all she's had. You, on the other hand...."

"Me?" I ask, unable to hide the wince when I stumble.

"Shit, sweetness. Is it your leg?"

"I'm okay," I tell him, but am unable to keep the pain out of my voice.

"Why the fuck didn't you wear your boots?"

"They don't go with this dress, and I wanted to look nice for you, Hunter." I shift my legs to try and keep the cramp from moving up my calf.

I was distracted. I didn't realize how much I was giving away. I want to instantly grab the words back, but when I look into Torch's eyes, I can't. His eyes are glowing with emotion, the likes of which I don't think I've seen because I can't name it. His hands come to my legs and he pulls me up on his body. My hands were linked behind his neck while we danced, so I tighten up my hold to keep from falling.

"What are you doing?" I ask, looking around. "People are watching! Put me down!"

"Fuck them. I'm holding my woman the way I want so I can enjoy dancing with her without worrying she's in pain."

I freeze. *His woman? Worrying about me?* What's going on between us, and why do his words make me want to cry? Still…

"Hunter, you forget, I'm not wearing *underwear!*" I hiss, trying to pull away from him.

"I didn't forget. I plan on enjoying that fact later." He grins, and that's worrisome in and of itself.

"What if they see? What if that thing…"

"Plug?"

"What if it falls out?"

His head dives down into the side of my neck where it meets the shoulder. His beard is so soft and it scratches against my neck, adding yet another layer of excitement to the way his tongue licks against the pulse of my neck. His lips ever so slowly move up my neck to my ear.

"I told you, sweetness. It's going nowhere. It will stay right there. In fact, when we leave here…" he whispers, his tongue sliding around the shell of my ear. His teeth capture the lobe and gently start to gnaw.

"Yes?" I ask, my body already on fire for him. Hell, I'm probably leaving a wet spot on his clothes.

"When we leave here," he repeats, still torturing my ear and sending hot sensations of need through my body, "I'm going to lay you down, and I'm going to slide my cock into your wet little pussy… and it will stay right there."

"Jesus."

"It will be like having two cocks inside of you at the same time, my naughty little Katie. You'll feel so full while I'm fucking you, you'll think your body is going to explode."

"Hunter…" I whimper needing him to stop teasing me with his words. "Let's go now," I beg.

"Anticipation, Katie. Trust me. It will be more than worth the wait," he assures me, carrying me back to the table.

"If you take me home now, I'll suck your cock all the way down my throat. You can even pull out and come all over my face, just like you've been dying to do."

"How do you know I've been wanting that?" he asks, pulling back to look at me.

"Because I'm not the only dirty one in this relationship, Hunter," I tell him with a smile, just as we make it back to the table with him carefully helping me stand on my legs.

He kisses me gently. "Later," he promises against my lips.

I hope I can wait for later.

Chapter 39
Torch

"She's never getting away."

"Can't you walk?" Angie's hateful voice hits us the minute we get settled back in our seats.

"I..." Katie starts, but I interrupt her.

"I hurt Katie's leg when we were house shopping."

"House shopping?" Angie repeats while Katie's hands bite into my leg. "But you live at the club?"

"Yes, but now that I have Katie, that has to change," I tell Angie, turning to look at Katie. Her eyes are wide, and I see the fear there, but I also see something else. I bring my hand to the side of her face, pulling her eyes up to mine. "We can't live at the club when the babies come. I want room for them to play." I watch as Katie shifts nervously, her muscles tightening. "We'll need plenty of room because I want our kids to be close to their nieces and nephews."

"Hunter..." Katie says, her nails biting into my arm.

"What? You said you'd never settle down!" Angie hisses.

"That's was before I met Katie. She's special. Things change when you fall in love."

Katie's eyes go large, and I can see so many different things charging through her. I kiss her lips soundly, pushing my tongue into her mouth to claim her while my hand tilts her head to get a better angle. Katie doesn't join in at first, but then her tongue finds mine and they dance. The kiss is charged with emotion and unspoken words. She's afraid to believe what I'm saying, and I know later she'll write it off, but it's true. I understand now what I didn't before. I know why Skull fell so hard and fast for Beth. I know why Sabre and Latch are completely wrapped up in Annie. I understand it because Katie is my downfall. She's *it*. The one. Now, I just have to keep Skull from going of the deep end and fucking it all up, keep Katie from running in fear, and make her believe that I'll never hurt her. That should be simple enough.

I pull away from the kiss when I hear Drake.

"Damn man! Way to spring the news on a man! Congrats! I didn't even know you were seeing someone steady. I have to say though, you seem like a hell of a woman, Katie."

Katie clears her throat and looks back at me before smiling at Drake. "Thanks," she says, her voice hoarse and barely above a whisper. Her cheeks are red and her lips are swollen. *Beautiful.*

"Where are you from, Katie?" Drake asks as we start eating.

"Montana, originally. My sister and I moved out this way with our parents when we were small."

"What does your father think about you hooking up with Torch?"

"My father's dead," she answers bluntly. "I'm sure if he wasn't, though, he'd want to kill him. Luckily, that just makes Torch more attractive."

Drake laughs, making Katie smile with that look on her face that drives me wild.

"So you started dating Torch to get even with your father?" Angie asks.

Before I can answer that, Katie sets her beer down and looks over at Angie. The look in her eyes would be enough to make a smart woman back off. I don't think Angie's that smart, but it's kind of fun to watch Katie in action.

"No. I had an itch. He was handy, and then, well… I'm sure I don't have to explain to you how good Hunter is in bed." She stops to look at me. "Actually, have we ever made it to the bed except to sleep?" she asks so sweetly I want to tan her ass.

Drake laughs his ass off. Angie is pretty much speechless, which is good for her; she should definitely try to be that way more often. Me, I just want to grab my woman and fuck her right here on the table.

"We have. Though, if you can't remember, I'll do my best to jog your memory later."

"Yay. Something to look forward to," she says with a grin, popping a bite of steak in her mouth.

Yep. Definitely want to fuck her.

"Torch, old buddy, you have met your match."

"Tell me about it," I say back to Drake with a grin.

Chapter 40
Katie

> "*Oh, crap.*"

My heart feels like it might beat right out of my chest.

I know Torch was probably just saying that stuff for Angie's benefit, but it felt like he was talking to me. It felt like he was being dead serious. It scares me. No. It *terrifies* me. I don't want that, do I? Why does it feel like part of me does? A *large* part?

"You okay, sweetness?" he asks me sometime later. Drake and *gag-me* have moved out to the dance floor. She's shaking her ass, bending down and touching her toes and sticking it up in everyone's faces. I don't see how Drake can be that clueless, but whatever.

"Yeah, just thinking," I tell him, trying to smile.

"I'd say *over*thinking."

"No, not really. I mean, I know that what you said, you said because of—"

"I said the parts that count because I meant them," he says, his hand coming back to cup the side of my neck, his thumb brushing along my chin.

"Okay." I wonder what parts he thinks *counts*.

"You're overthinking, sweetness."

"Is that a fact?"

"Mmm-hmm. I'm going to have to find a way to make you stop that."

"I miss your t-shirts," I confess, running a hand over the buttoned up shirt he wears. I don't know how a hot biker can manage to pull off slacks and a buttoned-up shirt, but he rocks it.

He smiles. "You don't say?"

"Yeah. I wanted to see what you would come up with next."

"I'll surprise you. Come here and give me those lips."

"I think I've given you too much lately."

"Is that right?" His face moves closer to mine. "I think you're going to give me even more. I think you're going to give me everything I want." His hand moves up my leg.

"Hunter." I try to protest at about the same time his hand finds my pussy.

"God, sweetness, you're *soaked* for me."

I wrap my hand around his arm in a weak attempt to pull him away, but then his finger skates over my clit. I'm already on edge and, with just that little touch, I'm primed.

"Let's go home," I tell him, unable to keep the pleading out of my voice. It doesn't even matter that I'm calling some hotel "home". It's a nice hotel, it's a suite, and it's close to a home. If I wasn't missing Gabby and my sister so much, I'd be more than happy to stay there.

He pushes a couple of his fingers inside of me, and I'm unable to tell him no. Right now, I just want more.

"Do you feel the way your pussy squeezes around my fingers, sweetness?" he asks into my ear. "Do you see how fucking full you are with that plug? Look around. No one here would even imagine that you're getting it in both holes right now. They have no idea that I'm finger-fucking you or that I'm about to make you come while they're sitting there eating their dinner."

"Jesus, Hunter…"

"Maybe I need to slide under the table and eat you. I bet my girl would like that, wouldn't she? Tell me, would you come loudly even in a room full of people?"

His words are more effective than any hands-on foreplay. They are enough to send me over the edge. I can feel my orgasm right there, just within grasp. That's when Drake and *gag-me* come back to the table. My entire body tenses up and I expect Torch to remove his fingers, but he doesn't. He keeps them lodged inside of me. He doesn't really thrust them, but he does slide them around. I shift uncomfortably, hoping he'll take the hint to remove them. Instead, his thumb pushes hard against my swollen clit.

"Hey, you two. You want some dessert before we call it a night?" Drake asks, motioning for a waiter.

"Actually, I could use a little taste of something sweet. What about you, sweetheart? Do you want something?" he asks, his face all innocent.

I wonder what he'd do if I told him I did want something: to come. Knowing him, that's exactly what he wants me to do.

"I could go for something," I answer stupidly. It's hard to think when he picks that moment to slide his fingers out of me and slide them over and over my clit. My dress is up to my hips now. I'm sitting across from Drake, who seems to be smiling a little too much. Gag-me is shooting daggers with her eyes. I feel like they know what's going on and I'm praying they don't look under the table. At the same time, I'm fast-approaching the point where I don't give a fuck. Torch's fingers are moving slowly over my clit, giving me a taste of what I want, but it's not enough. I'm busy trying not to thrust my hips or move in a way that might give away what Torch is doing to me. I didn't even realize he ordered cheesecake until he's holding the spoon near my mouth.

"Open up, sweetness," he says, pushing the spoon to my lips. My eyes are locked on his as I take the spoon in my mouth and suck the small bite of cheesecake inside. Its flavor dissolves in my mouth, but I barely notice it. The sweet taste is nothing compared to the look in Torch's eyes. That's a look I could get drunk on. His fingers pick up their speed. I look around, scared that he's giving us away. They have to know what he's doing. Drake is talking to *gag-me* and they're not really looking at us. I can't believe it. It feels like everyone should be watching. I bite down on my lips as I feel my pussy quiver. Torch's fingers move faster and faster over my clit in small circles, and upon the completion of each one, he pushes against my clit, pulling it to the side. My brain tries to keep up with the movement, but soon I can't. I feel the fire flood through my system. I'm going to come.

"More, Hunter. I want more." And there's no fucking way he could think I'm talking about the cheesecake.

In answer, he takes my mouth and kisses me just as I feel my release. My hand bites into his side to keep from screaming. He swallows my cries. The kiss lasts until my orgasm has somewhat died down. My body still feels as if it is on a razor's edge. I'm still primed for more, and nervous. When we break apart, Torch is smiling. It's not a cocky smile, not really, but he's happy.

"Fuck me, if cheesecake did that to Angie, I'd keep that shit in the house," Drake says, but I don't turn and look at him.

"Can we go home now?" I ask Torch.

"Absolutely, sweetness," he says, his voice hoarse with need.

Finally.

CHAPTER 41
TORCH

"Just when you think you have it all figured out..."

"Tell me, are you planning on making me wear one of these for the rest of my life?" Katie asks as I finish inserting the new plug, using the cloth to wipe the excess lube off my hands. This one is bigger, and she doesn't know it yet, but what comes next has nothing to do with a toy. That isn't what makes me smile, though. Hell no. What does that is how she automatically goes to "the rest of my life". That's different. Does she even know she's linking us together long-term? I doubt it.

I pull her skirt back down. This one is longer, falling to her knee. She bitched this morning when she couldn't find any jeans. I have them hidden. What can I say? I like what I like. She stopped bitching after I showed her the advantages of wearing a skirt. After her third orgasm on my tongue, she was more than happy with me. I'm thinking this may be my way of dealing with Katie from here on out. It's a solid plan. My genius is never fully appreciated. I flop back on the bed and Katie, who lies on her stomach, automatically puts her head on my chest. I can't stop myself from running my fingers through her hair.

"You're so fucking beautiful," I tell her.

She looks up at me, her arm loosely draped around my waist. Those damn gray eyes grab ahold of me yet again. If she knew how deep she had her hooks in me, that fear I see in her eyes would disappear.

"Don't, Hunter," she whispers.

"Don't what?" I ask, confused, my finger sliding down the bridge of her nose.

"Don't tell me lines. I don't need them."

"You think because I'm telling you you're beautiful that I'm automatically feeding you a line?"

"Listen, you're a player, I get that. But I don't need the lines. You've already bagged me. For the time we have left, just—"

"You need to shut the fuck up now, Katie."

I put a hand in her hair when she tries to pull away from me. That's not happening, not after what's gone down between us.

"Weren't you listening to me at dinner?"

"Well, yeah, but—"

"Katie, there's no buts. I'm not playing here."

"C'mon, Torch. We barely know each other. We agreed, one week, and—"

"Hunter."

She looks confused. "What?"

"I've noticed. When you let down your guard, you call me Hunter. When you're building up walls for me to break down or planning on saying something to piss me off, I'm Torch again. Let's clear it up right now. To you, I am now and will always be Hunter. No more fucking walls, no more jumping through hoops. Just you and me."

"We barely know each other," she repeats.

I pull her face closer to mine. "I don't give a fuck."

"Hunter, you have your club to look out for. Bethie explained to me how that works. I have my sister."

"You're not listening to me, sweetness. I said I do *not* give a fuck."

"You're being crazy," she says. "There's too much between us. It would make being together impossible."

"Do you care for me, Katie?"

"You were a one-night stand."

"Do you care for me, Katie?" I ask again.

"How are we ever supposed to make things work? I have to protect my sister, Hunter. I have to."

I won't stop asking. "Do you care for me, Katie?"

"Hunter…"

"Answer my question."

"I don't know how to do relationships!"

"Katie," I growl.

"Yes!" she finally cries out. "Okay! Yes! I do! But ... I *have* to put my sister and niece first, Hunter. Bethie risked everything for me. She saved me!"

"Sweetness, I told you that, whatever happened, Skull was not involved. You said he had a traitor who helped set Beth up before. Is it too hard to think that person is the one who sent Beth that note?"

"I'm not stupid. It occurred to me, to both of us. But, that was Skull at the movies, that was Skull in that picture, and Colin told us that Skull was working with him because he wanted his daughter, that he would stop at nothing to get Gabriella back."

"And you can trust Colin? And not me?"

"He had a recording of Skull swearing revenge."

My spine stiffens at this new bit of information. "You never mentioned this before."

"I was... Shit, Hunter, I'm not even sure I'm doing the right thing, talking to you now."

I rest my forehead against Katie's. "I know it's hard. I do. But I don't want to walk away from this. I want more of you. I want all of you."

"If you're playing me, Hunter, I will cut off your balls."

"I care about you. I don't want to give you up, not ever. I don't care if it's been days, weeks, or months. I know that you're *it* for me. Trust me, Katie. I won't let you down."

My club always came first—*until her*. Katie is an obsession I can't give up. An addiction I crave. She's a fire deep inside, a beautiful flame that leaves me burned with a heat that I keep wanting over and over. I will find a way to make this work. I don't have a choice because this woman *is* my future.

Katie watches my face closely. I don't even blink. I've laid it out. I have nothing to hide from her. She is my priority. Then, finally, she nods her head.

"Tell me, Katie."

"Okay, Hunter. I don't want to give you up, either."

Her voice shakes and I know how hard this decision was for her. I kiss her gently, conveying the hundreds of things I've told her and all the things I haven't yet. I will make this work.

I have to.

CHAPTER 42
KATIE

" Is this what it feels like to be ... normal? "

"Hunter! Let's get going, Romeo. Shake a leg!"

"I'm coming! Geez, woman. I had to fix my hair. It takes time for this perfection," he says, strutting out to the jeep.

I can't help but smile, watching him. It takes me ten minutes. Hell, he's been primping for forty. I can't say it wasn't worth the wait, though, especially when I get a look at his latest t-shirt.

"Seriously?" I ask him.

"What?"

His shirt is black, and on it, it has two figures in a square. The first square is a depiction of a woman like you would see on a restroom sign with the triangle dress. Under that square, it reads: *Your Girlfriend*. The next square has a naked woman with huge tits bent over and offering her butt, and it reads: *My Girlfriend*.

"You're ridiculous, you know."

"Just bragging on you, babe," he says. "What can I say?"

I ignore him with a smirk and hand him my duffle bag that has my clothes. "Remind me again why we're moving so early?"

"We need to make tracks, sweetness. I plan on getting you to Kentucky today."

"I'm not sure I'm as excited for that as you are."

He slides his hand under my hair and pulls my face to him. "I promise you, you'll love it."

"If you're wrong I'll—"

He puts a finger to my lips, hushing me. "I wish you'd quit threatening my balls. They love you. You hurt their feelings."

I smile despite the worry and stress I'm feeling. "I'll see if I can make it up to them later."

"I don't know. They're pretty upset. Still, a tongue bath might help them. They respond to physical attention."

"You're a freak." I place a gentle kiss on his lips. "Now let's go for food. I'm hungry."

Torch fake sighs. "Your wish is my command. Too bad you didn't wish for me to bend you over the hood. That would've been more fun," he complains, throwing our bags in the back of the jeep. He walks me over to the passenger side and helps me climb in, then secures the seatbelt around me like I was a little child. It should annoy me, but instead, I like it. I feel like he's trying to take care of me and I've never had that.

Thirty minutes later, we're pulling into a small restaurant that has a big sign up advertising breakfast twenty-four hours a day. He helps me to my seat, then slides in beside me instead of across from me.

"Couldn't we talk better if you're over there?" I ask, pointing to the empty seat.

"I like feeling you close to me. Plus, I can't sit with my back facing the door, sweetness. Too many years of training have taught me not to do that."

"I could—"

"That would leave *your* back exposed and *me* unable to protect you. Not happening. Besides, you'll like me eating next to you." He dips his head down and his lips find my ear. "And eating *you*."

"Pervert."

"You say that like it's a bad thing." He laughs, his teeth nibbling on the side of my neck.

"Hunter," I whimper, because I like it and don't want him to stop, but we're in the middle of a restaurant—yet again. "You can't be horny. There's no way, after the morning we had. Not to mention the night before!"

"You bring out the animal in me, Katydid," he murmurs near my ear. "What can I say?"

The waitress comes and takes our order and saves me from responding, which is good because I have no idea what I would say. Once we're alone again, Torch pulls me around so I can face him in the chair.

"Tell me about Gabby."

His question surprises me, but Gabby is a topic I love to talk about, so I immediately warm up to the conversation.

"She's amazing. She has these dark eyes that I swear glow they're so beautiful. And her laugh. I don't think there's a more beautiful sound in the world. She's quiet. I've never seen a child her age so quiet. She watches everything, takes it all in, you know? Plotting and determining. It's kind of scary, considering she's just two."

"Does she talk? What are her favorite things? Tell me."

I laugh, he seems so eager. Who would have thought he'd want to know about a child?

"She does talk," I admit. "I mean, not a lot. She's only two. But she says 'mom' and she calls me Kay-Kay. She knows 'juice' and 'nuggets'. She's always climbing, and she loves when people draw. She watches, entranced. I swear she's going to be a famous painter someday."

"You sound like a proud aunt," he says with a strange look on his face. His hand had been under the table, but he brings it up to run his thumb over my lip.

"You okay?" I ask, sensing something different from him.

Before he can answer, the waitress sets our food down in front of us, breaking the moment.

"Your leg seems better today," he says, changing the subject after he gets settled. Talking about my leg makes me tense up, as always, so I don't answer him. "Katie?" he nudges me.

I sigh, staring at my fork for a while before finally answering. "It's fine. I just ... used it too much the last few days."

"What does that mean?"

"Do we have to talk about this?"

"I want to know. I can't protect you like I need to, or even take care of you, if I don't know what's wrong. I've seen the scarring, so I'm assuming the leg isn't going to get better. I just want to understand."

"You're a nosey asshole, anyone ever tell you that?" I huff.

"You're so sweet."

I roll my eyes, take a breath, and decide to give in and tell him. I don't especially want to, but I figure, if this makes him react differently to me, it gives me just one more reason not to trust him. Since I've caved and pretty much agreed to try to build something with him, it'd be good to know if there's a reason I shouldn't. Right? It's like hedging your bets; you can't just jump in with both feet into the lake without knowing how deep it is, because you might drown. Bethie and Gabriella are counting on me, so I can't drown or let them get hurt, no matter what my hormones want from me.

"My leg doesn't have anything to do with my scars. I grew out of whack. One leg is like an inch or so longer than the other, and my back and hip is... misaligned. It's no big deal."

"So the pain comes and goes? There's nothing they can do?"

The pain is *constant*, but I don't tell him that. My leg is a weakness and I'm not about to reveal it. *I can't*. I'm also not telling him that my father could've taken me to a doctor when I was young and still growing, and help correct things. There's no point.

"No. It is what it is. Most of the time, I barely know it's there," I lie. "My father and grandfather hated it, though," I admit. "They saw it as a defect and blamed my mother's blood."

"Jesus, the family you grew up in," he growls.

"It was a laugh a minute," I agree. He doesn't even know the half of it. "My father couldn't stand to look at me after he found out. That's when he started looking for Beth. If I couldn't represent him in the family as the perfect daughter, perhaps my sister could. So, in a way, all this mess is my fault."

"Bullshit. Your father is a twisted piece of work, Katydid."

"That's one way to put it."

"How did you get the burn scars?"

"You're just full of questions today, aren't you?"

"Humor me."

"The snake wanted Bethie away from Skull. Roger came up with a plan and needed my help to see it through."

"The snake?"

"Oh, sorry. My *grandfather*. My father might have been evil, but he couldn't hold a candle to that bastard."

"How—"

"I think I've had enough of this episode of 'Ask Katie Anything'. How about—"

"Katie. I need you to get up and go to the back of the room where the restroom is," Torch says, and it's like someone flipped a switch. His entire body is rigid and his tone is dominating.

"What?"

"Do it now, Katie, and don't look behind you," he says, his voice tense.

"Hunter."

"Do it now, sweetness. I'll meet you by the bathrooms," he tells me again, this time giving me eye contact, but I can tell there's no room for arguments. I swallow nervously, wondering what in the hell is going on, and do as he ordered.

I pray my family isn't about to catch up with me.

CHAPTER 43
TORCH

"I can't catch a fucking break."

I watch out the window as three of the Chrome Saints gather around Katie's jeep. I got Katie out of here. I breathe as I watch her walk to the back of the room and down the small hall where the restrooms are. I've been here before and I know there's an emergency entrance off to the left. I motion for the waitress, keeping one eye on the men outside. As I watch them approach the diner, my heart rate accelerates. I'd face them down on my own without a problem—if Katie wasn't with me. I need to make sure she's protected at all times.

When I was last here, it was about six months ago on a gun run for the club. It's not our territory, though it's run by one of Diesel's allies, so we've never worried. However, the very reason for me being here is dangerous. The Donahues have lost a lot of clout in the last two years, but they're still the head of the Irish faction, and even if the Russians are slowly pushing them out of existence, no one wants to be on their bad side. This is why I've not worn my cut, and why I've not used my bike. It looks like that's not going to matter if I don't get out of here, because I recognize those fuckers, and one of them is Colin Donahue's cousin. If they catch me, the only escape is a fucking shootout, and no club, even if they are buddies of Diesel's, will stand for that in their territory.

The waitress finally comes over. I hand her a fifty dollar bill. "Keep the change, darlin'," I tell her. I get up and walk calmly to the back of the building, turning the corner just as I hear the bell ring, indicating the Saints have made it inside.

"Hunter? What's going on?" Katie asks when she sees me.

"I'll explain it when we get out of here, sweetness."

I take her arm and head for the back exit, only to find they've apparently made some security improvements since I've been here last. "Fuck."

"What? What is it?" Katie asks, confused.

"There's a damn buzzer on the door."

"So disable it."

"That would take way too long," I say back. "We'll have to find another way out. Maybe there's a window in the kitchen..."

I trail off as she slips a hand into her bra. To my surprise, she pulls out a pocket knife and pops it open.

"Where did you hide that?" I growl, because shit, if she's been hiding it this long, does that mean she had it when I first took her hostage?

"Beauty of having Double D's," she answers, not paying me much mind at all. "You can hide a lot of shit under them." Then, she uses the knife to pop off the face plate of the alarm.

"You seem to know what you're doing," I note, more than a little amazed. I'm good at technical shit. I can wire up a bomb and I can do anything you want to do using computers. But Katie's skill at disabling this alarm is scary good. Shit, I'd say she could outdo Briar at it, and he's the club's best at bypassing alarms by hand.

"It's just a cheap home security system," she mumbles, taking a pin from her hair. "If I hadn't learned to disable these, I would have never discovered boys." The next thing I know, she's got the door open and the alarm is completely silent. She's standing there looking at me like I've lost my mind. Hell, maybe I have. I know I'm standing there with my mouth open. "You, ready?"

I nod, shaking off my shock, then lead her to the jeep. We're halfway there when I see the guy they have posted outside. Trouble is, he sees me too. I toss Katie the keys.

"Get out of here, sweetness. Get the fuck out and once you get away, call the club in Kentucky and tell Skull the Chrome

Saints are after you. He'll protect you and help bring Beth in safe."

"Are you out of your mind?" Katie hisses.

I pull my eyes away from the man walking towards us. "No!" I say back to her. "Get the hell out of here while you can!"

"Hunter! That's *Levi!*" she says, naming Colin's cousin.

"I know, so get the fuck out and don't give me any lip!"

She shoots me a look like I've gone insane. Shit, maybe I have. I could have run for it, even though running doesn't sit well with me. Doing that, however, meant Katie also having to run, and she's not able to. I'm pretty sure I can take all of those motherfuckers myself, but if they join up, the chances go down. I picked the wrong day to leave my gun in the car. I didn't want to draw attention to us, so I just kept my knife.

Katie finally takes off, heeding my command. I turn my attention to the approaching man.

"Well, if it isn't one of the Devil's pussies," Levi says.

I'm going to enjoy messing his face up.

"Levi, I see you're putting on a few pounds. Did you have to trade your ride in for a *trike* so you can cart your ass around with the rest of you?"

"I'm gonna like beating your ass, boy."

"Carmen told me you preferred dicks. That's why she came looking for me," I tell him, talking about the bitch he claimed a year or so ago.

His face goes red, and he throws the first punch. I manage to dodge it, since he broadcast it for five minutes. I deliver one to his stomach, then his ribs, as he uppercuts me. The blow rattles me, but I shake it off and come back at him, finally scoring a good hit to his nose. Blood splatters everywhere and Levi goes back, falling on the blacktop parking lot. He's shaking his head, trying to get his bearings. When I hear footsteps running, I look up to see Levi's buddies head toward us. I'm preparing for a fight when Katie's Jeep suddenly slides to a stop in front of me. It moved so fast it comes close to tipping on two tires.

"Hop in!" she orders.

I don't have to be told twice. I jump in the Jeep, and we tear out of the parking lot, the trailer and my bike hooked on the back. I grab my phone and hit redial.

"Skull, we've got problems," I tell him the second he picks up the phone.

Damn it.

KATIE

" *I don't know what to do ...* "

"Someone needs to kill Colin, slowly and painfully," I growl, driving down the road.

"I'm pretty sure Skull's already making plans," Torch says and from the corner of my eye, I can see him staring at where he tossed the phone after hearing Skull go on for ten minutes.

"If he manages to do that, I might grow to like the asshole."

My mind churning, I don't know what to do. If Colin's flunkies find me, could they possibly be closing in on Bethie and the baby, too? *Shit.*

"He'll do it. It just might get real bloody. Step on the gas, sweetness. Levi and his assholes won't be far behind and I'd rather not have a shootout with you here between us."

Torch's voice is stressed and I can hear his worry... *for me.* That feeling hits my stomach again. Damn him!

"They won't come after us," I say.

"Trust me, they will."

"Not without stealing a car," I point out. "Even then, they'd have to change some tires."

"What are you talking about?"

I flip open the console between us and show him my Bowie Knife I keep there. "That's why it took me so long to pick you up. I slashed the front tires on their bikes and then slashed the four cars in the parking lot. Even managed to get the two on the side that I assume belong to the waitress and cook."

"Fuck me like a whore in church on Sunday!" he exclaims, then observes me. "I think I underestimated you, Katydid."

"Most people do," I admit without bitterness. It's just a fact of life. Torch shakes his head and looks out the window, growing silent. "What are you thinking about?"

"That if Skull hadn't killed your father," he answers, "I'd like to be the one to gut the asshole."

My hands freeze on the steering wheel. "Skull killed my father?"

"Yeah."

"Shit."

"What's wrong?"

"I didn't want to find something to like him for," I grumble.

"Where'd you learn all this shit, Katie?"

I tense up at his question. I keep my vision on the road in front of us and tighten up my hands. "What do you mean?"

"Don't play dumb, sweetness. We both know you're smart as a tack."

His words do a little more towards making my stomach feel weird and releasing that tight rein I have on letting Torch all the way in. It should scare me, but it's starting to feel normal. I'm starting to wish my walls were down. I want to let Torch in. No one has ever thought of me as smart before, except maybe Bethie, but she loves me.

"My father... was like two different men," I finally reveal. "When he and my mother were first together, he wanted to live a normal life. He tried to leave the family. Who knows? It might have worked out well."

"Why didn't it?"

"My mother was a money-grubbing whore, maybe? Can't say for sure. I'm judging from the many sermons my father gave while making sure his daughter didn't walk in her footsteps."

"What do you mean?"

"When my father left the 'family' for her, things were fine until my mother discovered that without the family, she wouldn't have summer homes in France, credit cards with no limits, no Mercedes, no maids or chauffeurs. In short, my mother hated everything about life in suburbia."

Torch processes this. "She made your father go back in?"

"If only it were that simple," I say with a sigh, wondering why some twisted part of me actually feels sorry for Redmond. I shouldn't; he beat whatever fucks I gave out of me long ago. "She decided, since Redmond wouldn't keep her in diamonds, furs, and private planes, she'd find someone who would."

"His twin," Torch says right on cue.

"Yep. Old Uncle Edmond was knee-deep and climbing the ranks in the family that Redmond had turned his back on. Isabel latched onto him and never looked back, even when my father told her he was taking the oldest daughter with him."

"But, you're twins…"

"Oh, see, but the family has a *system*," I point out. "Redmond came out first, so he had the position first. Edmond only got to be head of the family because Redmond didn't want it."

"So, by keeping you, Redmond was pretty much securing the next generation?"

"In his mind, yeah. Until he realized that having me would be a liability. Then, I was better off dead."

"And… that's why he said you died?"

"Yep. I went from being a liability to being a secret weapon."

"If that's true, then why did he push to get Beth back?"

By this time, I'm just driving down the road. I'm going on autopilot, lost in the memories and the pain. Torch thinks he's getting the whole story. He's getting the briefed-up, prettied-up version. He can't know of the pain of knowing that your father hated you, that he saw you as stupid and useless because you had one leg longer than the other that caused you to limp. Finding out I suffered from dyslexia and ADHD together was the final straw. I was stupid and deformed. That's when I was no longer a weapon, but a tool to get his *good* daughter back. That's when he came up with the plan to use me to trap Beth.

"Let's just say that a daughter with a bum leg—among other problems—was expendable. The heir to the throne, so to speak, had to be beyond reproach."

"What a fucking twisted…"

"Monster," I finish for him, because that's what my father really was. At his core, he was a complete monster.

"I'm sorry, sweetness." Torch reaches to squeeze my hand.

I don't know what I have going on with Torch. It has me constantly confused, but it feels… good. It feels right.

It feels safe. No wonder I want to keep him. Forever.

CHAPTER 45
TORCH

"I'm going to make it my mission to show Katie she matters."

"You look worn out," I whisper to her as I carry her to bed. I start at her feet, taking off her shoes, then her socks, letting my fingers and thumbs massage the soles of her feet.

"Been a long day."

"No kidding. I'm sorry, sweetness. I should have thought better and demanded that you let me drive."

"I could do it," she says. "Besides, it's not your job to think about my weaknesses, Hunter. I'll deal. I always deal."

"It's not a weakness, Katie. There's not a fucking thing about you that's weak," I tell her, and that's the God's honest truth. Katie might be the strongest person I've ever known. I can say that and don't even know half of the real hell she's been through.

"Hunter, I know…"

"You know nothing. You know what's been drilled into you by evil. That's it. Does your sister think of you as weak, Katie?"

"Hunter…"

"Because I've met Beth. She's an amazingly sweet and loving person, but she has nowhere near the grit you have."

"Bethie has this ability to see people and… and love…"

"I don't doubt it a bit, and it's a wonderful ability," I tell her, cutting her off. "But you, Katie, you have a will made of iron, grit, and determination that sees you through everything."

"Grit? Iron? You make me sound so sexy, Hunter. You're taking my breath away," she jokes. How many times has she used humor to deflect compliments because she doesn't believe them? I bet I couldn't even begin to guess.

I help Katie to stand, then start to unbutton my pants.

"Hunter?"

"Undress, sweetness. Bare yourself to me," I tell her.

She probably doesn't know it, but I'm not talking her body. She begins slowly taking her clothes off. Nothing else is said and nothing can be heard in the room but our breathing. Once we're both naked, I pick her up and walk to the small half-hall that has a small closet to hang clothes and a full-length mirror before moving into the bathroom. I stand her up in front of the mirror, then turn her around so she's looking in the mirror. I'm standing behind her. I can see her face staring back at me. Her face goes pink with embarrassment.

"Hunter," she whispers, confused.

I hold her hips and pull her back against my body so that our skin is touching from her back down to her legs. I pull her hair away from her neck and expose it on one side. I run my face against it, letting my beard tease her, and brush the tender skin. My lips find her ear and I place gentle kisses along the shell. My hands find hers and I place mine over them, moving them, palms flat, against the curve of her stomach.

"Look in the mirror. I want you to see what I see," I tell her, allowing my breath to be just one more thing to tease her.

"I need to lose weight. I gained—"

I bite her shoulder hard, knowing I'll leave my mark there, but I want her to stop.

"You're perfect," I correct her. "Look at how your stomach curves. So sexy. So feminine, it makes me hard just following the lines of your body." I move our hands up along her ribs. "Until you, Katie, I never realized the way a woman's ribs are formed that highlight and angle her body to make her fit perfectly against a man." I continue telling her this while I kiss her neck, letting my tongue follow the path my lips make.

"Hunter..."

"And your breasts," I go on, bringing our hands to cup them at the same time, slowly, carefully letting our combined touch be just one more thing to excite her. "Fuck me, sweetness, those breasts of yours are magnificent. Feel how soft they are? How they curve out from your body, looking so ripe and ready for the picking?" I bring our hands up so our fingers skate over her hardened nipple. With just the gentle touch, they contract further until they look painfully hard.

"Jesus, Hunter."

"I'm in love with your breasts, Katie. They've ruined me for any other woman. They're so receptive. The merest touch and they're begging for more. The sweet pink color of your nipples. The way they crave that tiniest bit of pain…"

As I tell her that, I use her fingers to grasp the large nipples. We roll them between her fingers, then I pull them. I drag my eyes from the reflection of her breasts in the mirror to find her face as her ass pushes against me. Her head leans into my shoulder. Her eyes are heavy as she watches the movement of our hands, her breathing turning erratic. Katie's face is still shadowed in pink, but now I think it has to do more with being excited than embarrassed, exactly as it should be.

"Oh, fuck…" she whispers, her voice dripping in need.

I smile. "Keep playing with your tits, sweetness. Don't stop," I whisper against the back of her neck.

"I won't."

"I love your back too, Katie. I love the delicateness of it. I love the way it's shaped, the milky-white color that makes me want to see my name inked on it. I love everything about it," I tell her, letting my hands move along the backs of her shoulders and slowly down until I reach her hips.

"Please, Hunter," she whispers. I drop down to my knees and place a kiss at the top of her ass. "Keep playing with those beautiful nipples, sweetness."

"I am… but I need more, Hunter."

I ignore her plea, letting my tongue drag across the cheek of her ass. "This ass, Katie. I love it. I have wet dreams about this ass, the way it plumps out in your clothes, making my cock beg." My hand reaches into the honeyed opening of her ass and finds the plug I inserted. I pull it out a little before sliding it back in.

"More," she whispers.

Oh, I'll be giving her more—*a lot more.*

I continue to fuck her with the plug, twisting it, pulling it almost out, and then ramming it back into her. Her ass pushes out, wanting more. I look in the mirror and find her eyes closed. She's playing with those juicy, hard nipples and I can't wait any longer. I have to have her.

I take the plug out, tossing it on the bed across the room. Her moan of protest is my reward. My hands bury into the cheeks of her ass. I grip them tightly, pulling them apart. I thrust my face into her ass, letting my tongue slide down that dark valley. I move my tongue over her opening, licking the outline, then slowly pushing in just around the rim and barely inside.

"I fucking love this ass, Katie. *It's mine.*"

"Yes. It is… It's yours, Hunter. Please, baby. Don't make me wait any longer."

I stand up then. Her cry of disappointment is even louder this time. "Shh, sweetness. I just want to show you what else I love," I tell her, bringing her hands slowly down her body.

"Jesus, Hunter," she complains, her ass pushing back and grinding against my raging hard cock. The damn thing has pre-cum running down the shaft. My balls are so fucking tight, I know this won't last long.

"This sweet, bare pussy," I groan into her neck, moving her fingers to her pussy. It's covered in desire. *So damned wet, it's like a fucking waterfall.* I guide her fingers past her lips and inside. I push her finger and mine, feeling the way her walls tremor against our entry. She's fucking primed. "This fucking pussy is unlike anything I've ever known, Katie. So sweet and addicting. It's like pure heroin to my cock. One hit, and I'm ruined for anyone else, Katie. You're all I want. Your body is all I want."

"Hunter, I need to come, please. Please let me come," she cries as I push our fingers back inside of her.

"In a minute, baby, I'll give you exactly what you need," I tell her, guiding her hand to her clit. It's almost pounding as hard as my dick. "Rub that clit for me, sweetness. Get it nice and needy for me, but don't come yet. Don't even think about it."

"Hunter!" she cries, but she does exactly as I tell her.

I turn her to the side, moving her free hand to hold onto the desk that's there beside the mirror. I pull on her hips until she's bent over at just the right angle. "Look in the mirror, Katie. Watch what I'm doing. See how hard my cock is for you. Realize how much you mean to me," I growl, my voice hoarse.

She does exactly that, her eyes glued to the mirror.

I push a finger into her ass. It gains entry so damned easily, I could almost shout in victory. On the second thrust, I add another finger and, again, it slides in without a problem. I stretch her, pulling my fingers apart. She's tight, unbelievably tight, but she's dying for more. I grab my cock. Honestly, I've been leaking so much pre-cum, it's probably all I need, but I can't resist sliding inside of her pussy one time. I push all the way to the hilt until my dick is scraping her womb, my balls pressed against her.

"Yes!" she yells, her walls squeezing my cock and trembling. She's a breath away from coming now.

I leave her tight little pussy for something else, though. Something I've been craving. Something I need from her. I line my cock with her ass, letting the head of my cock push into her so that it's just teasing through the tight ring of muscles.

"That's it, sweetness. Push back into me and give me your ass. It's mine. You're mine. I'll take care of you."

"Oh God, Hunter. I'm going to come."

"Not until I'm buried in your ass. Don't you dare, Katie."

"Hurry!" she cries, her body shaking with the need to fall over the edge.

That's all the encouragement I need. I thrust into that tight ass without stopping. It's so fucking tight, squeezing me so hard that my balls feel like they're on fire. I try not to move once I get seated all the way inside, but Katie isn't having that. Her body is quaking and it's urging me on as she cries out. I feel the orgasm take her, her hands moving so fast over her clit that she's shaking from that alone. I pull out and thrust back in. I fuck her ass, hard.

Once, twice, three times. On the fourth slam home, I can't hold it back anymore. Her muscles milk me, her body trembling as she starts a second orgasm, and I know I'm done for. Her ass is so tight that it's almost too tight, squeezing me so that I can't come, but I feel it, and my load is so big nothing can hold it back. I scream out her name as I empty inside of her. Her body greedily takes every drop. I stay buried inside of her ass, my hands going to hold her breasts as I try to calm my breathing.

"I could love you, Hunter," she whispers, like a dirty secret.

"I do love you, Katie. I'm never letting you go." I don't even blink saying the words.

"I'm not planning on going anywhere," she concedes, and I feel like I won a fucking war.

She's it.

CHAPTER 46
TORCH

"I fucked up."

"Where's Beth's sister?" Skull demands.

I'm standing in the bathroom at five in the morning and whispering on my phone like a fucking loser. It upsets me. Katie deserves better. For the last couple of days, I've been letting Skull listen to our conversations. From the one in the diner before the Saints found us, to the one in the jeep, and even the conversation last night before I claimed Katie. Anything that might give Skull information to find Beth, I've been feeding back to my brother. It's betrayal at its finest.

It would hurt Katie horribly, I know that, even if I am doing it to ultimately protect her, Beth, and Gabby. But Katie wouldn't see it like that. I want to give her time to come to terms with everything, to decide that letting Skull and Beth come together and work things out was the best for all involved. With the Saints out there, that time has run out. I need to get Katie back to the club so I can keep her safe, and we need Beth and Gabby behind those walls too.

"She's sleeping in the next room," I whisper. "Let's make this quick before she wakes up. What's the recon on the Saints?"

"Just as you thought," he answers back. "Colin called them in. They want both girls. The family is calling for their blood because they offed the old man. Half of them think that gives them ground to hang them. The other half are in love with them and want them to rule. Of course, the males want to claim them first. Jesus, that's the most fucked up family. It's no wonder Beth is such a goddamn liar."

"I don't think she is, Skull. Didn't you hear Katie? Their father used her to trap Beth."

"Bullshit. All she had to do was tell me the whole story."

"You expect a lot out of a young girl of nineteen who just found out her father wasn't the man she had always thought. Not to mention one that found out her sister was still alive after all this time."

"Just drop it, Torch. How I deal with Beth is none of your concern. She'll pay for taking my child away from me. She'll pay for lying to me. *For nearly destroying me.*"

"You need to make sure while you're making her pay that you don't destroy what you might find together now, brother. Love is rare. You have the child to think about now."

"What's making you so fucking philosophical?" he asks.

I could tell him it's because of what I've found with Katie. He's not in the frame of mind to hear it, though. "I just happen to think Beth was faced with… an impossible situation."

"Whatever. Do you have your computer there?"

"Yeah." I juggle the phone with my shoulder, trying to hold the laptop still enough to type. The phone falls as a result. I pick it back up, putting it on speakerphone and setting it on the sink. "You're on speaker so, for the love of God, speak quietly."

"You sure are awful concerned with some bitch you just met, *hermano*," Skull counters, his voice tense.

"I don't want to upset her until I get her home behind our walls. You don't know her like I do, Skull. She's a runner."

"Just how well do you know her, Torch? Been using your *polla* to keep her in line so she doesn't know we're using her as bait?" Skull asks.

His words make me sick. We're no better than Katie's dad, put like that. Sure, I'm doing it to protect her, but still I'm using her to get Beth. That's what it comes down to, even if I care for her. No, that's not right. I *love* her. She's the first woman I've met who makes me glad to have her around, who makes me smile, laugh, scream… She's it for me, and I have no idea how I'm going to make all of this right. I just know I *need* to.

"Boss, just give me the coordinates," I say, getting upset, more with myself than him. I don't know how I got in this situation.

He rattles off the coordinates that Diesel's crew gave him. It's supposed to lead to a piece of property that Colin's been using. He wants me to tap into the street cameras that the city put up. The property is on the Tennessee state line. It takes some hacking, but not a lot. I get it up on the computer. It looks like an abandoned business that has the gates closed and padlocked. You can't really see in, but there are armed guards at the entrances.

"They're definitely up to something, boss. I can run the feed through the system there," I tell him. "It might be worth having some men go check it out. Katie and I are about two hours away from the club. I can go later this evening," I offer, not wanting to, but I know I need to help bring an end to this shit. I need it behind us, not only for the club, but I want to keep convincing Katie of our future. I can't do that as long as there's more crap from the Donahues coming at us."

"No," Skull says as I finish setting the feed up so it will transmit into Skull's office. "You need to keep playing Beth's sister. You're doing good there. She's letting her guard down with you. I could tell while you were letting me listen in last night. Keep working her, do whatever you have to do. I want Beth found and back here. I could tell last night when you let me listen in that Katie was close to telling you where Beth was. A few more nudges by you, and she'll cave."

His words burn me from the inside. Jesus, fuck. Is that what I've been doing? I wanted to help Skull, but I thought by letting him listen to Katie talk, he could see what I see: that she loves her sister, that her and Beth aren't doing things to hurt Skull, that they've been abused and used by their family for so fucking long that they just don't trust anyone...

"Boss, it's not like that," I start, but that's when I hear the door slam. Katie's not only up, but she's heard this shit. "FUCK! Boss, I love Katie. You have them wrong. They aren't doing this to hurt you or—shit, boss, I have to go. Katie's been listening."

"Why the fuck would you let her hear—??"

"I didn't know! Okay. I was in this bathroom, hiding like a pussy and trying to do work for you when I should have just told Katie what the fuck was going on." I pull my shirt over my head.

"You better go after her! If she gets away, then—"

"Goddamn it, boss! Are you not listening? If she gets away, it's not *we*, it's *me*. *Me*. *I* love her! She's mine! This isn't some play to get your information. I love her!"

"Fucking hell," Skull groans. "Torch, man…"

"It's okay. I have the key. She can't get far. I'll get her back and—"

I'm heading towards the door with my phone and open it just in time to catch Katie zooming past our room in the jeep. She looks at me as she passes, flipping me off. She's moving fast, but even with that, I can see the pain and tears on her face. I see them and I know I'm the cause. She pulls out on the main road like a mad woman and I'm left standing there in my bare feet, holding a phone and a key and feeling like my world just exploded.

CHAPTER 47
KATIE

" Why did I ever let myself care? "

I stretch my body, feeling delicious pings zap through me. Torch... No, *Hunter*. Hunter loves me. Me. Even with everything wrong with me, he loves me. Well, he doesn't know about the dyslexia or my ADHD, but he knows about my leg and he didn't even blink. It didn't even make a difference to him. He asked for my heart. He asked me to let him in, to trust him, to take care of me and my sister. He'll protect Beth as his own, too, because she's important to him. The same with Gabby. I'm still worried, but he has been telling me over and over that Skull wouldn't hurt Beth. He's right. It's safer for her to be with us than out there where Colin might get to her. I was going to tell him that last night so we could go get Beth and Gabby together, but once I told him I loved him, we both kind of got off track.

I grin. Not that I would change a damn thing.

I sit up in bed, the chill in the room causing goosebumps to break out over my skin. I reach over and feel his pillow. It's still warm. The movement causes my body to tighten, soreness and delicious tingles of need moving through me. It seems weird without the plug he's been making me wear. Last night before I passed out, he said I was ready for him. I expected him to claim me then. He wanted me to sleep, though. I thought he'd wake me up this morning. It's barely dawn outside.

I stand up and look around for something to put on. His silly shirt is on the floor, so I grab it, bring it to my nose, and breathe it in. I love the way Hunter smells. His cologne is this scent that's definitely all man, but there's just something about the way he smells generally that makes me weak in the knees. It's this intoxicating aroma of outdoors, leather, and wickedness. I don't know how else to describe it. I just know I could get drunk on it.

I tiptoe to the bathroom, stopping to look at the mirror with a grin. My pussy clenches in memory, instantly wanting more. I need Hunter. Maybe he's in the shower. Mmm… shower sex. *Yes, please!* We can have some fun, then find food, because I'm famished! Then, I'll ask for his help in bringing Bethie and Gabriella home with us.

I'm about to open the door when I hear voices inside. It takes me a minute to realize it's just Hunter I hear. He's obviously on the phone. That explains why he's in the bathroom. He didn't want to wake me. I should reward him for being so thoughtful. A nice hummer in the shower. Heck, maybe I'll even swallow. Normally I'm not a swallower, but Hunter has made me like everything.

Before I turn the knob, I hear Hunter call me a runner. Then I hear how he wants me home before I can run. I thought I made it clear to him that I wasn't going to run anymore last night. I thought he realized I was surrendering to him… to *us*. I guess I'll just have to make sure he knows it now. I trust him. He loves me. That makes me smile.

Then I hear a new voice. *Skull's.*

I halt my movements, interested to know what they're talking about so early. He calls me a bitch. It's going to take a lot for me to like that man, despite Hunter's assurances that I will. What I hear next kills every trace of happiness I was feeling. It's cold and lodged inside of me now, choking me. When Skulls asks him if he was using his dick to keep me distracted, I want to scream. I fully expect Hunter to beat him down and stop him. Instead, he continues working on something, then offers to help him. No defending me. No denying that horrible claim. *None of that*. Skull's next words are what brings me to my knees.

"Keep playing Beth's sister, you're doing good there. She's letting her guard down with you. I could tell while you were letting me listen in last night. Keep working her…"

The words rip out my heart. They destroy me. Playing me? Using me? Will I never learn? Oh, God, Hunter... No, no, never Hunter.

Torch. *Torch* let Skull listen to us. My hands shake and I back away from the door like the Devil himself is behind it. And he is. The cruelest, most horrible...

He used me. I quickly find my pants. I get to my duffle bag, which has my clutch purse in it. I thought it was a sign of trust between us that Torch gave it back to me. I was an idiot. *He used me.* I feel the tears. They're there, but I refuse to give into them. I can't. *Not right now.*

I run outside and find the jeep locked. Torch didn't give me back my key or the spare. *That* should have clued me in on the whole trust thing. It doesn't matter. I know something about my jeep that he doesn't. One of the reasons I kept the older models is that they're easier to break into and use in a jam. For instance, the passenger side door of mine doesn't lock. The knob goes down saying it does, but it never actually locks.

I jump in on that side and climb over the gearshift. I push the driver's side seat all the way back and then maneuver so I'm hanging upside down. Under my seat are the only three things I've ever needed to get me out of a mess. I sure never needed a man. Not now, *not ever*. I grab the screwdriver, black tape, and the pen knife, and within a second I've got the cable-tied wires down from under the dash.

I've done this so often I could do it in my sleep. I find the starter wires and the power wires that come from the battery. A few flicks of my wrist and I've got the insulation stripped. I connect the wires. There's a sizzle, then a spark. I almost smile as the engine comes to life. I quickly tape up the ends of the start wire, resituate everything, then turn myself around. I adjust the seat and, before I can think about it, I jerk the car into reverse, squealing my tires and raking gears as I push it into second. I'm already in fourth, which is crazy for a parking lot when I whiz by Torch, who's standing at the opened door to our room. I flip him off and pull out onto the highway.

BURNED

It's only when I get three or four miles down the road that I realize I'm crying.

CHAPTER 48
KATIE

" I'll never believe in a man again. "

I drive for two hours straight before I'm brave enough to stop. The first thing I do is enter a store and buy a prepaid phone. Then, I dial Bethie.

"Katie? Are you okay?" Bethie asks. I can hear Gabby crying in the background.

I want to pour my heart out and tell my sister I'm not alright, that I'll never be alright. I want to tell her that I fell in love with an idiot who thought it would be fun to tear my heart out of my chest and stomp on it, but I don't give in to all that. Instead, I concentrate on her.

"Are you and Gabby alright? Where are you?"

"We're not in Tennessee yet. We should be there tomorrow. Gabby got sick."

"Is she okay?"

"Yeah. She has an ear infection. She'll be okay, she's just grumpy. It makes it hard to travel."

"Where are you? I can come to you. We'll change our travel plans. Maybe it's time we consider going across the border."

"Where? We both decided it would be easier to get lost *here* because we knew the land so well and didn't need additional documentation."

"I know, but... Canada is sounding better and better."

"We'll see. I really want Gabby to be close to—"

"That bastard doesn't deserve to have Gabby in his life."

"Katie."

"Listen, tell me where you are."

"Mississippi. I figured the safest bet was to travel in the opposite direction of you."

"Okay. Shit, I'm over a day away from you. Alright, I'll drive as far as I can tonight and then I'll meet up with you tomorrow. Do you need me to bring you anything?"

"No, I have Gabby's medicine and the hotel we're in has a kitchenette. I stocked up for a few days when we stopped," she says and then gives me directions to her hotel.

"Okay, sis. Call this number if you need me. Love you bigger than outer space," I tell her.

"Moon and back again. Be safe, Katie."

We hang up. Emptiness fills my heart. I hate being apart from Bethie. Since she found me again, we've been everything to each other. She's my confidant, my best friend, and my sister. She's also the only person I will ever be able to trust.

I shouldn't have forgotten that.

* * *

I'm killed when I finally pull into the Mississippi state line rest area. I couldn't go another step if I wanted to. I've traveled through the bottom half of Kentucky, from end to end of Tennessee, and finally hitting where I'm at now. With everything I've been through and all of the shit with Torch, I've got a migraine from hell. My leg is killing me, and my vision is blurry.

I'm a total train wreck. I didn't think I could even find a hotel. I doubt Torch is looking for me, but if he is, he'll scour the hotels. It'd be safest here, at least from Torch.

I get out of the jeep and limp towards the restrooms. There's a greasy-looking guy in a blue windbreaker eyeing me as I walk by. He looks like he hasn't bathed in a month. I don't look at him. No need to encourage the guy; he gives me the creeps. I keep my eyes straight ahead as I pass him. I feel prickles of awareness spread over my skin, and I know he's staring at me. I don't think I've ever been so glad to close and lock a door in my life. I do my business, then grab a rubber band from the three or four I have around my wrist and pull my hair up in a messy bun. When I leave, the greasy guy is still there. *Great.* I keep ignoring him, grab a water so I can down some pain pills, then head back to my jeep.

I take my medicine and feel instant relief that the guy hasn't followed me out. I was worried he would. I lock my doors. To secure the passenger side, I take a piece of sea grass rope and tie it from handle to seat belt cover. Once I'm sure that it holds tight enough that no one can get in easily, I stretch my seat back.

Sleep can't come fast enough.

CHAPTER 49
TORCH

"Time to man up."

"It was smart to put a tracker in that chick's boot," Shaft says.

Skull sent him down to pick me up after Katie left me stranded. The fucker's blathering on and on in my ear now as I drive one of the club's trucks down the interstate.

"Her name's Katie," I snarl, not bothering to take my eyes off the road.

I've been driving nonstop, which would be good, except so is Katie. Even with her leg, she's pushed through Kentucky, and in another twenty minutes or so, she'll have driven all the way across the state of Tennessee. When I see her again, I'm going to blister her ass. It will be so fucking red she won't sit down for weeks. She has to be miserable.

Jesus with a hangover, why wasn't I more careful? I should not have put Skull on speakerphone. What the fuck must she be thinking? Oh, that's easy. She's thinking that I'm an asshole and a moron, and she's *damn right*.

"Torch, brother. Look. Her car's stopped."

My attention goes back to the phone I have mounted on the dash. Fuck, it has. Good. Only problem is, it's stopped in fucking Mississippi. I knew she was a few hours in front of me, but I didn't realize she'd be *even more than that*. I step on the gas, hoping I can get there before it's too late. At best, it will be three hours before I get to her, and that's only if I peg the speedometer to get there.

My cell phone rings, making my track go blank. Even though it's a matter of pulling it back up, it's annoying as hell.

"What?" I roar, needing this conversation done.

I know it's just a blue dot on the screen, but when I see it, I feel closer to Katie and not quite so out of control. That's the major thing right now because I feel completely out of control.

"It's me," says Skull. "There's shit going on. I'm flying into Mississippi. I'll be there about the time you are. I got information back from our mole inside the Chrome Saints."

My heart stalls. *Fuck.* "What the fuck's going on and why Mississippi? That's where Katie is."

"I know, and apparently the Chrome Saints do, too."

"What? How?"

"They have a low jack planted on the jeep."

"Motherfucker! I saw them around it at the diner and I didn't even think to check. Fuck, I'm an idiot!"

"Too late, now. We need to hurry. They've been trailing it. They followed your girl into a store where she bought a phone. Unless I miss my guess, she's off to meet Beth."

"Motherfucking craptastic load of shit! I'm about two and a half hours out. I'll intercept her."

"The fuck you will! You'll not stop her from going to Beth and Gabby, and that's a fucking *order*."

"Boss, I can get there and protect Katie and—"

"And *nothing!* As mad as she is at you, she'd never tell you where Beth is, and I can't risk losing her again."

"I can't let something happen to Katie!"

"We'll have enough men there. Nothing will happen, Torch. Just don't fuck it up. I think a lot of you, but you try to come between me and my family and I *will* fuck you up."

The phone goes dead.

Motherfucker.

* * *

I drive the next three hours in silence. I drive as fast as humanly possible and I ignore every fucking thing that Shaft says. Not that he's said much. Ever since he asked me to stop two hours back so he could use the bathroom and I told him to hang his dick out the window and let it fly, he shut the fuck up.

I don't breathe normally until I'm staring at the exit for the rest area. I pull into it slowly, hanging back and trying to find Katie's jeep. As soon as I spot it, I park as far away as possible. Shaft jumps out at the same time I do.

"Where the hell are you going?" I ask.

"To the bathroom," he answers, "and fuck you very much, asshole."

I let him go. I'm glad he's leaving. I walk towards Katie's jeep, and that's when I see a motherfucker casing it out. I'm going to make sure she pays for worrying my ass. Anyone knows not to hang out at a motherfucking rest stop. I expect her to jump out of the jeep and confront the motherfucker. When she doesn't, I get worried. I see that the asshole's holding something, and then notice light reflect off of the silver blade in his hand. Now, I'm beyond worried. I inch up by the back of the jeep. I look inside and, from this angle, it's hard to tell, but it looks like she's *sleeping*. She needs to be punished for a fucking month.

I finish circling around the jeep. When the son of a bitch turns to go to the driver's side door, I come up behind him, wrap my arm around his neck, and cap a hand over his mouth. I pull him away from the jeep and behind another car, wrestling. It costs me because he cuts into my hand with that fucking knife. I don't stop until I have him completely pulled away.

Suddenly, he breaks away, spins, then comes at me with the knife. I deflect it, but I'm losing blood from my arm, and if I don't hurry and put an end to this, I'm going to get weak fast. I dance around him for a minute, then ram at him. I grab his arm, trying to keep the knife away from me as my other hand wraps around his neck and I slam him against a nearby pickup. I choke him, determined to keep him from getting air. The arm holding his shakes, and he slowly wins that battle as the knife gets closer and closer to me. He gets away from the truck and I back up a few steps, allowing it. I need to regroup. My fucking arm is losing blood pretty damn quick. This fight may get dirty.

I'm just about to junk-punch him with my knee, since my hands are a little busy, when the guy falls to the fucking ground like a piece of lead. Standing behind him is Shaft, who holds a big ass rock he just swung into the man's head.

Once he makes sure the motherfucker's unconscious, he drops the rock on the man's gut. The guy's body jerks, but shows no other signs of consciousness.

"About damn time," I growl, pissed off that I couldn't finish the motherfucker myself.

"If a son of a bitch had let me leak my lizard earlier, I would have been here, so shut it. What do we do with the son of a bitch?"

"Kill him."

"Wouldn't it be, y'know, smarter if we just tie him up and deliver him to the cops?"

"Not as much fun."

"Whatever, man. I'm not the son of a bitch who's leaking blood all over the place and starting to look like I haven't seen sun in a couple of years."

"Fine. Tie him up and we'll call 911 anonymously. There's a first aid kit in the car. I'll see about fixing my arm up."

"Got it. You going to get your woman?"

"Skull told me not to, so no, but we sure ain't letting her out of our sight."

"Joy," Shaft grumbles. "I'll be back. Gonna get some rope out of the truck."

I follow him after making sure that the asshole hasn't come around. He's still out cold, so I start walking back to the truck. I stop mere feet away from Katie's jeep. She's still sound asleep. She better be glad Skull forbade me to grab her tonight, because if he hadn't... *fuck*. I was already pissed. After seeing how close she got to some pervert raping her—or worse—I'm not sure how gentle I'd have been with her. I give her one more glance through the window of her jeep, then walk back down to my vehicle.

It's gonna be a long night.

CHAPTER 50
KATIE

> *"Bad luck seems to follow me.*
> *I think I'll name it Torch."*

Sleeping in my car was a lot more fun when I was younger. I think I'm sorer now than I was before I took my nap. I didn't mean to stay out quite so long. Apparently, Mississippi rest areas are safer than the ones I'm used to because no one bothered me.

I'm back on the road, headed to my sisters. I should be there any moment, which is good. Up ahead, I see a road sign that reads "HWY 3209" and take a small breath of relief.

Finally, I'll be with Beth and Gabby again. I go across a small, low-water bridge, take the right turn like Bethie explained, and start watching the odometer. She said the hotel was on the left about two miles. I cringe when I see it. It was probably a great hotel—*back in the early eighties*. I pull into the parking lot and take a breath. *I can do this,* I tell myself. Nothing to it. I'll just collect my sister and niece, then we have to get the fuck out of here before Norman Freaking Bates shows up. *Simple.*

I look around and it seems clear. I don't know why, but I've had this feeling all morning that someone's been following me. I could've sworn I saw the same truck a few times, but each time it would get lost in traffic or pass me. It's the interstate, and that shit happens, but I'm just being paranoid. I blame Torch. He got me to let my guard down and now I see enemies everywhere.

I go to the right door, then knock. It takes a couple of minutes before Bethie opens the door. When she does, she wraps her arms around me so tight I can't breathe.

"Let's get out of the open," I tell her, still unable to shake that feeling.

We retreat back into the room. She closes the door behind me. "Are you okay?" she asks at once, sitting down on one of the double beds in the room.

"I'll be better when we get on the road," I admit. "You got all your stuff packed?"

"All but Gabby's. She's still sleeping. She barely closed her eyes last night."

"Isn't she getting any better?"

"Yeah. You know I wouldn't put Gabby's health in jeopardy. She's just got her days and nights mixed up."

I walk over to the far bed that Bethie and her slept in. Little Gabby's curled up against a pillow, her thick black curls laying over her face. She looks like an angel.

"Hello, my sweet niece," I whisper with a smile. She makes everything better, just by being close. These two are all I need. I don't need Torch. You can only depend on family. God, that sounds absurd, coming from me. But Bethie and Gabby are the only *real* family I've ever had, so it's true.

"We need to get going," Bethie warns me. "How about I load up my stuff and move yours from the jeep? We'll put it all in my car. You can rest your leg and watch Gabby. Then, when I'm done, we'll load up the rest of her stuff and get the heck out of here."

I smile because that's Bethie, kicking into mother mode. I sit back down with a sigh. "Am I that obvious?"

"You're limping like crazy."

"Okay, it's probably a good plan," I concede, because I *am* in a lot of pain.

"And *I'm* driving when we hit the road," she insists, going to the nightstand and grabbing her keys.

"I'm going to miss my jeep," I complain.

"Too many people will be looking for it," Bethie reasons, "from what you told me on the phone this morning. I can't believe you and Torch…"

"Let it go," I say at once, "and please don't ever mention his name again."

"You'll wish you could get off that easy," she grumbles. "I'll be back in a minute. Throw me your keys."

"I'd love to, but I can't, don't have them. Had to hot-wire the vehicle to get away. It's unlocked, though."

"Katie ..."

"Don't start, Bethie. It's been a rough couple of days," I tell her, then lay back on the bed.

Gabby, the smart cookie that she is, must recognize that Bethie has left, because she wakes up just a few minutes later. I pick her up, loving how she fills my arms with her precious weight. She smells like baby lotion and powders.

I place a kiss on the top of her head. "Hey there, beautiful. Mommy just went to load up the car. We'll be on the road in no time and Aunt Katie will buy you some nuggies and french fries, and we'll listen to mommy tell us how that's not a nutritious meal and we'll laugh at mean ol' mommy."

"Kayyyyyyyytie!" she cries merrily, all smiles and rainbows this morning. Gabby's always been a happy baby. She starts wiggling, wanting down. I look at the floor of the room. She got some memory blocks in front of the kitchenette, which is really a mini-fridge, a hot plate, and a sad-looking coffee maker. I sit her down and start playing with her. Bethie knocks on the door a couple of minutes later.

"I'm gonna go let your momma in, short-stuff. Be right back." I groan at the added pressure it puts on my leg to get up from the floor. "You should have just left it unlocked, Bethie," I call out. "It was just a minute."

I open the door and look one last time over my shoulder at Gabby because she cries out. It's just because her tower of blocks fell over, but my nerves are shot.

"Hello, sweetness."

My body freezes into place right where I'm standing when Torch's voice hits me. I turn to him and the look on his face sends a shiver of fear through my system. His hair is tousled, his clothes wrinkled. His eyes are shining with anger. I'm scared, I can admit it, but there's a part deep inside of me that's glad to see him. He has on faded jeans that are so worn they're more white than blue. He has on a blue t-shirt that has a silhouette of a cat on it and a man with a whip. Underneath, it reads "Pussy Tamer". Maybe the most alarming thing is that he has his club clothes on again. His Devil's Blaze MC cut is staring at me and it makes my stomach turn.

I'd find something to say about that, if my brain wasn't racing. Did Bethie see? Is she…

That unasked question is answered when I see her in the arms of a big tall biker with blonde hair and all muscles. He holds Beth close, making it unable for her to get to me. She looks terrified and there's tears in her eyes.

Anger fires through me. I don't have time to think about it though, because I'm roughly pushed out of the way as another biker moves into the hotel. He's tall, his body covered in ink from his fingers and up his neck, the majority of them being skulls. He's big—bigger than Torch, though roughly the same height. His jeans have frayed holes in the knees and around the hips are smaller ones. He's wearing a Devil's Blaze cut, too, with a black shirt under that. He's got a piercing in his lip and a gage in his ear, and it doesn't take a rocket scientist, or the fact that his leather cut says Skull on it, to know this is the man Bethie is in love with. Jesus. When my sister, who is about as wholesome and good as they come, decides to taste a bit of the wild stuff, she doesn't mess around.

He doesn't spare me a word.

"Wait, what are you doing? You can't—"

"I'm taking my daughter," he growls, and I can hear Bethie crying in the background.

My heart is hammering in my chest and fear churns in my stomach. In all our time under lock and key at my grandfather's and then on the run, I've never known such fear.

I'm scared to death.

CHAPTER 51
TORCH

"She's not getting away again."

She's beautiful. Even when I stand here, worried about the confrontation coming up, mad as Hell at her *and* Skull, I still can't deny that my woman is beautiful.

She's also in pain. She's limping more than she ever did in front of me. Right away, I realize it's because she doesn't bother hiding things from Beth. Even when I thought her guard was down with me, I was wrong. When she goes to chase after Skull, I wrap my arms around her waist and pull her back into me. Right away, she starts kicking against me, her hands going behind to my head to wrap her fingers in my hair, pulling. She's wrestling like a wet mountain lion hanging on for dear life. Too fucking bad my patience is gone.

"Cut that shit out, Katie. We got company coming and I need you, Beth, and Gabby out of here before they get here."

"Like I believe you!" she cries out. "Let me go, you bastard! You used me! You lied to me!"

She's screaming, and one of her backward kicks manages to graze my fucking balls. I wince at the pain. I pull her around to face me, holding my hand around her neck and keeping her head still, even if the rest of her is fighting against me.

"You and I got shit to talk about, and we *will*, but right now Colin's men are headed this way. That means my job is to get you, your sister, and niece somewhere safe. So stop acting like a fucking baby and help me do that!"

Her eyes narrow down on me, her body jerking like I hit her.

"I hate you."

I throw her over my shoulder, fucking tired of her fit.

"I'm taking Katie back in Beth's car," I announce.

"You make sure you don't drag your fucking feet. I want all our men behind our walls before we attack," Skull says.

His voice is thick and I'd be blind not to see the tears he's shed. He's holding his daughter and her little hand is reaching for the hoop he has in his lip. They look so much alike it's freaking uncanny. I'm upset he didn't let me get Katie last night, even if I can understand why. My anger has settled some, though, because I have Katie back in my arms.

"We'll be there. Two days, max."

"I thought you said you were taking my family with us? I want Bethie and Gabby with me!" Katie growls.

I look over at Beth. She's crying, but her eyes are following every movement Skull and Gabby are making.

"My family will be with me," says Skull defiantly. "You've been helping to run interference too fucking long. If it wasn't for Torch, I'd leave you here for Colin's men to play with."

"Watch it, Skull," I retort.

He gives me a look. We're going to have words later. I get that he's upset, but Katie's mine, even if I'm mad as hell at her for running out and not giving me time to talk to her. This whole situation is fucked up, but it didn't come from the girls trying to take Gabby, or from willfully hurting Skull. I only hope in time he can grasp that. Right now, he's so angry I'm afraid he might do something he and Beth can't recover from.

I take Katie towards the car. Beth's voice stops me.

"The baby's bag with her food and clothes... most of it is in the room... but there's one bag in the car. I... Gabby needs it."

"I'll provide *mi hija* with anything she needs from here on out," Skull growls, still not looking at Beth.

"There are things in there she can't rest without. New ones wouldn't work," Beth's soft voice comes back. "I know you're planning on turning us back over to Colin, but please. Gabby. She shouldn't have to suffer because of—"

"Te tienes que callar la pinche boca!" Skull growls. "Torch, grab la pinche bolsa."

Katie has gone strangely quiet. I don't know if she's picking up on the undercurrents firing off between Beth and Skull or what, but I'm glad. I take her to the passenger side and get her in the vehicle. When she's sitting in the car, I notice the tears falling. Katie is so tightly wrapped up, seeing the tears physically hurts me. Jesus, having a woman is so damned complicated.

I pull the handcuffs out of my back pocket and click them over her wrist, connecting them to the handle above the door on the interior. Katie's head turns, looking at the handcuffs and back at me, and even in tears, she's shooting fire at me with her eyes.

"Remember these, darling?" I ask. "Get used to them because you aren't getting out of them any time soon."

"I hate you," she repeats.

"I've heard that one before," I remark, slamming the car door on her. I see the large colorful bag in the back that's covered by cartoon characters. I open the back door and grab it, taking it over to Beth. I kiss her cheek. "It'll all be okay, Beth. Hold tight. I'm going to take care of your sister, I promise."

It's not much, but it's my way of reassuring her. I just hope I'm right, for both our sakes. She gives me a weak smile through her tears, then I turn to go back to my woman. Everyone has loaded up and, as I look over my shoulder, Sabre's putting Beth in his SUV. It doesn't escape my attention that Skull still has Gabby and he's in a separate vehicle. Fuck, I hope I'm right. I go get my woman so we can get out of here before the Saints figure out we jammed their signal, fix it, then deduce our location. That's the last thing anyone needs.

Our plates are full enough.

" I wish I could hate him. "

We're almost back in Tennessee and we still haven't said a word to each other, which suits me fine, but when he reaches over and turns off the radio, I know my reprieve is over.

"I thought you had better sense than to pull the crap you've pulled. What the fuck were you trying to do, get yourself killed? Not to mention spending the night in a fucking rest stop!"

I know my eyes go wide. I guess it shouldn't surprise me that he knows everything, since clearly he's been tracking me. It does though, at least slightly.

"I was doing what I had to do to protect my family," I say in response. "And I was perfectly fine at the rest stop. It was safe. I know what I'm doing, y'know."

Torch mumbles something under his breath, his knuckles going white against the steering wheel, and I can see his pulse throbbing in his neck. Then, he turns on me and I swear if a man could breathe fire, he'd be doing it.

"You kidding me? Jesus on a Harley, you're completely nuts! You weren't safe! Nothing about the harebrained shit you've been pulling has been safe, and if it wasn't for me and my brothers being there this morning, Colin's assholes would have gotten ahold of you."

"Oh, they wouldn't have, either! If you hadn't been there to slow us down, we would be long gone."

"Jesus, you are clueless. The only reason they didn't get to you before we did is because we jammed their fucking signal when our intel let us know they were tracking the jeep."

"Whatever. I still say we would have been long gone. And what do you care, anyway? You and your brothers are just planning on turning me and Bethie over to Colin anyways."

He slams on the breaks and my body hurls towards the windshield. The seatbelt catches me and jerks me back, as well as my hand. The metal bites into my wrist.

"Are you fucking kidding me right now?" Horns are blaring and tires are squealing as they zoom past us and bow up behind us on the road.

"Will you watch it? Are you trying to get us killed? Hit the damn gas!"

"Fuck no! We aren't going another damn foot until you look me in the eye and admit that you know that there's no way in hell that I'm ever letting Colin or any of that fucking bunch get ahold of you!"

"Whatever you say."

"I'm not playing you right now, Katie. Admit it. Jesus Christ! How can you even say that to me after everything that's gone down between us?"

"You mean all of the lying? The taped conversations? The fucking backstabbing? You mean all of *that*, Torch?"

"Stop calling me Torch!"

"That's your name!"

"The fuck it is! You call me Hunter!"

"Are you for real?"

"Katie..." he warns me.

"Fine then, *Hunter*. Perhaps you should run to the hospital because I think you've had a stroke! Or you're just fucking insane!"

"You got that right, lady. Loving your ass has drove me completely insane."

"Don't say that," I tell him, my voice so quiet, I'm not sure he can hear me. I just know that when he uses those words, it hurts. No, that's wrong. When he uses that word, it *injures* me.

"Don't say what, Katie? That I love you? Don't you get it, sweetness? I fucking love you. I love you so much it's keeping me from strangling the fucking life out of you right now."

"Will you stop?" I scream, unable to hear that from him. His face jerks back like I've hit him, and I decide to just let out the rest. "I trusted you! I was letting my guard down, trusting you with the two things in this world that mean more to me than anything. They're the only reason I'm still alive! And you used me, planning to—"

"Planning to get *them* back to Skull. My God, woman! Did you even see the hell on his face when he saw Gabby? Did that even register, or are you and your sister so selfish that you think this is all about you?"

His words cut me. He doesn't know. He doesn't have any idea. He couldn't. I turn away from him then. A car comes up behind us and this time they don't go around. They just sit there with their hand on the horn, blaring it continuously.

"I'm going!" Torch yells, then finally jerks it down into drive, slamming his foot on the gas.

I just keep staring out the window and feeling like I might not survive this.

Chapter 53
Torch

"I don't know how to get through to her."

Silence. That's all it's been since our mini-screaming match. I say mini, because I'm pretty sure it's going to get much worse before I break through the walls she's trying to erect between us. I wish I knew how to get through to her. Some magical formula which could just end this shit. I don't. All I have to give her is the truth. I hope that's enough, because she sure as hell ain't going anywhere.

We get about halfway home when I decide to stop for the night. I pull into one of the big chain hotels. It's going to take a soft king-size bed, a Jacuzzi, and anything else I can find to make her happy. She's still not talking to me, so fuck it. I'll leave her chained to the arm-grip handle and get out. Her voice stops me right before I close the door, surprising me.

"Torch. Make sure you get two beds," she says.

I don't answer. There's no reason to. She's out of her fucking mind. She's sleeping with me tonight. No. Hell no. I'm sleeping *inside* her tonight.

Once I get us checked in and parked up, I unlatch her from the handle and help her out of the car.

"Can you walk?"

"I'm fine," she huffs.

I frown, but I'm too fucking worn out from the day to argue much with her. I latch her to my wrist and basically pull her with me to the back entrance. We get into the elevators and the minute the doors close, Katie decides to talk.

"You're such a fucking asshole."

I pinch the bridge of my nose and close my eyes, trying to remember why I wanted her to talk in the first place.

"Katie, don't push me anymore," I warn her. "You won't like what happens." I'm at the end of my fucking rope.

"Let me go, Torch. You have what you want. Just let me go."

"You'd leave your sister and niece behind?" I ask, pissed off and biting my fucking tongue to keep from asking her how she could leave *me* behind.

"No, but I'll get to your club on my own."

That does it.

"So it's *me* you'd leave behind. The fucking man who put everything on the line for you. The man who's dick is good enough to use, but nothing else."

"Don't do that! You don't get to do that. You don't have the right."

I push the button to stop the elevator. I grab her hand and hold it over her head, which lifts her other one, since it's still cuffed to mine, and I push into her tightly so she's trapped by me and the wall, unable to move.

"What don't I have the right to do, Katie? Tell me. Shouldn't I be upset because the woman I love is running from me and trying to push me away?"

"You don't get the right to act like I'm the one hurting you! I never promised you anything more than I gave you. I never used what we had together against you!"

"That's right, sweetness. You never promised me anything more than your pussy, right? That's all you ever invested. How can you use anything against me? I mean, all I was to you was a real life vibrator."

"You're overselling yourself," she hurls back. "My vibrator is *better*."

"We'll just see about that." My hand goes to her pants to undo them.

"What? What are you doing??" she shrieks.

"Giving you one last time to compare the two," I snarl back, pushing her clothes down over her hips.

"I am not making love to you!"

"Making love has nothing to do with what I am going to do to you."

"You're crazy! If you do this, it's rape!"

"And you're full of shit," I tell her, undoing my pants.

"I'm serious! Don't do this, Torch!"

"Stop calling me Torch!"

"It's your name! Stop it! Oh my God!" she hisses, trying to run away from me when I push my fingers through the lips of her pussy. Hot, wet heat gathers on my hand immediately. She's fucking drenched and I've done nothing.

"You might be saying no, but your body sure as fuck isn't," I tell her, my voice firm but quiet. "You're so wet, it's painted on the inside of your thighs."

"The bellboy we met in the hall was hot. It's all for him."

"Well, since he's not here, I'll just take it," I tell her, and for some reason, I'm smiling. Maybe it's because I thrust my fingers into her at that exact moment and my lips swallow the gasp that leaves her lips.

CHAPTER 54
KATIE

" Going down... "

Hunter's fingers thrust into me at the same moment he takes my mouth. His tongue wraps around mine and I try not to kiss him. I truly do. But, he's right. I do want him. I've wanted him from the first moment I saw him at the bar. I may always want him. I think my fate has been sealed.

He says he never means to turn me and Beth over to Colin, and I even believe that. Maybe I'm a fool. Maybe I'm completely and utterly fooling myself, but I believe him. So, maybe that's why I kiss him back. Maybe I just need his lips on mine and his tongue in my mouth. Who knows?

All I know is that with one touch, he sets me off. I pull on my hands, wanting them loose so I can touch him. He doesn't let me, though. If anything, his hold tightens. He breaks away from my mouth, and I'm panting when he looks at me.

"Give me the words, Katie."

"I hate you," I tell him, even though I don't, even though I'm pretty fucking sure I'm utterly and completely in love with him.

His fingers still inside of me, I tighten my muscles on them, nudging him with my hips to try and get more. I squirm, twisting and trying to get him to move. Nothing works.

"The words, sweetness, or this is all you get."

"You're an asshole."

"I know."

His easy acceptance trips me up. I wasn't expecting it.

"You hurt me."

"I know that too, Katie, and I'm so fucking sorry."

Something else I wasn't expecting from him. It annoys me that he's being this way. I don't want it. It would be easy to walk away from him if he remained an ass and all of this just boiled down to sex. With that, I might be able to forget what we shared the night before I left. The night before his words... destroyed me.

"Are we going to have a heart-to-heart with your fingers inside me?"

"If that's what it takes," he mutters.

"I'd rather you fuck me."

"That's going to happen too, eventually."

"You let Skull hear things I told you. *Just you.* You betrayed me."

"I was just trying to reach Skull, sweetness. I thought, if he could hear the reasons behind Beth's choices, then... *Fuck!* I don't know what I was thinking. I was trying to help. I needed for Skull and Beth to be okay, because—"

"Because?" I prompt, knowing that what he says matters. What happens between us hinges on what happens here in this elevator.

"I'm not giving you up, Katie. I'm not letting you go. If I have to keep you chained to me for the next twenty years, that's exactly what I'll do."

"What does that have to do with Skull and Beth? We aren't them!"

"Exactly! You would give the world hell and face anything head-on with me. Beth didn't do that. That's on her. Her choices destroyed Skull, and the shit he's pulling, that's on *him!* They're tearing each other apart and I wanted to try and fix it because I knew!"

"Knew what?" I ask, softer this time.

I'm confused and wondering how in the hell we are having this conversation with his fingers still inside of me and my pants down around my knees.

"I knew you would choose her," he finally answers. "I wanted to try and fix it so I could still be part of your plan. I knew you'd be just like Beth. You'd choose her over me. Hell, I gave you my *all* that night in the hotel and you still wouldn't tell me you loved me. You still wouldn't hold onto me. You ran. Maybe I'm wrong," he says, taking his hands away.

My body instantly misses his fingers, but I try to concentrate on his words. I need to hear them.

"Maybe we are just like them," he goes on, "because you ran, just like her…"

He drops his hands, letting go of my free one. He unlatches the handcuffs, then stuffs them in his back pocket. I stare at him a minute, rubbing my wrist. Then I look at him, *really* look at him. My cocky biker with the horrible t-shirts and the easy smile. The eyes with wicked promises glowing in their depths. All of that is gone and, in its place, is just a man. A man who, even though his brother has what he wanted, is still trying to be with me. A man who claims he loves me, even when his side has won. A man who claims to love me when he's seen me at my weakest.

A man who… *I* love.

He reaches over to start the elevator back. Now is decision time. Do I keep running? Do I repeat the mistakes that my sister made?

My hand goes to the elevator and I stop it again.

"What are you doing?" he asks.

My hands go to his belt, undoing it and unlatching the button and zipper on his pants. I push them out of the way, thanking the stars my man is a free-baller.

"Claiming you," I answer, my eyes watching his as I stroke his cock.

It might be my imagination but I thought I saw a tremor run through his body.

"Get off your knees, sweetness. You'll hurt your leg."

"Stop worrying. My leg is fine. I'm loving on my man."

"Am I your man?" he asks.

I keep stroking him, but I angle my head under him so I can run my tongue over his balls and suck on them, toying with them. His balls are already hard and the heated skin sends waves of need through my body. "Katie?" he asks, his voice quiet and full of desire, of need, of something else… something more tangible.

I release him from my mouth with a pop, then use my hand to rub his balls one last time before I lick my way up his cock. My eyes are on his the entire time. When I reach the head of his cock, I slide my tongue around it, gathering his pre-cum.

"Katie," he prompts.

"The only one I'll ever want. I'm not running, Hunter. Not anymore."

I slide my mouth over him, taking him inside. I keep going until my lips meet my hand, which circles the base of his dick. I use my tongue to love on his dick as I take him all the way in, licking the large vein that seems to be pulsing. Slowly, I move back up, releasing his cock from my mouth. Even more pre-cum slides from his head and leaks down on my hand as I move up and down the hard length of his shaft.

"Sweetness…"

I move my tongue back down, using his pre-cum and my mouth to make his dick shine, coating it. I look up at Hunter. He's watching everything I do. His hands are in my hair, but he's not demanding; he's letting me play.

I suck him all the way back in my mouth, making his huge cock disappear and hollowing out my cheeks. I repeat this and use my hand to stroke as I go back and forth, working in unison. His cock is so wet now, strands of pre-cum stringing from the head of his cock to my lips. I watch his face as my tongue gathers them into my mouth, all while my hand keeps stroking him.

"You taste so good, Hunter."

"Jesus, sweetness…"

I use my lips to kiss his head, my tongue sliding between them to curve into the small opening and demanding more of his pre-cum. I tighten my hand on him and continue to stroke. His hand tightens in my hair, silently demanding more. I don't give into the urge to give him what he wants. Instead, I flatten out my tongue and use his hard cock to paddle it, slapping the dick so it spanks my tongue. His heavy cock bounces back and forth, pre-cum splattering on my lips and the side of my face.

"Mmm…" I moan around him as I take the head and suck in more of his taste. His body quakes as the vibration of my voice hums against his dick.

"Jesus. Fuck!" Hunter growls. His head goes back against the wall of the elevator. "Seeing my cum on you… It's a fucking dream come true, sweetness. You're mine. Tell me you know that," he all but moans out.

My other hand pets his balls and I can feel the way they've tightened even more. I know he's close. His words serve as inspiration. I move my hands to his cock. It takes both of them to completely engulf them. Just acknowledging that makes my pussy tremor.

That's for later, though. Right now, it's all about Hunter.

I keep the head of his cock on my tongue as I use both hands to continue stroking him, holding him tight. My hands slide up and down his shaft easily, it's so slick. His head pulses against my tongue. I get faster with my strokes, loving the way he's giving me his pre-cum, a little at a time, but I know what's coming. I know even before he growls out my name. *Mine.* He's proud it's me. He *wants* me. After a lifetime of feeling like I don't measure up, that settles in my heart, and it fucking blasts away the damage all of the negative has done.

"I'm coming, sweetness. Oh, fuck, I'm going to—"

His words hit me almost at the same time his cum starts pouring into my mouth. Stream after stream is ejected from his cock, splashing on my tongue, along the side of my face, and down my chin. I can even feel it running down my neck. He groans as his eyes shut. The way his body quakes, combined with the way his hand slides against my hair caressing it, is my reward.

When it's over, I go back to licking his semi-erect cock, cleaning it up, then kissing it with soft, barely-there touches from my lips as he recovers. It takes him a few minutes, but he reaches down and pulls me up. I resist to put one last kiss on his cock.

He half-buttons his pants, leaving the zipper and belt undone. Then he pulls my clothes back up over my hips, leaving them undone.

"You're never leaving me, Katie. We're together no matter what or *who* tries to come between us. Say it."

"I'm right here, unless you do something to fuck it up," I tell him instead.

He looks at me, then rips his shirt off his head, using it to clean off my face and neck gently. "What am I going to do with you, Katie? Always giving me shit."

"It's a gift, but if you're going to keep me, you should get used to it," I tell him as the elevator takes off. We didn't hit the button, I guess it has an override.

"I guess I will," he agrees, and he's smiling. It's a beautiful smile.

"I love you, Hunter," I finally say, letting it out. "I've only said that to two other people in my life. Bethie, and my niece. But I love you. You're right. I should have screamed at you, not ran. I'll never do that to you again. I'll fight to keep us. Does that work for you?"

The look of happiness in his face deepens. "I think that's perfect, Katydid. Just perfect."

"You look awful happy for a man whose woman just told him she was going to spend her life screaming at him," I tell him, trying to joke my way around the swell of emotion I feel in my chest.

"That's because I'm fucking ecstatic," he admits. "Especially if all our shouting matches end like this one did."

I don't say a word. I let him gather me up in his arms and hold me close as the elevator door dings, signaling our arrival. I hold his discarded shirt against my stomach as we walk down the hall, ignoring the stares from the other guests who were waiting for the elevator. It doesn't escape my notice that he cleaned me up with a shirt that declared him a pussy tamer. I kind of have to agree, as long as it's *my* pussy.

Chapter 55
Torch

"FINALLY!"

I carry her to our room. She's biting into the side of my neck, raking her teeth against my skin. We pass people in the hall that stare, but my little wildcat never misses a beat. I open the door and kick it shut with my foot behind us. I stand her up by the bed and hold her while she kicks off her shoes. Then, I pull her shirt up over her head and unlatch her bra. Next comes her pants and underwear. I bend down and pick up her panties, bringing them to my face and breathing them in. I look over to Katie while I'm still taking in the green lace that covers her.

"I want to yell at you for wearing these damn things, but I find myself dreaming of having them wrapped around my cock while I watch you make yourself come," I tell her, the pink tint of her embarrassment heating up her face.

"I can't believe you just smelled my panties," she says.

I put them down on the nightstand with a grin. "Honey, if it was possible, I'd eat the damn things," I tell her, picking her up and tossing her on the bed.

"Err... Einstein? The head of the bed is up there," she says. The way I tossed her, her head is at the foot of the bed—which is exactly where I want her.

"True, sweetness," I tell her, taking out the handcuffs from my back pocket. "But the headboard is just leather mounted on the wall. Now here at the foot is an honest-to-God post I can use to my advantage."

"What are you doing?" she asks as I latch one of her wrists in the cuff. "I told you, I wasn't going to run anymore." I run the handcuff around the post, pulling her other hand up to attach it, then stand back to look at my handiwork. Her hands are secured above her head and there's no way she's going to get loose. The position causes her breasts to jut out, moving slightly with each jerk of her body. "Hunter?"

I hear the hint of arousal in her voice. "Sorry, sweetness. I was just admiring my new toy."

"Toy?"

"Mmm. Yes, definitely. You see, Katie," I tell her, starting to undress. Her eyes follow everything I do, and when she licks her lips, my cock jerks against my stomach. The fucker should be down for the count after the blowjob he got earlier, but that just got his engine started. Katie may kill me, but Jesus Christ on steroids, what a fucking way to go. "I plan on you being at my mercy all night long."

"Hunter, I don't—"

"Don't worry, baby. I'll make you like it," I promise her, moving down to the other side of the bed and sitting at her feet. "Did you know that there is a huge debate about how many erogenous zones a woman has?"

"Oh, fuck."

"I mean, there's the normal, and those are great. We'll get to those for sure. The head, the pussy, the breasts... but I think there are more. I think there are areas on every single part of you that will make you beg to come. What do you think, sweetness? Do you think I'm right?"

"Hunter, I..." Her voice breaks off as I pick up her foot and begin massaging the balls of her feet. I lick around her ankle and nibble on the back of her calf. Her body jerks in response and she gasps as I continuing massaging her feet, letting my fingers manipulate the muscles.

"What do you say, Katydid? Do you think the feet should be included as erogenous?"

She whimpers, but doesn't reply. So, I move up. My tongue finds the back of her knee as I raise her leg up enough so I can slide under.

"I've always thought the knees were particularly sensitive," I tell her, licking along the backside of her knee while my hands massage the leg gently because it's the one that gives her so much trouble. I bite the side of her leg, moving up to her thighs. "Or maybe you'd rather I concentrate on your thighs? They are beautiful, and there's so many places for me to bite, lick, and tease…"

"Hunter!" she growls as I bite the inside of her thigh. I can smell her sweet pussy, and from where I'm at, I can see the cream gathered on the lips. I turn so I'm looking up at her, just a breath away from her pussy.

I pull myself up to sit on my knees as I watch, putting her legs over my shoulders. "What is it, sweetness? Don't you think the thighs are worth my time?"

"Please," she whimpers her hips trying to thrust up off the bed. I grin, stroking my cock. I meant to take my time. Of course, I have all night, and she's not moving, so…

"Maybe the most overlooked erogenous zone for you is your fucking cervix," I growl, thrusting hard into her pussy and not stopping until my balls are pushed up against her. With her legs over my shoulders and her ass raised up, I'm scraping her walls and pushing up against her womb. She cries out, demanding I fuck her, and I can't even think of denying her. I'll have to play later. Instead, I pound the hell out of her pussy, fucking her harder than I ever have, and I don't stop until I come deep inside of her while her body is still rocking from her own orgasm. I don't leave her, then. I stay where I'm at. I want to stay here. I want my cum to stay here. I make a note to make sure she stops taking her birth control. I'll bind her to me every fucking way I can. She's never getting away.

CHAPTER 56
KATIE

" *Love. Faith. Hope.* "

"Are you staring at me, Katydid?" Hunter asks, those beautiful green eyes slowly opening.

"Maybe. Good morning, sleepyhead."

He stretches and I feel his body move against mine. "Morning, sweetness," he says, his hand coming to my neck and holding it while his thumb moves back and forth along my jaw. "Have I told you that I love you?"

"I can't remember," I joke, kissing his chest.

"I love you, Katydid. So fucking much."

"I love you too, Hunter." I stare into his eyes and let my fingers tangle into his hair.

"You ready to go back to Kentucky today, baby?" he asks, and I feel a moment of fear run through me before I push it aside.

"You really think Bethie will be okay?"

His face goes serious for a minute and his finger combs through my hair. He stares off into the distance before coming back to me.

"Skull has a lot of anger to work through, and it might not be pretty for a while. I promise you that he will love his daughter and be good to her."

My muscles tense up and the fear returns. "But he won't be to my sister?"

"They have to work it out, Katie. It's their life. I can promise you that he won't hurt her, at least not physically."

"That's not reassuring, Hunter."

"I can't offer you an answer to something I don't know,

sweetness. We just have to have faith. I know that the way I love you tells me that you and I are forever. No matter what comes up I'd move Heaven and Earth to keep you, to keep what we have."

"I feel the same."

"So, do you really think Skull and Beth won't fight to find what they had?"

"Maybe. If the anger doesn't..."

He puts his finger to my lips. "We can't do it for them, sweetness. You be there for your sister. That's all you can do."

"Then I guess I'm ready to go back to Kentucky... well... after?"

"After?" he asks with a smile.

"I thought I'd be a good girlfriend and serve you breakfast in bed."

"Is that a fact?"

"Mmm... Hmm..." I moan, rolling over on my back and looking over at him with a lazy smile.

"And what am I having for breakfast?" Hunter asks unnecessarily, because he's already rolling over and sliding between my legs.

"Me," I tell him, spreading myself open to give him more room, my hands reaching behind me to hold onto the bedpost, my eyes closing as I feel his tongue slide against my clit.

He's right. I'd do anything to keep what we have together. I'm never letting him go. I hope Beth and Skull get even half of the love I feel in my heart for Hunter.

"I'm never letting you go, Hunter," I tell him, because I can't keep the words inside. "I love you."

"I love you too, sweetness," he murmurs against my pussy as his fingers thrust inside of me. "You're my forever," I hear him say before his tongue dives back in.

He's right. What we have is forever. He's my forever, too.

EPILOGUE
PART ONE
BETH

> " *Heaven help me.* "

Sabre drives me to a small airfield about an hour away from the hotel. In that time, he doesn't talk to me, and neither does Latch who rides beside him. They barely even look at me.

I feel so ostracized. *Dirty.* I'm missing Gabby. Since she's been born, I've never been away from her. The longest has been an hour while I ran to the store. Will I get to see her before he turns me over to Colin? The thought of never seeing Gabby again crushes me. I can't stop the tears. They haven't stopped since the minute I walked out of the hotel and Skull grabbed me.

"Hello there, *mi puta esposa*," he'd snarled. The coldness in his voice as he grabbed me when I went to get the stuff out of Katie's jeep will be something that sticks with me until the day I die, which I guess won't be that long once Colin gets me, so I should be grateful for that at least.

There's no talking when we stop, or when I'm pulled onto the small airplane and pushed into a tiny bathroom. Not one word is exchanged. The only sound is that of the door as it locks behind me. The room is dark. I just sit there, doing my best to not give into the fear that swamps me. I'm terrified of the dark, too. It's one of the things grandfather used to his advantage during my hell in France. I can feel the chill bumps spread over my body and I hug myself close, trying not to give into the panic. Instead, I close my eyes and picture Skull and Gabby together. I don't understand it. He pushed me away from him, but there's no mistaking the love I saw coming from him when he was holding Gabby. Gabby will have his love. If I have to die, then at least I can go knowing that. And maybe... *maybe* if Torch and Katie work out, she will be able to help care for her. That's good. That's really good. Gabby adores her aunt. She's young. She'll barely miss me. I feel my way to the floor and slide down against the wall, curling into myself. I feel safer against the wall. Nothing can come at me.

* * *

I don't know how much time passes before the door opens. I'm so lost in my panic that I didn't even notice we landed. At first, the bright light that shines in hurts my eyes. I blink, trying to adjust, but before I get a chance to, someone grabs my wrist and pulls me out of the room. I struggle to stand. My knees scrape against the hard metal door frame. I don't know this person. His jacket reads: "prospect". I guess I don't warrant a full-fledged member of the club at this point. I'm dying to ask where he's taking me, but it probably doesn't matter.

No one talks to me as I'm pulled off the plane and towards the main building. The property used to be an old airfield, from the looks of it. Minutes later, I'm being taken through the club. I ignore all the eyes I can feel on me, even though I'm dying of embarrassment. He takes me to the area where the members have bedrooms. I'm not taken to Skull's room, though. The man pushes me into a room and slams the door. I sit on the bed, afraid to touch anything. I must sit there for an hour. I feel like I'm going to go insane. Is this part of Skull's torture? Make me wait for my death? Or is it Colin who's just dragging his feet?

My heart is in my chest when Skull enters. How can I think he looks amazing and dread seeing him at the same time?

"Where's Gabby?"

"She's being cared for," he answers. "That's all you need to know."

His voice is colder than I can ever remember it.

"Don't I get to see her before you send me to Colin?" I know my voice sounds pleading. I can't help it. The thought of never getting to touch my child again...

Skull stops, his dark eyes looking over me, and I feel like the dirt underneath his fingernails.

"I'm not turning you over to Colin. He wants you too much. I hate him almost as much as I do you, *mi esposa*. Why would I do anything that gives him pleasure?"

"You're not giving me away? Well, if you're not doing that, then... What are you going to do with me?" I ask him, my brain so stressed out that I'm having trouble piecing any of it together.

"That answer is easy. Whatever the fuck I want. Here's your food. I must get back to *mi hija*," he says lifelessly, leaving a plate of food on the dresser.

"Whose room is this?" I ask, not wanting to be alone again, even if it means having someone who obviously hates me in the room with me.

"Pistol's. It seemed fitting, one traitor for another," he shrugs, his voice trailing off.

"I'm not a traitor. I only ever tried to save you—"

"We see things differently," he says, walking towards the door. He's almost out before I can find my nerve to speak again.

"Can I see my daughter?"

"Maybe I should make you wait years, like you did to me. Maybe you will never see her again. Haven't made up my mind."

My body shakes from the unexpected reply. "You can't... You can't just take her from me!"

"I can do whatever the hell I want, Beth. You're in my home. *My rules.*"

"Skull, don't do this. If you do this, we'll never be able to work together to raise our daughter."

"I'll be raising *my* daughter," he says coldly, and fear slides through me at his announcement.

"You can't mean to keep me away from Gabby."

"Why not? You didn't have a problem keeping her away from me."

"I tried! I thought you wanted us away from you, Skull! I tried to make it back to you!"

"You never would have been away from me if you had told me everything from the beginning. I never would have had a traitor in my ranks. You never would have taken my child away from me," he adds, and with each statement, he advances on me until finally I'm backed up against the wall and there's nowhere for me to go. He wraps his hands around my neck, exerting enough pressure that I think he might choke me. My eyes go wide and I'm afraid to move. This is not the man I remember. This Skull, he's cold, hard, and deadly. This Skull is full of hate, and it's all directed at me.

He leans in close, his breath filtering out against my ear and down my neck. It sends shivers through me, a mixture of fear and need. "If you had told me the truth, my beautiful *tigresa*, none of this would have happened."

"I did it to protect you."

The pressure on my throat increases until the air refuses to come. My hands go to his in reflex. His black eyes are shining with emotion, but instead of the love or need I've dreamed of seeing there, they are full of anger.

"Instead, you made me a *tramposo!* You had me cheat on our wedding vows!" His hands clench before letting off the pressure. I take the air back into my lungs, but concentrate on his words.

"We were never married!" I scream out, not wanting to think of Skull with another woman, the idea nearly gutting me. Doesn't he know how much it cost me to let him go? Doesn't he care that I tried to protect him and keep him safe? How did this get to be all my fault? I've been without him for years, too, and I didn't go to another man. I didn't even think about it.

"We never will be, now. I would not have you now even if you begged me, Beth. *Me das asco,*" he hurls at me. He doesn't know I've learned Spanish since I've been gone, or he doesn't care. Probably the latter. But I know. I know, and his words still any fight I have inside of me.

I disgust him. As he walks off, slamming the door and locking it, I sink to the floor and do what I've done all day.

I cry.

" No puedo respirar. "

I close the door on Beth's cries. Her tears won't do her any good. I'm not the man I was. I will never be him again. I go to the nursery to check on Gabriella. Gabriella. She named *mi hija* after my mom. Was that just a trick, too? A card she could play when her back was against the wall?

Gabriella is sleeping in her crib. My daughter. My hands shake as I reach out to brush a stray curl from her forehead.

"She's beautiful," Annie says, coming up behind me.

Sabre and Latch brought her here to keep her safe, but to also help me make sure Gabriella is taken care of when I can't be with her. I wasn't grandstanding talking to Beth. I have so much anger at her right now that I want to punish her. I want her to hurt like I hurt. *Like she made me hurt.*

"*Si.* She reminds me of *mi madre.*"

"She looks just like you."

I smile at the words as pride slides through me. She does. She looks like me. It feels good having that acknowledged.

"Did you put the monitor in my room?" I ask her.

"Yes, just like you asked. But I'll be here until Sabre and Latch get back with Lucy."

"Thank you, Annie. You are a *diamante* among *inmundo perlas*," I tell her, but I don't wait around for a reply. Instead, I leave and head out of the building.

I make my way to the club's garage. Once inside, I open the trapdoor to the basement. I climb down into it and turn on the light. Standing in front of me chained from the ceiling by his hands and dangling a good two feet from the floor is Pistol. His face is a bloody mess, swollen beyond recognition. His knees have been taped and semi-repaired by Dr. Torres. She's a fucking hot piece of work. Why couldn't I have fallen for someone like her? Hot sex, uncomplicated... if only I could feel any of that beyond the pain I feel right now.

The florescent fixture buzzes and then clicks before lighting all the way. Pistol is naked. He's missing most of his toes now, and his ass has been cut by a mixture of my knife, broken bottles, and other objects. I figured, if he's going to fuck with me, I might as well show him how to take it like a man. Blood has run and dried down his legs. His ribs are purple, but nowhere near as scary-looking as it was last week. I know a couple are broken, but he's still breathing, so they must have not punctured a lung.

I stand there watching him, taping my hands up. I think he opens an eye. It's such a fucking mess, who could be sure?

"*Mátame*," Pistol says, the word coming out barely more than a soft whisper. I might not have heard it, except he begs for the same thing every time. It's monotonous. He should figure out by now that he dies when I'm done, not before. Now that my hands are taped, I circle his body.

"I met *mi hija* tonight, *cabron*. The *hija* you helped steal from me," I growl, slamming my fist into his rib. "The *hija* who is two and does not even know who I am," I tell him, pummeling him again and again. "The *hija* I never would have known existed if you had gotten your way," I add.

I pound into him over and over, each time telling him I know what he tried to do. I don't stop. I go a little too far when blood spews from his mouth and his body heaves with the force it takes for him to gasp. The thought of not having him to take my anger out on again is what makes me stop. I use my hands to stop his body from spinning listlessly. I tear the tape from my hands and go to recline against the wall, watching as the blood trails down his neck to his chest, and right there, just below his collarbone, I see it: a bit of unmarked, unblemished skin. *That can't happen.* I use the phone on the wall, hit speaker, and dial the number.

"Yeah?"

"I need you again."

"When I said I would help you out, I didn't know I would be keeping a man alive just so you could kill him," Teena's voice comes over the phone.

"Are you coming or not?"

"I'll be there."

"I'll be waiting," I tell her, ending the call.

I light a cigarette, letting the smoke circle around me.

"*Dejame morir*," Pistol wheezes, more blood dribbling from the corner of his mouth.

Let me die. How many times did I pray for that very thing? Ask God for that very same thing? How many times did it go unanswered? Not as many as Pistol's will. That, I can promise.

"Not tonight, *carbon*, not tonight." I take my cigarette and, finding that one untouched spot around his collarbone, I push the lighted end of the cigarette to it and curl my nose at the smell of burning flesh. Pistol barely moves, this pain hardly detectable under the deluge of other pain he endures. That thought brings me a very small sliver of peace—*for now*.

No. He will not die tonight. He will not die until I can breathe again.

THE END . . . FOR NOW

LOOK FOR **RELEASED**, THE FINAL BOOK
IN THE TRILOGY, NOW AVAILABLE!

BURNED By JORDAN MARIE
FINAL NOTE

I hope you guys enjoyed Burned. I felt this book needed to bring Skull and Beth up to the present so we could deal with everything coming in Book 3. A break from the angst, I guess. I will have Conquered, Book 3 out to you as soon as possible. It will be April. I hesitate to name a specific date, as I am dealing with some health issues that have put me behind. To keep up to date with the release and everything though you can join my newsletter or follow my Author pages. While this book was dedicated to a wonderful lady whom I shall forever miss. Special shout out goes to my Street team the Badass Bitches #BB4L - I love you ladies. Thank you to the Dirty Girls who have been helping me bounce off my thoughts and making this journey so amazing. I'm keeping you girls forever. Also a special shout out to Gabby Landazuri and Teena Torres, for lending your names to the book and letting me play with your toes.

Peace Out till next time!
Xoxo
J
www.jordanmarieauthor.com

GLOSSARY OF TERMS

Cabron	Dumbass
Cielo	Sky
Diamante	Diamond
Hermano	Brother
I puta la odio	I fucking hate it
Inmundo perlas	Unclean pearls
La pinche bolsa	The fucking bag
Mátame	Kill
Me das asco	You disgust me
Mi hija	My daughter
Mi puta esposa	My fucking wife
Mujer	Woman
No puedo respirar	I cannot breathe
Polla	Cock
Que es un hecho	For a fact
Querida	Dear one
Te tienes que callar la pinche boca	You need to shut your goddamn mouth
Tigresa	Tigress
Tramposo	Cheat

CPSIA information can be obtained
at www.ICGtesting.com
Printed in the USA
LVHW04s1403140918
590032LV00001B/79/P